KIWI

KINGS OF RETRIBUTION MC LOUISIANA

CRYSTAL DANIELS

SANDY ALVAREZ

TWO PENS-
CRYSTAL Daniels
Sandy ALVAREZ
-ONE STORY

1

KIWI

ELEVEN YEARS AGO

The warmth from the rays of the sun as morning light creeps across my plush king-sized bed wakes me from sleep, which is soon followed by a knock on my bedroom door.

As I stretch my arms above my head, Catalina, my father's housekeeper, enters the room. "Mornin'." I scrub my hand down my face, feeling the lingering effects of partying from the night before.

"Your father wishes to speak with you before he leaves this morning," she informs me, her voice neutral, and her Ukrainian accent thick.

What I've gathered from the year I've been in the States, living with Donovan, my birth father, is that Catalina has worked for him for many years. She doesn't speak much. Keeping to herself, she looks around the room for anything that may need tidying up. I'm not one to leave messes, and I damn sure don't expect someone to clean up after me when I'm more than capable of doing it for myself. With nothing to do and no more to say, Catalina quietly walks out of my room, closing the door behind her.

Tossing the bedsheet aside, I rise, swing my legs over the side of the bed where my feet press against the cold wood floor. Inhaling, I gaze out the massive floor to ceiling window that spans the perimeter of the room—one of the perks of having a penthouse suite. Standing, I retrieve the pair of jeans draped across the chair arm beside the bed, stride over to the glass, and open the sliding door leading to the balcony, and step out into the warm Las Vegas air.

A year of living here, and I still can't get used to the heat. Growing up in Raglan, New Zealand, our average highs hover anywhere between forty-nine and seventy-two degrees. I close my eyes and soak in the sun. It's been months since I've seen home. Raglan is a coastal town. I love everything about it: the people and the community. I was born in Auckland, where my mother lived all her life until she met and married Benjamin Cooper, my stepdad. I wasn't quite two when he came into the picture, and never once treated me as anything but like his own flesh and blood. Not long after he and my mom got married, the three of us moved to Raglan.

I start thinking about the rest of my family. After marrying Benjamin, mum couldn't wait to have more kids. Now, nineteen years later, I have three sisters, Frankie, Molly, and Poppy. All three of them look just like my mum with their dark blonde hair and blue eyes.

Making my way inside, I head for the en suite bathroom and turn the water on in the sink. Leaning over and cupping my hands, I splash cold water on my face. Green eyes connect with my reflection in the mirror. I stare at someone who looks nothing like my mum, but the replica of Donovan Black.

As long as I can remember, I was always curious about my birth father. Who was he? What did he look like?

Mum never gave too many details about him. Only his name and where he lived at that time in her life. To be truthful, she didn't know enough about the man herself. What the two of them had wasn't a relationship, but a one-night stand. She had gone on a trip with girlfriends to the States, celebrating her best friend's bachelorette party.

And, as they say, what happens in Vegas, stays in Vegas. Only mum left with a consolation prize.

Shortly after my eighteenth birthday, I sat mum down and told her my thoughts and plans on connecting with my birth father. She wasn't sold on the idea of my traveling alone, and she worried he might reject me. The rejection was something I was prepared for but had to face it and find out for myself. I wanted to get answers to all the questions I had swirling around in my head. In the end, it was my stepdad who convinced her I would be fine. The following day Ben sat me down, and handed me an airline ticket, then said, "You're my son. Nothing will ever change that. Your mum and I support everything you do. That's an open-ended ticket. Take as much time as you need." Then he handed me a credit card. "You need more, let me know."

Donovan may be my birth father, but Ben will always be my dad, and never replaceable.

Striding to my closet, I yank a shirt from the hanger and pull it down over my head. It's been almost a solid year since I got on that plane, leaving New Zealand. It took a few days to track Donovan down, but one thing I'm good at is being resourceful and persuasive. Call it what you will, a bullshitter, a smooth talker—people like me. I'm an easy-going guy if you don't piss me off.

A few minutes later, I'm walking through the kitchen, where I find Donovan sitting at the table, staring at the newspaper in his hand. He folds it, then lays it down. Looking at the diamond-encrusted Rolex on his wrist, he says, "I'm hosting a party for a huge client down at the club tonight. Think you can rustle up some eye candy?" His eyes lift to look at me, and I can't help but flashback to the day we first met.

I walk right up to him in his club, where suited men and scantily dressed women surround him. "Who the hell are you?"

"Tai Cooper. Your Son." His poker face never wavered.

"Prove it."

"Shit," one of the suited men laughs, looking between the two of us. "What proof do you need? He could be your twin."

I stare at my birth father, which feels like looking into a mirror: same tanned skinned, dark hair, and green eyes. The only difference being he's older. I could even tell he keeps himself in shape, though his physique is a little more muscular and broader than mine.

"What do you want from me—money?" He reaches into his jacket, pulling out a money clip, then tosses a hundred-dollar bill at my feet. "I'm feeling charitable today. Go buy yourself a burger and some cheap pussy."

Picking the money up off the floor, I tear it up, then throw it at his face. "How about I shove this money right up your arse." Two broad men step into my peripheral vision as I take a step forward.

Donovan raises his hand. "We're good here." He eyes me. "Sit," he orders, but I stand my ground. "The rest of you get your asses out of here," he barks.

It's not until the group he is sitting with disperses that I finally sit down across from him.

We talked for a couple of hours and, as I figured, he wanted a paternity test. Once I convinced him I wasn't looking for money, he eased up a bit, but never let his guard down. Neither did I. Before I knew it, weeks turned into months. Eventually, he offered me a job—a promotional position. I spread the word about his clubs and hustle up business. My mum wasn't entirely sold on the idea. She wanted me to go to college. Not that I was against it, but I was having fun. Donovan was kind of taking me under his wing, showing me another side of what life had to offer. The lights of the Las Vegas Strip are bright as hell. I was drawn to the lifestyle he was offering. Like an addict, I wanted more.

"Tai," Donovan barks, snapping me back from my memories. "I need girls for the mixer. They flock to you like flies on shit." Giving me a little extra incentive, he reaches into his pocket and pulls out the key to his custom Lamborghini. "Here," he tosses the keys in the air, and I catch them. "Use my car to get around town. The party is exclusive. VIP only, so be sure to hand them the black business cards. They won't get in without one." Standing, he lifts his suit jacket from the back of the chair and slips it on. "I want you there tonight. There are a few clients I'd like you to meet."

I stare blankly at him because I usually don't attend his VIP parties. He glances my way before making his way to the foyer but says nothing more about the matter. Shrugging, I turn toward the counter, grab some bread out of the breadbox, and pop a couple of slices in the toaster. Once done, I smear some butter and jam on them. As I'm eating, I realize the date and the fact that my oldest sister has a birthday soon. I smile and pull out my phone. Five minutes later, I have scheduled a flight home due to leave in two days.

Almost four hours later, I've passed out at least thirty VIP cards. Before returning to the penthouse, I decide to do a little shopping, and hopefully find something special to take back home as gifts.

Just as I'm placing my hand on the handle of the car door, I feel someone behind me. As I go to turn, a deep voice says, "Don't fuckin' move." Of course, I had to go and ignore his demand. Throwing my head back, I bash his face with the back of my skull, then quickly duck. Pivoting my body, I come up, throwing my shoulder into the guy's gut, knocking the attacker off his feet, slamming his big arse into the concrete wall behind him. The big son of a bitch clocks me in the side of the head with the weapon in his hand, causing my vision to blur. Another set of hands grasp me from behind as I stumble back a few steps. I raise my head to get a look at the man in front of me, but his face is hidden behind a mask. Struggling to break loose of the hold on me, I lift my feet off the ground, kicking the attacker in front of me in his nuts. I watch him fall to one knee, coughing, just as a thick arm wraps around my neck, restricting my airway.

"Goddamn, you're a wiry shit." The one with a hold on me grunts as I continue to struggle against him. His grip tightens. My vision grows fuzzy around the edges until I fade into darkness.

My lids feel heavy as I blink them open, and my fucking head is throbbing in pain. It takes me an extra second to get my bearings and realize I'm in a darkened room, with a dim light hanging above my head like a spotlight. My body is restricted, tied to a chair, with my hands bound behind me. I flex to gauge the tightness of the ropes, finding no wiggle room.

"You won't get out of here unless I let you go." A different voice from earlier breaks through the silence in the room. The screeching sound of a chair being dragged across the floor causes my skin to crawl. From out of the shadows, a man appears. I keep my eyes fixed on his bearded face as he straddles the seat. "You've got fight in you; I'll give you credit for that. Few have put my brother to his knees." He smirks a little, his accent thick, but I can't place it—southern maybe?

"Motherfucker kicked my dick." A tall black man steps into the light, his arms crossed over his chest.

"Who the fuck are you?" My eyes stay on the man sitting in front of me.

"Let's make this quick because I have shit to do." He opens the manilla folder in his hand, pulling out a stack of paper. He holds them three inches from my face. One by one, he shows images of me, standing and talking with various young women. "Every one of these young ladies went missing not long after these pictures were taken."

I feel all the blood drain from my face. *Missing?* "What? Listen. I don't have anything to do with those girls' disappearances."

The man looks at me for a few seconds. "I believe you."

I stare at him, then shift my eyes to his friend, who looks uninterested.

The bearded man sighs. "I know all about you, Tai Cooper from Raglan, New Zealand. Mother's name is Kora Cooper. Stepdad is Benjamin Cooper."

I interrupt him. "Dad. Benjamin is and always will be my dad. Not stepdad," I correct him, narrowing my eyes.

He continues, "You have three sisters. Graduated with honors, 4.0 GPA, loves to surf, helps his dad on weekends at his mechanic shop, and is tech-savvy," he pauses. "Should I continue?"

"So, if you know who I am, and know I don't know what happened to those women, then why the fuck am I tied to this chair while you interrogate me?"

Standing, he tosses the photos in his hand on the seat. Reaching into his pocket, he pulls out a cigarette and lights it. "You've unknowingly played a part in their disappearance." He takes a long drag from his cigarette. "Donovan Black is not who you think he is, and all these VIP parties he hosts are nothing more than a way for him to give his clientele what they want. You just so happened to come along, giving him the perfect opportunity and resource to make his entire operation easier."

"He used me, how?

"Good lookin' young man attracts a lot of attention from pretty young women. Convenient for him, wouldn't you say?" I'm doing my best to absorb what he's telling me. "Sorry, kid. You were a pawn. Our intel has your father being one of five men running a major sex trafficking ring."

My gut churns, and I feel like I may throw up. "How many?" I ask. When he doesn't answer, I look him in the eyes. "How many?"

He shakes his head. "You looking for a specific number since you've been in the picture? At least thirty."

His words sink in. How could I have been so fucking stupid? All this time, Donovan used me? What is more messed up is knowing that I have no one to blame but myself. I hang my head. How did I not see any of this? What will my parents think of me once they discover the world I've been living in for months? Corruption and lies. All of it right under my fucking nose, and I had no fucking clue. "What can I do to make things, right?" I ask, straightening my back while looking at both men.

"Helps us."

I don't hesitate. "I'm all in." Then he holds out his hand.

"My name is Riggs," he jerks his head toward his friend standing at his right, "and this is Wick."

"Cops?" My eyes dart between the two. Riggs scoffs, then Wick starts removing my binds, and I rub my wrists once freed.

"We need you to get us into that party tonight," Riggs presses.

"I can do that."

"Good," he scrubs his palm over his face. "He's grown to trust you. That being said, can you gain access to his personal office?"

"He doesn't allow anyone in his office, including me."

"Shit," Riggs grunts.

"We need those files, Prez," Wick blows smoke in the air from the cigarette he just lit.

Shifting in my seat, I lean back, realizing I can help, or at least try. "I need a computer." The two of them eyeball me. "You want my help, right?" Wick moves across the room into the shadows. I briefly hear a rustle before he returns, holding a laptop. Wick holds it out to me. Opening the computer, I get to work. What I'm doing is technically illegal. Back in high school, a buddy of mine taught me how to hack into damn near any computer-operated system. I've never used the knowledge personally, but I'm damn happy now that I paid attention.

"What are you doing?" Riggs asks as I type away.

"Trying to hack dear old dad's files," I inform him, which is proving to be more challenging than I thought. He must have plenty of security measures in place to keep unwanted threats out. I run through every trick in the book before finding a backdoor. My window of opportunity is small, so I act fast. Creating an export point to an encrypted file on the laptop, I download whatever files I can, mostly what looks to be money transfers.

Riggs and Wick stand behind me, looking over my shoulders. "Impressive. I knew you were good with computers but I didn't know you were a hacker."

"I'm not," I pull up the download of the files to the hard drive.

"Sure as shit looks like it to me," Riggs states. He grabs the computer and starts scrolling. "Shit, kid," Riggs says with amazement. "Look, brother," he shows Wick. "Send this shit to Cowboy. Have him comb through everything." A hand clasps my shoulder. "Thanks."

The guilt of everything starts weighing on me, more so than before. I swallow hard, my mouth suddenly dry. The screech of a chair knocks me from my thoughts of regret and turmoil to see Riggs has pulled his chair beside me.

"Listen, after tonight; you'll need a place to lay low for a while."

"I'll go back home," I tell him.

His heavy sigh makes me uneasy. "I strongly advise against it. If shit goes south, hell, even if it doesn't, you could potentially put your family in danger."

I run my hand through my hair. "I have nowhere else to go," I admit. "But, I could definitely use a change of scenery."

"I don't have much, but I can offer you a room and a job," Riggs offers, and I'm shocked.

"Why would you do that for me?"

Riggs shrugs. "You're helping me, so I'm helping you. Plus, I have a good feelin' about you, kid."

"That simple?"

"Yep."

What other choice do I have? Once I help them apprehend Donovan and whoever else he is involved with, I won't have a place to lay my head in Las Vegas. Donovan was the only person tying me to the City. And I'll do whatever it takes to keep my family safe. I won't let Donovan Black or his filth stain any part of their lives.

2

PIPER

PRESENT

Shoving the last of my clothes into the suitcase, I slide the zipper closed, then haul it off the bed and roll it over toward the door, sitting it next to the boxes I packed the day before. Turning, I let my gaze linger on the small dorm room that has been my home for the past year. I never thought I would find myself hundreds of miles away from my home and the people I love, but I have come to learn life can be an unpredictable shit show sometimes. I chose to handle my unsettling set of circumstances by pretending they didn't exist. Like the fact that my birth mother decided to show up after eighteen years, suddenly wanting back in my life. I'm not ready to deal with my mother and listen to her excuses for why she abandoned me. I don't know if I ever will be. Besides, moving away from home has given me a chance to spread my wings; to find who I am outside the club. Here, I am just Piper, not the daughter of a member of The Kings of Retribution MC. I adore my family though. And lately, missing them has made me more and more homesick.

A year ago, my decision to come to Texas was not an easy one.

During my senior year of high school, I got a job working for Doctor Lillian Channing DVM. She owns a veterinarian practice in New Orleans. My job was helping tend the animals, feeding them, cleaning out their cages, and walking the dogs. I soon fell in love with the animals I was helping and became enthralled with what Doctor Channing was doing. Doctor Channing noticed my interest and took me under her wing when I mentioned wanting to know more about what she does. She even helped me when I was researching colleges. By the time I graduated high school, I had accepted the chance to attend a University in Texas. My dad had been blindsided with my announcement to go to school out of state. He and the rest of my family had assumed I would stay close to home. I felt guilty for not talking with him sooner. But being the great guy he is, my dad shoved his feelings aside and supported my choice. The truth is, I didn't know the career path I wanted until working at the clinic. I was never one of those kids who knew what I wanted to do with my life at an early age. Dad always said it would come to me when the time was right.

My phone vibrating in my back pocket pulls me out of my wandering thoughts. A smile tugs at my lips when I see who the caller is. Swiping my finger across the screen, I answer. "Hi, Dad."

"Bean," he grunts. "You should have been on the road an hour ago if you want to make it home before dark."

I chuckle. "You do know I have driven at night before, right?"

"It's not safe to drive at night after you've been on the road all day."

"I'll be fine, dad. If I get tired, I'll find a hotel to crash at for the night."

"It's not..."

I roll my eyes and finish his sentence. "Safe."

I hear him sigh over the phone. "Piper."

"Dad, I'll be on the road in an hour, and I'll be home before dark. I got eight hours of sleep last night, so I'm rested. Should I need to stay in a hotel, I have my pepper spray and my taser. And don't forget that I've mastered the perfect ball shot. I promise any would-be assailant will be left without the ability to reproduce."

"I don't know if I should tell you to stop busting my balls or to be proud of you," he grumbles.

A second later, I hear my little brother Jaxson crying in the background.

"I have to go, Bean. Promise has court this morning, so it's just my boy and me. Call as soon as you leave, and when you stop for gas, check-in. No texting and driving either."

"I know the drill, Dad. Love you. And give my baby brother a kiss for me."

"Will do, sweetheart. Love you too, Bean."

When I hang up with my dad, there is a knock on the door, followed by my best friend barging in. "Look, I know we said our goodbyes yesterday, but I woke up this morning already missing you." Jia throws her arms around me, nearly knocking me over.

"Damn, Jia," I laugh. Jia is tiny, but she's a powerhouse. My best friend stands at barely five feet tall, has long, sleek black hair that she gets from her father, who is Korean. Jia is a rambunctious, fearless, spontaneous, little spitfire, and I love her. I met Jia on my first day on campus when dad, Uncle Abel, and Uncle Malik rolled up to the school on their bikes. Three large men riding Harleys on a college campus has a way of attracting attention. Dad said the guys wanted to come help get me settled. I didn't buy it. I was proven right when I caught them making faces and growling at any guy who dared to look in my direction. I've moved past the stage where my dad and uncles embarrass me. I mostly ignore their boorish behavior. On the other hand, Jia found the three hulking men that followed me across campus toward my dorm, swoon-worthy. She proved it by strolling up to me out of nowhere, saying, "Nice entourage. Know where I can get my own alpha bodyguards to follow me around? Your badass, biker eye candy puts the pink Polo wearing preppy's around here to shame."

"This is only for the summer, Jia. You do know we'll see each other again in a couple of months?"

Jia releases me. "I know.

"My offer to come along still stands. My dad and stepmom said it was okay."

Jia sighs. "Yeah, but I promised my mom and dad I'd visit them at our beach house in Florida."

Jia's family is loaded. Her dad is a successful businessman, and her mom is your typical trophy wife—her words, not mine. From the way she talks, she and her parents are not close.

"Well, if you decide to cut your visit with them short, hit me up."

I've been on the road for two hours, and already my stomach is in knots. I would be lying if I said the situation with my mom and wanting to be a veterinarian were the only deciding factors that led me to leave New Orleans, but they're not. Tai Cooper, or better known to the club as Kiwi, is the number one deciding factor in my decision to leave New Orleans. I'm in love with a man who is not only forbidden but a man who doesn't even know I have breasts. To Tai, I am like a sister. He came into my life when he was nineteen, and I was eight. It didn't take long for me to care for Tai like I did the rest of the club guys, but my feelings changed somewhere around seventeen. And they intensified shortly after when someone attempted to assault me at a rally the club was hosting not long ago. While my dad was trying to murder the dirty son of a bitch who put their hands on me, Tai was the one who swooped in and carried me away to safety.

I'll never forget the way his arms felt as he wrapped me in his embrace or the smell of his leather cut and his cologne when I buried my face against his neck. Or the way he looked at me the moment he brushed my hair away from my face and used the back of his hand to dry my tears. I could have sworn the heat I saw in his eyes said he wanted to kiss me. Our lips were inches apart, and his breath skirted across my lips. My heart was about to beat out of my chest, but I wanted it to happen. I closed my eyes and waited; I waited for a kiss that never came because a second later, Tai had distanced himself from me. He still comforted me by keeping his arms around me, but he wouldn't even look at me after that moment. I was mad at myself for acting foolishly. All Tai was trying to do was calm me down after a man had attempted to violate me, and there I was embarrassing myself by trying to kiss him. Thank god he never spoke of that awkward moment, and neither have I. After the incident, we went back to being the friends we've always been toward each other.

Spotting the sign for a gas station, I pull off at the next exit. When I park at the pump, the first thing I do is reach back and grab my purse from the back seat in search of my cell so I can text my dad.

Me: I'm alive. I stopped for gas and food.

Dad: Smartass.

Me: You love me.

Dad: You're lucky, I do.

Me: Love you, dad.

Dad: Love you too, Bean.

I shake my head and smile. It takes a minute for the last text to come through. He's too dang predictable.

Dad: Check-in at the next stop.

God, I love that man.

After I have paid for my gas and loaded up on snacks, I walk back out to my car to see two men standing near the trunk looking down at the ground. When I get closer, I notice they are staring at the back tire on my car, which is flat. I let out an audible sigh. "Great."

"Hey there, sweet thing." A guy with a beer belly and greasy hair addresses me. "This your car?"

I hold my eye roll and give him a polite smile as I open the car door and toss my snacks on the seat. "Yep." I keep my purse that has my taser in it on my shoulder and my keys, which has my pepper spray on it, in my hand. These dudes are giving off bad vibes, and I'm not taking any chances.

"Looks like you're in a bit of a bind," the equally creepy friend adds.

I shrug. "Just a flat tire, nothing I can't handle. Thanks for your concern, though." I dismiss the two men. I'm no damsel in distress. I knew how to change a tire by the time I was ten. Dad made sure of it.

"If ya need a ride somewhere, we'd be happy to give you a lift."

My back goes straight, and I no longer care about being polite. These two creeps are about to learn; they cannot pull one over on me. Reaching in my purse, I pull out my taser. Opening the car door, I toss my bag inside and make my way to the back of the car, where I proceed to open the trunk. I don't miss the way both men eye the weapon in my hand. "Like I said before, gentleman. A flat tire is nothing I can't handle." I make sure to keep my eyes trained on them as I speak.

The big guy with the gut holds up both hands and sneers, "Suit yourself."

Both men walk away, climb into an old pickup truck, and drive off. Once they are out of sight, my shoulders relax, and some of the tension leaves my body. I then go about hauling the spare from the trunk of my car and set it down on the ground. Crouching down next to the flat tire, I take a closer look. The tension that left my body moments ago returns. Those assholes sliced my tire. What were they expecting? That I'd be a poor defenseless female, and I would jump at their offer to give me a ride? My stomach churns at the thought of those men preying on other women. Pushing my anger aside, I get busy changing the tire, cursing those fuckers the whole time.

Thirty minutes later, I'm placing the jack back in the car when my phone rings from the front seat. Jogging around, I pull open the door, swipe the phone from the console, and answer. "Hello."

"Piper." My dad's voice sounds urgent. "What's wrong? Why are you still at the gas station?"

My dad has a tracker on my phone, so he must have checked my location and seen I haven't moved in almost an hour. "I'm okay. I had a flat tire." I try masking the pissed tone in my voice but fail.

"Piper, what happened?"

I rest my back against the car, tilt my face up toward the sky and let out a heavy sigh. "Some assholes sliced my tire when I was inside the store. They tried to help and offered me a ride."

"What!" he roars over the line, and I wince. I could have kept this situation from him, but I'm not good at lying, especially to my dad.

"Dad, calm down. I handled it. They're gone, and I just finished with the tire. I was about to get back on the road when you called."

"There is no fuckin' calm when my baby girl tells me two assholes slit her goddamn tire and then tried to lure her away with them. I'm comin' to get you."

"No!" I cut him off. "I'm literally an hour away. By the time you get here, I can be home. I'm okay, dad. I promise."

The line is silent for a long moment. "Fine," he grits. "I'll be tracking you. Stay safe and alert. Keep watch in your rearview mirror for any signs of being followed."

"I will. I'll call you if I need anything."

"Alright. Love you, Bean."

"Love you too."

The sun is starting to set as I pull into the driveway of my home. I smile when I see my dad standing on the porch, waiting for me. Promise is standing beside him with Jaxson on her hip. My heart melts at the sight of my baby brother. I park, and before I turn the car off, dad is at my door, pulling it open. And in the next second, I'm in his arms. "Jesus fuckin' Christ, Bean. You are determined to give your old man a heart attack."

I squeeze him back. "Good to see you too, dad."

Pulling back, dad flicks his steely gaze over me from head to toe, inspecting me. His eyes land on my hair with a grunt.

"What, you don't like it?" I give him a grin as I run my fingers through my locks.

"You're always beautiful, Bean." My dad's voice is soft. He leans down, kissing the top of my head.

"Oh my, god! Piper, you look fantastic! I'm digging the new you," Promise boasts as she comes bounding down the steps. Jaxson reaches for me, and I nearly burst with anticipation to have my brother in my arms.

"Come here, little man," I gush. Jaxson is the most adorable baby. "My goodness, you're getting so big!" I nuzzle my face into the crook of his neck, making him giggle. "I'm going to eat you up." I pretend to make chomping noises as I hold him up and blow raspberries onto his chubby tummy. All the while, my dad and Promise are looking at me with matching grins. "What?" I ask, smiling at them.

"You're a goof," dad teases. "Come on, let's go into the house and get ready."

I place Jaxson on my hip and follow dad and Promise. "Get ready for what?"

"We're takin' ya out to dinner."

"Okay. Let me shower and change first. I feel grimy after being on the road all day, and I have grease on my jeans from changing that tire."

I hand Jaxson off to my dad and don't miss the tick in his jaw at the mention of what happened earlier. I make a mental note not to bring it up again. I don't want him getting upset any more than he already is. What's done is done. At the end of the day, nothing happened. However, I'm not too fond of the thought of those men doing something like that to some other unsuspecting woman.

An hour later, I have showered and dried my hair, opting to wear it down in loose waves, and just finished applying a touch of mascara and my favorite red lipstick. Knowing dad will not take us anywhere fancy, I choose to wear a lacey, emerald green bodysuit, paired with skinny jeans. After slipping on some gold sandals, I make my way downstairs, where dad and Promise are waiting.

Together we load up into my dads' truck, and I climb into the backseat where Promise is strapping Jaxson into his car seat. I still can't believe how big he has gotten, and I feel like I've missed so much already. Sadness washes over me at the thought.

"I'm going to stop at the bar for a minute. I left some paperwork in the office," dad says from the cab of the truck as he pulls up in front of Twisted Throttle, the bar my Uncle Abel owns. My brow scrunches, wondering why the bar is empty. This time of night, the bar is usually packed.

Promise unbuckles her seatbelt. "I'm going to take Jaxson in and change his diaper real quick. Piper, do you want to wait in the truck, or come inside?"

I unbuckle as well and open the truck door. "I'll join you."

3

KIWI

It's late afternoon. I have a cold beer in my hand, good music in the background, and the entire club, along with their families, are gathered inside the bar. We're waiting for Piper's arrival. Nova's daughter has been away, attending college in Texas for close to a year. Moving away from home was a difficult choice for Piper to make. She and I talked about it often before she left. I understood where Piper was coming from, and the desire to discover more about life—about yourself. Sometimes you have to leave home to figure out who you are. Piper has always had a zest for life. She thrives on helping others and lives for her family, but she needs to live for herself too. The only problem was, once Piper finished high school, everything changed. Her mother wanted back into her life, and that alone was enough to make her want to leave so that she could breathe again. She tried to get away from it all—her feelings. Piper wanted to quiet the storm inside her. She was looking for peace. I knew she needed to leave home because she wasn't finding solace in Louisiana anymore. And I won't lie. Even though she's been home a couple of times since, her absence hasn't gone unnoticed.

Nova walks through the front door as I lift my beer to my lips. At his side is Promise, holding their son in her arms. Then, in walks Piper..*Holy shit*. My chest tightens. Is that Piper? Long platinum blonde hair replaces her once brunette, falling in waves over her shoulders. I take her in, following the curves of her body. The emerald green bodysuit she's wearing compliments her sun-kissed skin.

I can't take my eyes off her.

Breathe.

Her eyes lock with mine from across the room. She smiles, and I swear to God, my soul leaves me. My heart pulsates, matching the rhythm of the music playing from the speakers behind me, as I watch her embrace everyone in the bar. The moment Everest wraps her in a bear hug, welcoming her home, my body heats with an overwhelming urge to bury my fist in his fucking face for touching her.

What in the hell is wrong with me?

Get your shit together, Tai.

It's Piper for fucks sake.

Throwing her head back, Piper laughs as Wick lifts her feet from the ground when he embraces her. Even that shit pisses me off. I should be making her laugh—be the reason she is smiling. My hand tightens around the bottle in my hand. I close my eyes. With everything in me, I fight what I'm feeling.

Rage.

Want.

Need.

Because she's mine.

"Tai." Aside from my parents and siblings, Piper is the only one who calls me by my name. Her voice's mellow tone creates a physical pull, and I open my eyes to her, standing in front of me. I take her in once more. Her bright hazel eyes are sparkling. She's so different, yet the same. Piper throws herself into my chest, her arms wrapping around my waist. The sweet scent of honey blended with jasmine engulfs my senses as I embrace her.

"Fuck, you always smell good." At my comment, I feel Piper smile against my chest. I mentally kick my arse for saying that.

"I missed you," Piper says.

There is a shift in the core of my soul—an audible crack in the universe. With those three words, I realize I'm screwed.

I want this woman to be mine.

"Missed you too," I clear my throat, "we all did." Then kiss the top of her head. "Welcome home."

"Feels good to be home."

Pulling back, I reach out and touch her hair. "This is different." Her strands slide between my fingers.

"I needed a change. Something drastic and bold." Piper nibbles on her lower lip, something she often does when something is on her mind. "You like it?"

"Yeah, babe, I do." Fuck if she only knew the thoughts running through my head right now. Thoughts I shouldn't have—accompanied by feelings I shouldn't be feeling for her. Stepping back, I put a little extra space between us.

Looking past her shoulder, I take notice of Nova walking in our direction. He comes to a stop at his daughter's side, pulling her to him. Nova eyes me as he speaks to Piper. "Bean, I need to speak with Kiwi for a moment. Why don't you give the women a hand with the food that was just delivered?" Then kisses her forehead.

Piper flashes another smile my way before heading across the room to where the women are busy setting out dinner. Nova jerks his head. "Let's talk in the office."

I follow him toward the back of the bar, closing the door once we've both entered the room. His demeanor changes, becoming intense. For a moment, I believe he must have seen something in the way I looked at his daughter. Quite frankly, I wouldn't blame him for losing his shit. I'm pissed at myself as well.

"I need a favor." The sharpness of his words put me on alert, and I give him my complete attention. "A couple of men harassed Piper earlier today." I feel my body heat, and my fists clench at my sides.

"Where?" I struggle to keep my anger in check.

"A small mom and pop gas station just outside Baton Rouge."

"They touch her?" I ask and pray like hell, for their sake, that they didn't.

"Piper says, no. Either way, I don't give a fuck." Nova pauses a beat, and I can tell he's fighting mad and struggling to contain it. "She found her tire slashed when she came back out of the store."

"The fuck!" I growl.

"I know the place, but I want to see the bastards' faces."

He doesn't have to say it twice. My ass is in the chair, staring at the computer screen. The longer it takes me to trace down the location, tap into the system, the more pissed I get. "There." I stop when Piper's vehicle pulls up to the gas pump. We watch her climb out, then walk inside. One of two ugly-ass motherfuckers who was standing by the corner of the building makes their way over. He squats, hiding his body between the car and the trash bin nearby, so we can't make out in detail what he is doing. "He slashed the tire," I state, as the dirtbag walks away, shoving his hand into his pocket. Piper exits the store several minutes later to find the two men are already standing beside her car when she walks up. They strike up a conversation with her, then point out her flat.

"I've seen enough," Nova grits.

"What's the plan?"

"You up for a ride?" he asks.

After a quick word with Riggs, Nova and I slip out the back. An hour later, we roll up to the gas station. After talking with the older man, who owns the place, he was more than happy to help us identify the men we are looking for, saying the two do nothing but cause him problems. The older man points toward the rundown trailer park across the street. "The Thibodeaux brothers. They live there, Lot number 32, I believe. Nothin' but two sorry pieces of trash if you ask me. Fuckin' grown-ass men still livin' with their momma, who, I heard, is currently in the hospital. They steal every penny of that poor lady's disability check every month to feed their alcohol addiction." The old guy shakes his head.

"Appreciate your help, old man," Nova says.

"You got it." He shuffles behind the counter. "By the way," he catches us before walking out of the store, "Those boys are gun owners. They won't hesitate to shoot," he warns. Pulling my cut open, he catches a glimpse of my weapon strapped in the holster at my side.

"I wish a fucker would try," I state, then walk out of the door. "We should leave our bikes here," I suggest to Nova once we are outside and scan our surroundings. We are damn near in the middle of nowhere. There's not much to this little town if you can even call it that. I hear a buzzing, and Nova pulls his phone from his pocket. He shakes his head as he taps at the screen. "Everything okay, mate?"

"Just Prez checkin' in." He shoves his phone away. "Let's get this shit takin' care of so I can get back home to my family."

Night has fallen and it's dark as shit once we enter the trailer park. Not one damn streetlight works, only the soft glow from a few trailers with porch lights. Rocks crunch beneath our feet as we travel down the unpaved road, stopping once we reach lot number 32. A couple of broken-down trucks are sitting in the short driveway, and noise from a TV coming from an open window—Nova motions for us to check the perimeter. Circling the small single-wide trailer, I peer into the windows, then meet Nova at the porch. "One of those assholes in the back bedroom gettin' his dick sucked," I tell him.

"The other asshole is passed out in the living room," Nova says, retrieving his gun. I do the same, walking up the rickety steps to the front door. He wraps his hand around the knob, twisting it, and pushes open the door. The stench of stale beer and rotten food hits us. Quietly, I close the door behind me as Nova crosses the room. He presses the end of his barrel into the guy's open mouth, stifling his snoring, and the fucker gags as he pries open his eyes. Nova warns the guy as he becomes aware and tries to reach between the couch cushions. "Move again, and I'll blow your fuckin' head off." The guy raises his hands, and his eyes dart over to me, then back to Nova. "Hey, brother. I've got this one. What do you say you bring the other one to the party?"

I move through the kitchen to my left, then down a short hallway toward the back bedroom and open the door. The filthy son of a bitch who slashed Piper's tire is sprawled out on his back, still getting his half-hard dick serviced, and never hears me enter the room. The woman who is bobbing on his knob stops, causing him to open his eyes. He rises on his elbows to look at her.

"Bitch, did I tell you..." his words fall short once he sees me, then shoves the woman, causing her to scream. I have to give the bastard some credit. His reaction is swift. Jackknifing from the bed, he reaches for a revolver I spot lying on the nightstand. Unfortunately for him, I'm quicker and plant my heavy boot between his legs. Holding his dick, he screams in agony. I lift my gun, aiming it at his head.

The guy looks down at his crotch, lifting one of his hands, sees blood, and judging by the unnatural angle his manhood is currently in, I would say his day just went from bad to worse. "I need a doctor," the asshole screeches at the sight of his broken dick.

I look at the woman, who has slunk off the bed and frozen in fear. "Out," I bark. Scrambling, she snatches her bag from the floor and runs past me. I turn my attention back to the guy. "Get up." When he doesn't attempt to move, I grab a fist full of his greasy hair and jerk him off the bed. Still holding his dick, he stumbles out of the bedroom door.

Upon entering the living room, I shove the naked asshole to the floor. He falls to his knees, blood trickling to the floor from between his legs. "Who the fuck do you think you are?" The brother Nova has at gunpoint spits.

Using his weapon, Nova cracks the guy across the face. "Let's see if we can jog your memories. This morning, a young woman stopped for gas across the street, and you slashed her tire."

"What fucking business is it of yours?" The skeezy brother kneeling in front of me on the floor spits as he shoots daggers between Nova and me.

His attitude earns him a blow to the head, and he falls to his side. "You picked the wrong woman to prey on, motherfucker." I don't stop there and begin stomping the fuck out of him, burying the toe of my boot in his ribcage numerous times, until he's spitting blood and coughing for air.

"Shit, man. Stop before you kill him," his brother pleads.

"You're lucky we don't shoot you dead," Nova growls.

"Consider this little visit a warning. You and your brother are on our shit list. Prey on another woman again, and all you'll have to worry about are the maggots eating your corpses." Nova knocks the fucker out cold, his body falling to the sofa. My brother glances at my feet, where the other cocksucker lays in the fetal position, moaning. "Let's get the hell out of here."

The following morning, I'm in the barn working on a bike. The fat orange tomcat that has been hanging around since I moved into the place jumps from the overhead rafters. He swats at the sweaty bandana draped on my knee, stealing it as I tighten a frame bolt. "What the hell, Tom?" The cat looks at me like I've offended him in some way. He picks it up in his mouth, then totters away with his goods. "Damn thief. That's the fifth one you've stolen this week." Using the back of my hand, I wipe the sweat from my brow. "My cat is a damn klepto." I shake my head. Not only that, but the damn cat also brings me dead mice—only the heads. He leaves them on the front porch, right on the welcome mat, so that I won't miss them. I'm convinced he's part of some feline mafia or some shit. I don't know if he's plotting my murder or it's just his way of being nice.

Standing, I wipe my palms down the front of my jeans and walk outside. The goats make noise the moment they see me. Yep. Nubian Goats, to be exact. They came with the property and the house I bought. I was getting such a good deal on the house that the animals being part of the asking price didn't deter me. The only problem is, now that I have them, I don't know what the hell to do with them. Leaning against the fence, I watch the two babies climb around on the old barrels and tires. The roar of a Harley causes me to turn my head. Wonder what Riggs is doing out here this morning? He rolls his bike right up to the barn, where he parks it. "How's it goin', Prez?"

"Good. How about yourself?" He gets off his bike and stretches his back. "I see you're makin' progress on the bike." Riggs walks in through the open barn doors. He takes a bandana from his back pocket and wipes his forehead. "Even Satan's sweatin' today," he remarks.

I stride over to the cooler beside my toolbox, lift the lid and grab a couple of cold beers from the ice bath. "It's the hottest day of summer yet," I agree with him and hand him the beer.

"Thanks, brother." He pops off the top and takes a swig. "Goddamn, that hits the spot."

"What brings you out here?" I ask, taking a drink of my beer.

"I've got a proposition for you." Riggs leans against the old tractor. "I got a call from Jake this mornin'. He would like to expand Kings Custom, and possibly open a shop here in New Orleans."

"That sounds like a great idea," I tell him.

"Exactly. And we would like you to manage the place."

I drop the beer from my lips. "You're shittin' me?"

Riggs grins. "No bullshit." He gestures to the bike I'm working on now. "It's already a side job for you anyway. You are a great mechanic, Kiwi. There's no one better qualified than you." Riggs downs his beer. "So, what do ya say, brother?"

"Hell yeah, brother. Where and when do we start?"

4

PIPER

Walking into the kitchen the following morning, I find Promise standing at the stove cooking eggs while dad sits at the table beside Jaxson, who is sitting in his highchair. "Morning, dad." I kiss the top of his head.

"Mornin', Bean," he says just before taking a sip of coffee.

"You look like crap. I'm surprised to see you up since I didn't hear you come home until nearly sunrise. You know, dad, you're getting old. You shouldn't be out partying with the guys so late." I giggle, and he glares at me over the rim of his mug.

"I'm not old." He rubs a hand down his face. "Besides, I wasn't kickin' it with the guys. I was handlin' club business."

When dad mentions club business, I know the subject is over —moving across the kitchen, I fix myself a cup of coffee.

"So, Piper, did you have any plans today?" Promise asks. "I thought we could hang out and catch up. I was going to take Jaxson to the park for a picnic."

Sitting at the table, I reach over and tickle my brother's belly, making him squeal. "I'd love to hang out with you guys. What about you, dad? Are you coming to the park with us?"

He shakes his head. "I'm meetin' with Kiwi today. He's almost finished with that bike he's been working on out at his place, and I want to check it out. I told him I might have a buddy who wants to buy it from him."

At the mention of Tai, my tummy flutters. Being around him last night was hard. All the feelings I've spent the past year trying to bury rush back.

"But don't worry," dad stands and places his mug in the kitchen sink. "I'll be back in a few hours. I want to spend some time catching up with my baby girl. I want to hear all about college life." He kisses the top of my head, does the same with Jaxson, then goes over to Promise, wraps her in a hug, and murmurs something in her ear, making her blush. I love seeing the two of them together. I love seeing my dad so happy.

A little more than an hour later, Promise and I are sitting on a blanket under a large oak tree at the park, watching Jaxson try to crawl around after a ball. "I feel like I've missed out on so much this past year. Jaxson has gotten so big. I hate that I missed some of his first milestones." I sigh. I was home on break when he was born and have been home a couple times since. But still, it's not the same. "If it weren't for Facetime, my brother wouldn't know who I am." I start picking at the blades of grass in front of me. Promise stays silent; she only nods and hums. "I'm contemplating whether or not I want to move back home."

"Is that what you want? Is this only about your brother, or is there more?"

I cut my eyes to her and huff. "Since when is there not more?" Promise and I have grown close since she came into my dad's life. She and I have talked about many things, and she probably has a good idea as to my reasons for leaving New Orleans. She's just never called me out on them.

"Can I be real with you, Piper?"

"I want you to always be real with me, Promise."

"I understand needing to escape, needing to get away and clear your head. You've been through a lot in your life. Being a part of the club is not easy. Then your mom showing up threw you for a loop. I'm not going to pretend to know what you're going through, sweetie, but I do know that keeping all that heartache bottled up inside and not working through the situation will only cause the hurt to fester. If you choose to come home, do it for you. Do it because it's what you need and because you are ready to face your fears, so you can move on with the rest of your life. Don't let too much time pass, because if you do, you will end up with a hell of a lot of 'what if's' that you'll never have the answers for."

Promise doesn't say anymore, and neither do I. The two of us sit together, quietly watching Jaxson play while I let her words roll around in my head. I spend the next two hours soaking up every second with my brother, riding down the slide with him tucked close to my chest, pushing him on the baby swing, and listening to his laughter. Soon, Jaxson becomes cranky. "It's time for his nap. How about we pack up and head home?" Promise suggests as I help her gather what's left of our lunch and pick the blanket up off the ground.

"Sounds good. I wanted to go by the clinic and say hi to Dr. Channing."

As Promise loads Jaxson into his car seat, I'm popping the trunk of her car and packing our stuff in when a strange feeling of being watched washers over me. Peering over my shoulder at the opposite end of the parking lot, I see a familiar white sedan. It's my mother.

"Is that?"

"Yup," I say, cutting Promise off as she too looks in the direction my eyes are trained. "She must have heard I was back in town. Although, I'm not sure how she found out."

"Do you want to go over and talk to her, or call your dad?" Promise asks.

I shake my head. "No. She never approaches me. She just randomly shows up when I'm out. Like that time at my graduation and a few times last summer, or when I come home to visit."

Promise cuts her eyes to me. "You know about that?"

"Yeah."

"Why didn't you say anything? Your dad and I saw her that day too, but we didn't think you had noticed."

I shrug. "She told dad she would let me come to her when I was ready. It might sound stupid, but I kind of like that she checks up on me."

"That doesn't sound stupid at all, Piper."

Turning my attention away from Promise and back over to my mother, I can't help but notice the hopeful expression on her face. That look quickly morphs into defeat when I turn on my heel and climb into the passenger seat of Promise's car.

Luckily, Promise remains quiet on the ride home. My head is filled with a jumbled mess of conflicted emotions. I desperately want to know the answers to my many questions on why my mom decided to abandon me, but at the same time, I'd like things to go back to the way they were before she found her way back into my life. From what dad told me, Hell's Punishers and The Kings have no beef with each other, and both clubs show respect to one another. My dad's number one rule he made clear was that my mother and nobody from the club she is associated with approaches me. Today is the first time she has been alone too. All the other times, she has checked on me from a distance, Crow was with her. The first time was at my high school graduation. A few other times were during the summer before I left for Texas. Sometimes I would be out having lunch with friends and hear the rumble of a Harley. I know she has good intentions. The club wouldn't allow her or Hell's Punishers to step one foot into New Orleans otherwise. I'd bet anything that my dad knows of every single time they road through town.

Nothing goes on in New Orleans that the club doesn't know about.

Lost in my thoughts, the ride home passes in a blur, and we are pulling into the garage.

"Are you still wanting to go to the clinic?" Promise asks.

"Yeah, I miss that place," I smile. "I'll be back home in time for dinner. Dad said he was going to make his famous beer-battered onion rings and grilled steaks. I don't want to miss out."

"Alright, sweetie. I'll see you later." Promise lifts a sleeping Jaxson from the backseat while I grab my purse, make my way over to my car, and climb in. On the way to the clinic, I come up to the tactical store the club owns, and spot my dad standing outside talking to Fender. With a smile on my face, I turn into the parking lot. My dad returns my smile when I step out of my car. "What ya doing, Bean?"

I throw my arm around his waist. "I was on my way to the clinic when I saw you out here. I thought I'd stop and say hi." I look from my dad to Fender. "Hi, Fender."

"How's it goin' darlin'?"

"Going good. I'm happy to be home."

Dad squeezes me. "And we're fuckin' happy to have ya home."

I'm about to open my mouth to respond when Tai strolls out of the front entrance of the tactical store. I suck in a sharp breath at the sight of him. Tai stands at 6 feet 2 inches tall, has brown hair that has grown out a bit since the last time I saw him, has a week's worth of scruff on his face, and has the most beautiful green eyes I have ever seen on a man. Wearing a pair of faded jeans, a gray t-shirt that stretches tight across his broad chest, and black motorcycle boots, Tai makes his way over with a woman dressed in a police uniform following behind him. I've never seen her before, so she must be new to the force. The woman looks to be in her late twenties to early thirties. She's tall and has her brown hair pulled up into a ponytail. She's also currently making goo goo eyes at Tai. A sick feeling settles into the pit of my stomach. I have to bite my tongue to keep from saying something. The last thing I want is the green-eyed monster known as jealousy making an appearance. The only thing that manages to tame the wild beast is the fact Tai is blatantly ignoring the woman. In fact, I can feel his gaze directed at me. I do my best not to let my satisfaction show by keeping my eyes cast downward.

"So, I'll see you Tuesday?" At the sound of the officer's sultry voice, I snap my head up to see her batting her lashes at Tai. He takes his eyes off me and addresses the woman.

"Fender handles the orders," he says, his tone flat.

"Well, I just thought..."

Tai cuts her off. "Thought what?"

I almost feel bad for the woman when she becomes crestfallen and starts stuttering over her words. "Oh, well, okay. Sure, I'll be back Tuesday to pick up that order then."

By the time the woman goes to leave, Tai's attention is back on our group, and the pretty new officer has become an afterthought.

"Damn, brother." Fender slaps Tai on the back and chuckles. "Did you have to be such an ass? I mean, the newbie is a little desperate, but she's not bad to look at."

Tai shrugs while taking a cigarette from his cut, lighting it.

Deciding to take my leave, I give dad a nudge. "I'm going to take off. I'll be home in time for dinner. Are you still cooking?"

"Yeah. I promised you beer rings and steaks, so that's what you'll get."

Dad jerks his chin toward Fender and Tai. "You two want to stop by the house later for supper?"

"I wish I could, brother, but I have plans. I need to pick one of the kids up from the Rec Center and take him home. Sawyer's mom has to work late, and I'm going to help her out."

Dad nods and looks at Tai. "What about you?"

Tai takes a drag from his cigarette, flicks his eyes over to me, and then returns to my dad. "Yeah, brother. I'll be there."

Walking through the door of the clinic fifteen minutes later, I scan the room to see Erica, the girl who replaced me when I left last summer, is not sitting behind the reception area. I hear barking coming from the back, along with Dr. Channing shouting. "I'll be right with you!"

A second later, she bustles around the corner from the back, looking a bit frazzled and a lot overwhelmed. In her late fifties, Dr. Channing is about three inches shorter than me, has dark brown hair sprinkled with a little grey cut into a short bob, and is one of the sweetest women I know.

"Piper! Oh my god! What are you doing here?" She walks up to me and pulls me in for a tight hug.

"I'm home for the summer and wanted to come see you. How are things here? And where is Erica?"

Dr. Channing puts her hand on her hip. "She quit last week. No notice or anything."

"You're kidding—just like that?"

"Yep. Not that it mattered. She was a crap receptionist. Honestly, I was going to fire her before she quit. My calendar is a mess. The poor girl didn't know her ass from her elbow."

I chuckle. "Do you want me to rescue you? I'm not doing much while I'm home for the summer."

"Piper, don't play with me, child. Are you serious?"

"Yes. I would love to come back. I've missed this place."

"Oh, Piper, I've missed you too. The place is not the same without you. I'll only need you in the mornings until about two in the afternoon. I hired this sweet kid. His name is Mathew. He's a high school student attending summer school. He comes in after class."

"That will be perfect. What about today? Want me to take a look at your calendar and get you sorted?"

"Yes, please. Thank you, Piper."

"You got it, Dr. Channing. But first, can I go back and see the fur babies?"

"Of course. I just let Rocky outside."

Rocky is an English Bulldog who was found on the side of the highway last summer. We think he was dumped there on purpose and suffered in the heat for some time. He was severely dehydrated, and the pads of his paws burnt, which can happen to animals when the pavement gets too hot during the summer. Rocky is also old and not very trusting of people, which has made it difficult for him to be adopted. I'm not surprised he's still here.

As I make my way into the kennel area, I go straight to the largest kennel in the back where she keeps Chance. Chance is a beagle who was rescued from a puppy mill a year ago. Many of the one hundred plus dogs rescued have found their forever home, but unfortunately, several had to be put down. One of those that was almost euthanized is Chance because his back legs are paralyzed. It was Dr. Channing who heard about the situation and swooped in to take him on. Dr. Channing knows a guy in Mississippi who makes wheelchairs for dogs, and he didn't hesitate to help. I love Chance and bonded with him on my first day working here. I hated leaving him behind when I left for Texas. If it weren't for school, I would have adopted him myself.

As soon as I step up to his kennel, I find it empty. I scan the other kennels to then turn to Dr. Channing. "Is Chance outside with Rocky?" I ask and start making my way to the door that leads to the small back yard behind the clinic.

"Nope," she replies, her voice chipper. "He's been adopted."

"What?" I ask, my tone sounding a little disappointed.

"Chance was adopted soon after you left for Texas. A guy came in here and asked for him specifically."

My brow scrunches as I try to think of who would have known about Chance enough to ask for him by name and then adopt him.

Dr. Channing takes in my expression. "Oh, Piper. I assure you Chance went to a great home and is very happy. I would never let him go otherwise."

"I know. I trust your judgment. I just wish I could have taken him."

"I know, sweetie, but I promise he's in a good place. Besides, his owner is bringing him in next week for annual booster shots. You can see him then and meet his new owner."

A couple of hours later, as I finish going through the clinic calendar that Erica screwed up, I can't help but think about Chance and wonder who adopted him. Taking care of a disabled dog takes time and dedication. Not that I am not happy for him. He deserves to be in a home and not spend his days here. And like Dr. Channing said, I can meet Chance's new owner next week.

With my work done, I log off the computer, grab my purse from the filing cabinet beside me, fling it over my shoulder, and walk back to Dr. Channing's office. I stick my head in the door. "Hey. I'm all finished. I was able to fix everything, and you even have three hours free tomorrow after lunch. Erica had managed to double book some of the appointments. I deleted those duplicates and moved a few things around so that you can get caught up."

Dr. Channing looks up from the paperwork in front of her and beams. "You're an angel, Piper, Thank you."

"You're welcome. I'll see you in the morning."

5

KIWI

I'm closing the tactical store early today. After my usual rounds, before locking up the store, I make one more sweep through the building before grabbing two bags of trash then walk out the front door. Dropping the plastic bags at my feet, I lock the door and set the alarm. Lifting the garbage, I stroll to the corner of the building, where my bike is parked, stopping briefly to toss the trash in the dumpster along the way. It's almost 7:00 pm. With my keys in hand, I swing my leg over my 1997 Heritage Softail Harley. The setting summer sun beats down on my back as I pull onto the street, ending the same as it began—hot. Figuring I should clean up a bit before heading to Nova's, I head home.

Thirty minutes later, I turn my bike down an old dirt road, lined with old pecan trees. I still find it hard to believe I pulled the trigger and bought a piece of land and a house. To be honest, staying in the States for as long as I have was never part of my plan. A couple of years at the least was how I imagined it would go after Riggs first offered me a haven. The cords in my neck tighten, thinking back at the reason I came to Louisiana in the first place.

To this day, I think about the part I unknowingly played in my birth father's underground empire. The fact that his sorry arse is still alive, in hiding makes my blood boil. We still can't figure out how he managed to give Riggs and his team the slip during the nightclub's takedown that night. A few days after all hell broke loose, the FEDs raided his office building and his penthouse.

Rolling to a stop, I park my bike and head toward the front door. The moment it opens, a happy howl from Chance greets me. "How ya doin', boy." Kneeling, I give him scratches behind his ears. His tongue flops out the side of his mouth. "Who's a good boy?" Standing, I slap the side of my leg and head for the kitchen. Chance may not have use of his back legs, but he keeps a steady pace at my side. Tossing my keys on the counter, I lift the lid of the treat jar, then throw a peanut butter dog biscuit in the air. Catching it, Chance follows me on my way to the bedroom. He totes his treat to his dog bed, where he hides it under an old flannel shirt he confiscated the first week I brought him home.

About two weeks of being alone in this house, I decided that what I needed was a dog. For the longest time, I laid my head at the clubhouse. For the years I've been in New Orleans, it was my home, and with the girls staying there and the other guys coming and going, I always had company.

Remembering the vet Piper worked for before leaving for college, I decided to swing by there first before hitting the local animal shelters. From what Piper mentioned in the past, Dr. Channing was always receiving strays. I chuckle to myself when I think back at all the times Piper tried talking Nova or one of the other guys into keeping yet another animal. Piper has the most caring heart. From the moment she started working at the clinic, Piper was on a mission. Birds, dogs, cats, turtles—you name it, she was determined to rescue them and find them all homes. Chance watches my every move as I strip from my sweat-soaked clothes.

Once Dr. Channing introduced Chance and me, I knew I was taking him home. It was him being paralyzed, which made finding him a forever home difficult. Few people were willing to adopt a dog with special needs. I don't understand why. Chance's disability doesn't seem to slow him down. His perseverance and lovable nature were all I saw, and I couldn't ask for a better friend to come home to at the end of the day.

Walking into my small bathroom, I reach into the shower, turning on the water. It doesn't take long for steam to fill the room, fogging up the mirror over the sink. Chance settles down on the bathroom rug as I step into the tub. It's hot as hell outside, but the heat from the water as it pelts my skin feels good and begins to relax my muscles. Why did I agree to dinner? Why this time, out of so many others, am I finding myself reluctant to sit at my brother's table? Maybe because ever since Piper walked through the door of the bar, all grown up, I've done nothing but think about her. Not once in my life have I been consumed with thoughts of a woman. And, as much as I keep telling myself Piper is a woman, I'm also conflicted with the fact I have watched her grow from a child into the woman she is now. Not to mention, first and foremost, Nova is my brother, making her off-limits. Beads of water roll down my face as I replay how Piper looked at me and how her body felt against mine during our embrace the other night. I swear nothing has ever felt so right. Rolling my head, I try to work out the tension in my neck and shoulders.

My Mum's words come to mind as I battle my emotions. *"Everyone's journey is different. Sometimes the road is long—sometimes it's not. Eventually, we end up where we are meant to be, and with the person we are destined to share our life with. Trust the journey, even when it doesn't go your way. Even when it hurts, the secret is never to give up."*

I feel my soul grasping at her words now more than ever. In a perfect world, wanting Piper and having her be mine would be as simple as taking a breath of air. But perfection is not my reality. Pursuing Piper has consequences. Forcing those thoughts aside, I finish with my shower, take care of a few house chores, then get on my bike and ride.

A short time later, I'm pulling up outside Nova's home. The smell of food cooking on the grill wafts in the air as I park my bike. Pocketing my keys, I stride toward the backside of the house where music and laughter are coming from. I find Nova manning the steaks on the grill, Promise sitting at the patio table beneath the umbrella with their son Jaxson bouncing on her lap, and Piper swimming laps in the pool Nova had put in a few months ago. I force myself to look away.

"Hey, brother. I was beginning to think you decide to skip out on us tonight." Nova spots me as I walk onto the deck. Reaching down, he flips open the cooler at his feet and lifts a cold beer from the ice.

"Since when have I turned down a free meal?" I smirk as Nova hands the longneck bottle to me. "Thanks, mate." I pop the top off with the ring on my finger and take a long swig.

"Kiwi," the sound of Piper calling my name has me turning my head. She waves at me, smiling as she emerges from the pool wearing a crimson red bikini, showing off all her curves. Snatching a towel from a lounge chair, she walks in my direction.

I swallow hard, trying like hell to keep my cool around my brother. "How's it going?" I answer Piper.

"I almost didn't think you were coming." Piper mimics what her dad just said, then plops down in a chair beside Promise. Her baby brother instantly reaches for her, and she gladly takes him.

"I had to swing by my house first."

Piper looks at me, and her jaw drops. "Did you say your house?"

I grin. "Sure did."

"You never mentioned you bought a house." She seems shocked, and maybe a little hurt by the fact I never told her about it. Not even when she came home to visit did I tell her about it. I mean, she's been wrapped up in college life. Buying a house is no big deal.

"I closed on it almost a month after you left for school," I tell her.

"How are the repairs comin' along?" Nova asks.

I take a drink of my beer. "Slow. I swear I don't know what I was thinking when I bid on the place." I keep stealing glances at Piper, my eyes drinking in the curves of her breasts.

"Piper, do you mind helping me with Jaxson while I set the table for dinner?" Promise asks. Piper, who is staring at me, tears her eyes away to answer.

"Sure," she gives Promise a weak smile. With her brother in her arms, Piper follows Promise inside.

Nova reaches for a tray sitting on the patio table. "I've been meaning to ask if you've checked in on the Thibodeaux brothers." He takes the perfectly cooked ribeyes off the grill.

"I gave the old man, by the way, his name is Otis, a call early this morning. He says there haven't been any signs of the assholes since the other day."

"Good." Then Nova chuckles. "That was the first time in my life I've seen a broken dick." He shakes his head and closes the grill lid. "Never want to see one again."

"The fucker reached for his gun. Since I was told not to kill him, I stomped the fucker on the dick." I chuckle a little myself.

"Well, the bastard is goin' to be pissing sideways for the rest of his life." With the tray in his hands, Nova turns toward the back door. "Grab us another beer." He walks inside and I follow behind.

The rest of the evening goes by smoother than expected. Although Piper and I exchange glances, the steady flow of conversation manages to distract others from noticing, or so I hope. I listen to her talk about campus life and her academic progress. When she speaks about her experiences so far, she does so with a genuine smile on her face. I haven't seen her this stress-free in a long time.

"So, Kiwi. I heard the club was opening a Kings Custom Bikes shop, and that you'll be running the place." Promise sways in her chair, soothing a very sleepy Jaxson. Piper looks my way again.

"That's fantastic news, Kiwi." Piper rises from her seat, rounds the table, and hugs my neck. I stiffen for a split second, then quickly relax. It's not like Piper hasn't hugged me before and in front of a club member. *Jesus, get a grip.* "I'm so happy for you." Piper releases my neck and sits in the empty chair beside me.

"I'm stoked. Riggs' realtor already found a few properties. We looked at them just the other day."

"Oh yeah?" Nova grabs a whiskey bottle from the center of the table and pours a couple of ounces into his glass. "What's the verdict?" he offers me a drink, but I decline. I don't plan on crashing at Nova's house tonight.

"We had the realtor put in an offer on the building down on Parker," I tell him.

"No, shit? That's the one right down the road from the youth center, right?" he asks.

"Yep. Since it used to be an old tire and oil change shop, the set up is perfect. All the paperwork is signed. Utilities are on already too, so we're ready to roll."

Promise stands. "Well, I'm going to lay this little guy down, run myself a bubble bath, and pour a glass of wine. Kiwi, I'll see you later," she smiles at me then exits the dining room.

"I'm gonna head out," I tell Nova.

"You can crash here if ya want," he offers, but I decline.

"Thanks, brother, but I have an early day tomorrow. I have to get shit rollin' at the shop. Believe it or not, we plan to open soon.

Hell, most of the shit we ordered for the place was purchased before we bought the building. In a few days, we should have everything we need to get going."

Nova pushes away from the table. "I think I'll go help my woman wash her back," he grins, "I'll catch ya later, brother. Stay safe."

6

PIPER

The bell over the door chimes and a teenage boy with shaggy hair and glasses walks into the clinic. I immediately know who it is. "Hi, are you Mathew?" I smile.

The boy freezes in place, and his cheeks turn a light shade of pink. Mathew gives an awkward wave. "Yeah, hi."

"Dr. Channing said you just started working here in the afternoons. I'm Piper and will be helping out for the summer."

"Uh, that's cool," he stutters. I find his shyness cute, and it causes my smile to widen.

"Well, I'm going to get out of your way." Standing, I grab my purse and step out from behind the reception counter. "It was nice meeting you, Mathew."

"Yeah, yeah, nice meeting you too."

Leaving Mathew, I make my way down the hall and to the back to find Dr. Channing in one of the exam rooms with an orange tabby cat and its owner Mrs. Howard. She's attempting to give the large cat his allergy shot, but the way the furry beast is hissing and batting its paws at my boss, he is not having any of that. "Need some help?" I ask, already setting my bag down on the counter next to the door.

"Yes, please. Thank you, Piper."

Walking up to the opposite side of the exam table, I gently clutch the cat who has now turned his murderous glare away from Dr. Channing and has his sight set on me. She uses the moment of distraction to give the cat his shot quickly and effectively. As soon as we finish, the feline's owner scoops the cat into her arms. "Did the big mean doctor hurt my baby?" the old woman coos. Dr. Channing and I share a look and roll our eyes at each other. Mrs. Howard is a seventy-something year old woman who is grumpy as the day is long. She also treats her cat better than she treats humans. I can't argue with that, though. Animals, in my opinion, are better than most humans.

"You can make your follow-up appointment with Mathew, Mrs. Howard," Dr. Channing addresses the woman.

"Yes, yes. I know the drill." Mrs. Howard ushers her cat inside his carrier and shuffles out the door.

"Thanks again for your help, Piper," Dr. Channing says. "I swear that cat has put on another five pounds since the last time he was here. And every time I mention the word diet, Mrs. Howard gives me the stink eye."

I chuckle. "Oh, yeah. He is bigger than I remember."

"Are you headed out for the day?"

I nod. "Yep. I'm heading out now. Oh, by the way, I met Mathew. He seems like a sweet kid."

"He is. I bet he blushed and stammered up a storm when he saw you. The boy gets all flustered around pretty girls. But I like him, and he's great with the animals."

Twenty minutes later, I pull up to the house and spot a familiar bike parked next to my dad's, and my tummy erupts with butterflies. When I walk through the front door, I see Promise sitting at the kitchen table feeding Jaxson, who is happily babbling in his highchair. "Hey, is dad around?"

"Yeah, him and Kiwi are out back."

Grabbing an apple from the fruit bowl on the kitchen counter, I take a bite and make my way out of the sliding glass door and across the backyard toward my dad's shed. Dad has been creating and selling blown glass art for years and is currently working on a piece when I step into the shed. My eyes sweep over to Tai, who is perched on a stool drinking a beer. My skin prickles at how his green eyes roam over my body and dilate as if he notices the effect he has on me. Tai quickly tears his focus away when my dad speaks. "Hey, baby girl. Good day at work?"

"Yeah. It was good. The usual," I shrug. "I uh, actually wanted to talk to you."

Dad stops what he's doing, places his tool down on the metal bench, wipes his sweaty brow with a bandana, then sticks it back in his pocket. "What's up, Bean?"

Tai doesn't make a move to leave. Honestly, this family and the club don't have any secrets. I toss my unfinished apple in the trash bin and rub my palm down my pant legs. "I've been thinking, and I have decided I want to see Madison. Do you think you can call or get Uncle Abel to call and get an all-clear for me?"

My mother is the old lady to the President of Hell's Punishers. Me being a part of The Kings, I would assume we need to get permission. I can't just show up at another clubs' compound.

Dad studies me for a beat. "Are you sure, Bean?"

I nod. "Yeah, I'm sure. It's time."

Dad strides over, stops in front of me, and kisses the top of my head. "I'll talk to my brother and get shit sorted. How about we plan for next weekend? I have some shit to handle for the club. We can roll out next Saturday mornin' since it's a bit of a drive."

I take a step back. "Dad, I kind of thought I could go on my own. Plus, I was hoping I could go tomorrow. I'm afraid I'll change my mind if I wait."

He shakes his head. "Absolutely not. We don't have beef with this club, but no way in hell am I sending my little girl out to another MC's territory alone. Not fuckin' happenin'."

"Dad, I'm not a little girl. I can handle it on my own. Besides, I need to do this for myself. You and Madison have a strained history. I don't want this visit to turn ugly."

"I will not budge on this, Piper. You either have me take you next week, or one of the brothers can take you tomorrow. Your choice."

I huff. "Fine."

Dad then turns to Tai. "Can you take Piper up north tomorrow? Fender and Everest have shit going on."

I go to open my mouth and protest, but Tai responds to my dad before I can. "No problem, brother. I got Piper."

My dad gives Tai a chin lift. "I'm going to head to the clubhouse and talk to Riggs. One of us will make a call and let Crow know you two are coming out tomorrow. Crow told me last year, Piper was welcome at any time, but I want to make sure her arrival runs smoothly."

As soon as dad walks out of the shed, I turn to Tai. "Listen, you don't have to take me. I can just wait until next weekend. I know the last thing you want is to babysit me."

Tai stands from his stool and strides across the shop, stopping directly in front of me. He's so close his chest nearly brushes against my breasts. My heart rate picks up as I tilt my head back and look up at his face. I watch as he runs his tongue over his bottom lip. "I'm taking you."

My breathing increases and I quickly realize I need to put some space between us, so I take two steps back. "Fine. Can you be here by seven in the morning? We can take my car."

"I can be here by seven, but we're not taking your car. Tomorrow you'll be on the back of my bike."

"Tai, I..." I go to protest only to have Tai eat up the space between us once again, and this time he leans down, putting his face a breath away from mine.

"Your gorgeous arse will be on the back of my bike."

"Tai," I breathe. His eyes drop to my mouth, and I lick my lips. His nostrils flare, and a heated look flashes across his face. My nipples harden to stiff peaks, and if he moves a single millimeter closer, he will feel the effect he is currently having on me. The moment between us lasts only a few seconds before Tai breaks away, leaving me feeling lightheaded and confused. I am once again left feeling like the attraction between us is one-sided.

"I'll be here at seven in the morning," he tosses over his shoulder as he walks out of the shed and away from me.

Later that night, after my shower, I'm sitting in my room in front of the mirror, trying to tie my hair into a braid when there is a knock on my door. My dad pokes his head inside. "Hey, Bean."

I turn and smile. "Hi."

He walks into the room and comes to stand behind me. He takes the brush from my hand. Neither of us speaks for several minutes as he goes about French braiding my hair. I close my eyes and enjoy the feel of his rough but gentle fingers as they work their magic. My dad is an expert at braiding. When I was a little girl, he took me down to the salon in town and had the lady who owned the place show him how. My big, tough, and rugged father didn't balk at learning how to take care of his little girl's hair. I wanted braids, so he had done whatever it took to learn.

"No matter how old I get, I will never get tired of this," I tell him.

"And it doesn't matter how old you get; you'll always be my little girl."

After tying a band at the end of the braid, dad sits on my bed, and I turn to face him.

"You understand why I can't have you going alone tomorrow?"

I get up and sit down beside him. "I understand. And I'm sorry I was a brat."

"You know you can turn around and leave at any time? If there is any moment you feel uncomfortable, or Madison makes you upset, tell Kiwi. I've already talked with Crow, and he assures me they will follow your lead."

I nod. "Okay."

"You sure you don't want me to come with you?"

"No. I need to do this without you. It's time I face my mother on my own."

"Alright, baby girl. You know the rules. Kiwi is always to stay with you. Though Crow has given me his word that you will be safe, I still need you to keep your guard up."

"I know, dad. I'll be careful. As you said, Kiwi will be with me the whole time."

"Have you thought about what you want to say to your mom?"

I sigh. "Honestly, no. I mean, there is the obvious question, like why, but other than that, I have no clue."

"Make sure you are doing this for you, Piper, and not her. You don't owe her anything."

"I'm doing it for me. It's like I'm stuck in limbo, you know? I need closure. We'll see after tomorrow. I'm not saying this visit will give me what I need, but I have to try."

Dad puts his arm around me, and I snuggle into his embrace. "I'm proud of you, Piper. Not just with the situation between you and your mother, but with school too."

"Thanks, dad." I kiss his cheek. "We've both come a long way, haven't we?"

"We sure have, Bean, and it's been one hell of a ride."

Dad stands, and I do the same. "Promise bought a movie for Jaxson. The damn thing has a fuckin' talking donkey. You up for a movie night? Don't make me sit through that shit alone."

I giggle. "Yeah. I'll watch it with you guys. And don't be trashing Shrek."

I don't think I got an hour of sleep last night. I was up before the sun and ended up watching Jaxson when he woke up at five, so that Promise could sleep in a bit longer. It's now a quarter to seven, and I'm sipping on a cup of coffee while sitting on the front porch as my brother happily plays with his toys beside me. The screen door creaks, drawing my attention. I look over my shoulder, to see Promise steps out of the house.

"Good morning, sweetheart."

"Morning."

Promise sits in the rocking chair beside mine. "Thanks for letting me sleep. Your dad usually gets up with Jaxson on the weekends, but he headed out early."

"Yeah, I heard him leave around four."

The two of us are quiet for a beat before Promise asks, "Where's your head this morning? How do you feel about today; about seeing Madison?"

I let out a deep sigh. "My head is good, but I am nervous. I still don't know what I'm going to say."

"I don't think you'll know what to say until you are face to face. You can't rehearse anything like that. All you can do is be honest with how you are feeling at that moment. There is no right or wrong here, Piper."

I look over at Promise when she reaches out and squeezes my hand.

"You're right. All I can do is take one step at a time."

A few minutes of silence pass before Promise speaks again. "Your dad said Kiwi was taking you today."

"He is," I say just before taking a sip of coffee.

"Do you want to talk about that?" Promise asks with a knowing look. I'm sure Promise is the only person who suspects I have feelings for Tai.

I shrug. "There's nothing to talk about."

Promise snorts. "This is me you are talking to, sweetheart. Your dad and the other guys might be oblivious to what is going on between you and Kiwi, but not me. That storm has been brewing for over a year; probably longer."

I look at Promise and shake my head. "There can never be anything between Tai and me. Not only would dad lose his shit, but Tai doesn't see me the way I see him. I'm sure he still sees me as a little girl. I thought at one time there was something between us, but..."

"What do you mean?" Promise asks.

I fidget with the cup in my hands. "A little over a year ago at the rally after that guy tried to attack me, Tai was comforting me. I misjudged a moment we shared. I thought he was going to kiss me. Nothing happened, though. All I did was embarrass myself."

"I don't know, Piper. I notice the way Kiwi looks at you. He most certainly doesn't look at you as a little kid."

Just as those words leave Promises' mouth, I hear the familiar rumble of a motorcycle making its way up the drive toward the house. A second later, Tai appears. Cutting the engine, he climbs off his bike and makes his way up the porch.

"Good morning, Kiwi," Promise greets him.

"Mornin'," he jerks his chin then trains his eyes on me. "Ready?"

I stand. "Yeah. Let me grab my bag." Turning, I make my way inside, drop my cup in the kitchen sink, and then grab my purse sitting on the table. I take a few deep breaths to calm my nerves before heading back outside. When I step back out on the porch, I can tell Tai and Promise were speaking, but both fall silent as soon as they see me. I decide not to ask any questions. Ignoring the weird tension, I stroll down the steps and wait for Tai to follow. When he does, I wordlessly hand him my bag to stow away. I chance a look at Promise, who now has a warm smile on her face. "You guys, be careful." I return her smile, and Tai nods.

After tucking my purse away, Tai grabs the spare helmet and proceeds to place it on my head. He's standing so close I can't help closing my eyes and breathing in his scent. He smells of laundry detergent, whatever cologne he wears, and motor oil.

"You good, babe?" he rasps in a low tone only I can hear once the helmet is secure. I open my eyes to find his green ones staring back at me.

My words get caught in my throat, so all I can do is nod.

Turning, Tai straddles his bike then holds his hand out for me to climb on behind him. Once I am on, I do my best to keep some space between us, only if it's an inch. Being on the back of his bike is torture. A friendly hug here and there is one thing, but being pressed against his body while on the back of his bike, is another. I don't miss the side glance he gives me or the way his jaw flexes with irritation just before he starts the bike. Thank god for the roar of the engine, or he'd hear how hard my heart is currently beating. How in the hell am I supposed to survive this long ride to North Louisiana?

We've been riding for what seems like hours, but in reality, it's only been forty minutes. Tai white-knuckles the handlebars to his bike, and I can feel how tightly wound his body is. I don't know what the hell his deal is but between my acting weird and his moody behavior, we are in for a long trip. Or so I thought until Tai flips his blinker and pulls into a gas station, parking beside a gas pump. As soon as he cut the engine, I climbed off and mumble, "I have to pee." I go to retrieve my purse from the saddlebag when suddenly Tai's hands are around my waist, and I'm spinning around to face him. I gasp when his knee pushes between my legs as he forces my back against his bike. I have no choice but to brace my hands on his chest as he cages me in. "What are you doing?" my question comes out breathless.

"I want you to stop what you're doin'."

I swallow. "I don't know what you're talking about."

"Don't play dumb. It's not a good look on you, Piper."

My lip curls up at his comment, and I push him away. "Look, I don't know what the hell your problem is. If you didn't want to make this trip, then you shouldn't have told my dad. The last thing I need today is you being an asshole." I walk away without waiting for his reply.

When I walk back out of the gas station, Tai is sitting on his bike, smoking a cigarette. I don't say anything as I swipe the helmet from the seat. Tai takes the helmet from me, grabs my hand, and brings me to stand beside him. "I'm sorry for being a dick. You have enough going on today, and me actin' like an arse doesn't help. Today we will focus on you and your mum. Later you and I are going to talk about this thing between us."

My breath catches in my throat. "Us? We don't have anything to talk about, Tai. I just want to get through today. After that, I'll make sure you're not tasked with being my keeper anymore." Tai chuckles, and the throaty rumble of his laugh sends a tingle straight to my core.

"There you go again, lying to yourself. That's okay, babe. You're going to see just how much of an 'us' there is."

The rest of the ride is done in a haze. I keep replaying what Tai said inside my head. I'm so confused. I've gotten signals crossed in the past when it comes to him and me. No way do I want to make that mistake again. It will only lead to heartache.

I'm so far lost inside my head that before I know it, we are pulling up to a large ten-foot iron gate. Tai brings his bike to a stop, and a young guy wearing a Prospect cut approaches us. The man is tall, slim, and has shaggy red hair. He gives Tai a once over then cuts his eyes to me. Suddenly my nerves pick up. I press myself further against Tai's back and clutch the front of his chest. Tai doesn't take his attention off the prospect, but he does give my thigh a reassuring squeeze.

Once the man sizes us up, he presses a code into the gate's keypad, and it opens. Tai rolls on through, and we park in front of the Hell's Punishers clubhouse. I look over my shoulder and see the prospect jogging up behind us.

With my nerves hitting me at full force, I climb off the bike onto shaky legs. Creep, the man who attacked me at the rally, was a member who belonged to this club. And even though Creep is long gone, just coming here makes me uneasy. No way my dad would have let me come here if he felt I wouldn't be safe. Luckily, Tai senses my mood and is at my side within seconds, wrapping his arm around my waist, pulling me close for support.

With our arrival, we draw several club members' attention as they pour out of the clubhouse. The first to greet us is the President and Madison's old man, Crow. As Crow starts striding in our direction, the prospect who was at the gate steps up to Tai. "I'm going to need your piece."

Tai pushes me behind him and stands to his full height, which is at least four inches taller than the redhead. "And I'm going to need you to fuck off."

"Prospect," Crow grinds out as he grabs the guy by the back of the neck, making him wince. "I suggest you get back to your post before I let my new friend put a bullet in your ass for disrespecting him and scarin' my old lady's daughter." The prospect pales as

Crow shoves him. The guy stumbles, barely catching himself. He doesn't spare Tai or me another glance as he tucks tail and scampers back toward the gate.

"Sorry about that. I'll deal with him later." Crow offers his hand to Tai.

"No worries, mate." Tai takes the President of the Hell's Punishers' hand.

Crow looks over Tai's shoulder at me. "Good to see ya again, Piper. Madison has been lookin' forward to your visit."

I give Crow a little wave but don't say anything.

"Why don't we go inside."

With a nod, Tai takes my hand in his, and we follow Crow into the clubhouse. Upon entering, I take in my surroundings. Their clubhouse is a bit different than The Kings'. There is a bar on the far-left side of the room, and to the right, there are two pool tables where a couple of club members are playing. There is also an area with a large flat screen tv surrounded by a leather sofa and two leather chairs. Occupying those chairs are a couple more guys with barely dressed women sitting on their laps. The one thing that stands out the most in a cool vintage-looking jukebox. When I bring my attention back to Crow, I see him no longer looking at me, but a woman standing just inside the opening of a hallway. My mother.

She looks a little unsure, but with Crow giving her a look of encouragement, she slowly makes her way toward us. Crow places his arm around Madison, and I notice the gentle way he handles her. It's so different from the way he interacts with his men. It reminds me of how my dad is with Promise and how Uncle Abel is toward Luna. There is no doubt of the love he has for her. I don't know how long the two of us stand here, staring at each other, but finally, Madison works up the nerve to speak. "I'm so happy you came, Piper. You'll never know how much this means to me."

I give her a small smile. "Thank you for agreeing to see me."

"Baby," Crow leans down and kisses Madison's temple. "Why don't you and Piper talk in my office? I'm sure you two would like some privacy."

Madison beams up at Crow then looks at me. "Would that be okay with you, Piper?"

"Sure, I'd like that." I turn to Tai. "Will you stay close by?"

Tai places his finger under my chin, "I'll be right here."

Madison leads me down the hall and into Crow's office. We both take a seat on the sofa. I can't get over how much I look like my mom. She is tall and has long wavy brown hair, much like mine was before I changed it.

"You look beautiful, Piper. The blonde is gorgeous, and it suits you."

I run a hand through my long locks. "Thank you."

The two of us fall silent again, both unsure of where to start. I rub my palms up and down the tops of my thighs.

"Piper, I want you to know you can ask me anything and I will answer as honestly as possible. I've made so many mistakes in my life, and I want to own up to them. You'll get no excuses from me. I will accept whatever today's outcome will be. Today is not about me; it's about you."

"I guess I want to know why. Why did you abandon me, and why did you stay away for so long?"

Madison lets out a heavy sigh. "When I found out I was pregnant with you, I knew I had to protect the precious gift given to me. Darkness surrounded me my entire life, Piper. I won't tell you the details of my childhood because it's the stuff of nightmares, but I will say I lived in the kind of dark that swallows you whole with no chance of clawing your way out. Your father and I didn't know each other that well. I was good at hiding my drug and alcohol addiction, and he was so busy with his path in life that he wouldn't have noticed. But when I found out about you, I knew that bringing you into this world would be my only chance at seeing the light. The day you were born was the only time I had ever felt what it was like to fall in love and be kissed by the sun. It didn't take long for the darkness to seep back in, and when it did, I did the only thing I knew to do. Had I not left you with your father, I would have dragged you down into the abyss with me, and there was no way I could let that happen. There was not a day that went by I didn't think about you, that I didn't long to hold you in my arms, to rock you to sleep at night, to watch you take your first steps, to wipe away your tears when you had a bad dream, to hold your hand on your first day of school, to comfort you through your first broken heart." Silent tears stream down my face as Madison continues. "I walked away because I love you, Piper. I stayed away because even when I got better, I knew I would never be worthy of your light. Until one day, I met a man who saved me. Crow saved me, and not only did he love me, but he taught me how to love myself. He made me realize that if I didn't at least try to mend things with you, I would regret it for the rest of my life. I hope that one day you can forgive me, Piper. There is nothing I want more than to have you in my life."

Wiping the tears from my face with the back of my hand, I croak, "I think I would like that too."

Scooting closer to me on the sofa, Madison puts her arms around me, and for the first time in nineteen years, my mother hugs me, and it feels incredible.

Over the next couple of hours, Madison and I talk about anything and everything. She tells me about when she met Crow, and I tell her about school. She asks me how my dad is doing and seems genuinely happy when I tell her about Promise and Jaxson. Soon, I look down at my watch and note the time. "Wow, I should probably get going."

"Do you and Kiwi want to stay for dinner?" Madison asks.

"I'd love to, but it's getting late, and we have a long drive. If it's okay with you, I'd like to call you and plan a day for me to come back, or you can come to New Orleans."

Madison beams at my suggestion. "Absolutely. I'll come to you next time."

"Great. Can I call you in a few days?" I ask.

"You can call me anytime, Piper. Even if it's just to say hi."

The two of us leave Crow's office and make our way out to the main room. I come to a dead stop when I see Tai sitting in one of the leather chairs talking to Crow and perched on the arm of the chair with her tits practically pressed up against his shoulder is one of Hell's Punishers club girls. I get a sickening feeling in the pit of my stomach at the image in front of me and the smile I have on my face vanishes.

"What's wrong, Piper?" Madison places her hand on my shoulder. She looks at me then to where my eyes fixate. Without a word, she marches over to where the guys are hanging and addresses the woman. "Sherrie, dinner is not going to cook itself. I suggest you hop to it."

At the sound of Madison barking orders, Tai twists in his seat to find me standing behind him. Not wanting to let on that what I just witnessed bothered me, I keep my features neutral and turn on my heels, walk across the room and out of the clubhouse.

7

KIWI

The instant Piper storms out of the Hell's Punishers clubhouse, I'm hot on her heels. The bright sun hitting my face blinds me as I burst through the door. Scanning the yard, I find her standing with her arms crossed beneath her breasts.

Loose gravel crunches under my boots as I stride in her direction. "Mind tellin' me what that go to hell look was all about?"

Lifting her chin, Piper turns her head, avoiding eye contact. "Nothing. Please take me home. I came here to see my mother, not for you to score with a Hell's Punishers' club girl," Piper sasses.

I try to hide my amusement, but a smile tugs at my lips. "You're jealous."

Piper gasps. "Of whom—her?" she points toward the clubhouse. "Please," she crosses her arms once more. "I'm not jealous of anyone. Who you sleep with is your business—not mine."

Invading her space, I cage her body between myself and my bike. Her scent invades my senses. Like always, she smells of jasmine and honey. It's intoxicating. Gripping her chin, I bring her face to mine. "I'm not fuckin' anyone, and Crow's club girl

60

doesn't mean a damn thing to me. There is only one woman I want."

The sun shines on Piper's face as she stares at me. The specks of gold around the irises in her beautiful hazel eyes hypnotize me and the way her skin glows, caused by the hot, humid air. "Who?"

"You," I confess, then lightly brush my lips against hers, before realizing what I am doing. Just as her body leans into mine, I step back and shake my head. "Shit. Piper, I'm sorry." Reluctantly, I walk away, leaving her standing next to my bike with a look of hurt and confusion on her face. *What the fuck was I thinking?* I can't keep giving her mixed signals. I can't keep hurting her.

With her taste still lingering on my lips, I push myself to continue putting distance between Piper and me. I acted on impulse—a knee jerk reaction to the emotions swirling in my gut to make her realize that I am blind to everyone but her. I wanted her to feel what I feel. I wanted her to know she is mine. I run my fingers through my messy hair as I stomp away.

I feel like I can do anything—be anything for Piper.

At the same time, she is my biggest weakness.

"Everything alright out here?" Crow's gravely voice catches my attention.

As I look at him, I notice his old lady walking toward Piper, who's eyes lock with mine. "Yeah, man. We're good." I offer him my hand. "Appreciate you for allowing us to pay a visit."

"No problem." Crow grips my hand. "Piper is welcome here anytime. It does me good to see them get to know each other. Madison is in a good place. Her sobriety is in a good place. Getting the chance to make amends with her daughter means the world to her—and me." Crow and I look on as mother and daughter embrace. It took Piper a long time to get here. Giving her mother a chance wasn't an easy choice for her to make. I can only hope her mum doesn't take the opportunity for granted.

Sensing it's time to go, I speak. "We're gonna head out. I have your number. As soon as I look into the parts, I'll give you an estimate on restoring that old Panhead," I tell Crow.

"Sounds good." He scratches his beard, nodding.

Shoving personal shit aside, I cross the yard, striding toward Piper, who has already settled onto the backseat of my bike. Madison pauses on her way past me, her hand touching my forearm. I stop and look down at her.

"Don't hurt her." Her eyes are soft, but her words are sharp and stern.

For a split second, it pisses me off. Where does she get off giving me a warning after the years of pain she inflicted on her daughter? Just as quickly, I let the anger go. She cares and is determined to show it now. That alone matters, and I give her credit for having the guts to say something to me. Instead of words, I respond with a tight nod. Satisfied, Madison walks off.

Once beside my bike, I look at Piper. With her eyes shielded, hidden behind sunglasses, she keeps her face forward, and her lips tight. Her body language is clear that this shit between us is far from over. That talk I mentioned before needs to happen sooner than later. I swing my legs over the bike, then slide my glasses over my head. "Let's go home," I tell her.

An hour into our ride, I need to make a pit stop, so we pull up to a truck stop gas station. "Bathroom break," I tell her after shutting off the engine.

"I'm good," she says, her words clipped.

"Either way, you're not sitting out here by yourself. Let's go," I tell her and hold out my hand. I would never leave a woman alone, to begin with, but after the trouble she experienced on her way home several days ago, I sure as shit won't take any chances. This truck stop is crawling with men. Not to say all men are seedy, but you can't trust anyone either. Not giving me any lip, Piper allows me to help her off the back of the bike. Keeping hold of her hand, we walk together into the store. Several sets of eyes fall on us as we make our way to the back of the building where the restrooms and trucker showers are located. Good. I need them to notice Piper is with me. "Wait here," I tell her, and she leans against the wall in the hallway, still not saying a word. Her silence pains me, but I can't fault her for it.

Finished taking care of business, I walk out to find Piper missing. Just as I'm about to lose my shit, she walks out of the women's restroom. She's pushed her sunglasses to rest on top of her head. Her eyes lock with mine. Her small smile instantly relaxes me, and I smile back. "We good?"

"Yeah," she says.

"Let's get back on the road. You thirsty?"

"I could use some water," Piper concedes, and I snatch one from the refrigerated section, along with a sports drink for myself.

Once at the counter, a display case sitting near the cash register, with heart-shaped keychains, catches my eye. I reach into my pocket, retrieving my wallet. "Let me have one of those, too," I gesture to the case. The guy behind the counter unlocks it and plucks one from where it hangs. I smile and hand the cashier some cash, and he slides back my change. I don't know why I buy these damn things. Maybe it's something I picked up from my mum. She was always buying small souvenirs from her travels or places we went on family vacations. Shoving my wallet into my back pocket, I turn, handing the metal heart to Piper.

She looks at it, then smiles. Damn, I fuckin live to see her smile. "It's pretty." She moves her hand in the sunlight, watching the colors shift from gold, blue then to purple.

"Thank you, Tai." Her lashes flutter against her cheeks as she stares at it.

Grabbing her hand again, in mine, we step out into the scorching summer heat. Taking a moment, the two of us down our drinks. Just as we are mounting the bike, my phone rings. Pulling it from my pocket, I answer the call. The owner of the Harley sitting in my barn, who is a good friend of Wick's, is in town and wants to swing by to pick it up. After talking with him briefly, I hang up and slide my phone back into my cut. I look over my shoulder before starting the engine. "Mind if we make a quick stop by my place before taking you home?"

"Are you kidding?" Piper squirms, adjusting herself on the seat. "I've been dying to see your place since you mentioned it the other night."

Forty-five minutes later, I steer my bike down the long dirt road leading to my house. Piper slides forward, and her breasts press against my back. My cock swells against the zipper of my jeans from the warmth of her body. She speaks close to my ear. "Oh my God, Tai. You bought a farmhouse." I don't answer. Instead, I enjoy the feel of her body close to mine until rolling to a stop. I help her off the bike. Her eyes light up. "You bought old lady Ruth's place?"

"It's not much, and needs a shit ton of work done to it, but it's home," I tell her as I park and we climb off my bike. "Come on. I'll give the grand tour." Piper follows me up the steps onto the porch. "Watch your step. Most of these boards need replacing," I warn her as I unlock the front door. Immediately I hear the clatter of Chance's toenails, tapping against the wood floors as he moves towards us.

"Chance!" Piper says with shock, then kneels to the floor. Chance throws his head back in a howl, just before he's lapping at Piper's face. "You are the guy who adopted Chance?" She scratches his head. Chance flops to the floor and rolls over to his back, waiting for belly rubs, which Piper is happy to oblige.

"Hey," I jest. "Where is my welcome home?" Chance cocks his head and looks at me, as Piper continues to love on him. I laugh. "Traitor."

Standing, Piper takes a few steps in my direction, then wraps her arms around my waist. "Thank you."

"For what?" I hug her back.

"For giving Chance a forever home. I watched people pass him by so many times while working for Dr. Channing. It broke my heart." She finally releases me, and I let my arms fall to my sides. "Okay. Show me the rest of the house." Piper smiles.

It takes all of ten minutes to walk her through the whole house. "Come on. I need to push the guy's bike out of the barn. Wick is driving him out this way, and is due to arrive at any moment." On our way to the barn, Piper spots the goat pen.

She throws her head back, laughing. "You have goats too?" She runs to the wooden fence, and the goats flock to her, making their usual goat noises.

"Yeah," I rub the back of my neck. "Unfortunately, they came with the place. It turns out, the old lady used to sell goat milk products, like cheese and soaps."

"I think I remember seeing Mrs. Ruth at the county fairs selling her stuff." Reaching over the fence, Piper pets them. "What are their names?"

"Beats me," I tell her. "I don't even know what to do with them. I was thinking of sellin' them or something."

Piper looks at me. "This is their home, Tai." Then she turns her attention back to the babbling goats. "Don't sell them."

With a smile on my face, I sigh. "I'll think about it." Shit. Only for Piper would I keep the damn things around, so that I could watch her fuss over them like she is now.

I pull open the heavy barn doors. Inside, I lift the tarp covering the motorcycle. Cranking her up, I let the bike sit and idle for a few minutes. Piper walks in, holding Tom, the yellow tabby cat that apparently came with the place too. "I see you've met Tom."

Piper nuzzles his face against hers, and the fat shit eats the affection up. "He's a sweetheart. Did you adopt him too?"

"Naw. I think he belonged to the old lady. He keeps me

company when I'm out here working, and Chance doesn't seem to mind him either."

Looking around, Piper spots a small wooden stool nearby and sits. Tom jumps from her arms, slinks my way, and rubs his side against my leg. Piper props her elbows on her knees and rests her chin onto her knuckles. She watches me as I take a cloth and wipe down the bike, making sure I don't leave any grease marks on the paint or chrome.

I cut the engine. The air in the barn feels heavier than usual. When I look at Piper, she's chewing on her lip. "Piper, we need to talk."

"I agree." Piper stands, slowly walking toward me. "You're giving me whiplash, Tai. One minute I think you want me—the next..." her words trail off.

"Piper," I swallow hard when her fingertips trail up my arm. "You have no idea how bad I want you."

"I want you too," she confesses.

"Shit," I whisper, leaning my forehead against hers. "I wish it were that simple." I thread my fingers through her hair, gripping the back of her head.

Piper's finger grips my biceps. "It is."

"No, babe. It isn't."

Piper's grip tightens. She's smart and, without me saying it, knows what is at stake if we pursue this. "What do you want more, Tai?"

I know what she's asking.

Closing my eyes, I fight like hell not to kiss her. In the end, I'll have to choose between her and the club—between her and my brother. "You Piper, so much it scares the fuck out of me. Yet, here I am, wanting you anyway."

The sound of a vehicle approaching pulls us apart. Looking past her shoulder, I watch as Wick's truck comes into view. He rolls the vehicle to a stop in front of the barn. Wick and Sean step out of the truck and make their way toward me.

"Sean," I extend my hand, gripping his. "Good to see ya again, mate."

"You too, man." He walks over to his bike and whistles. "Damn. It looks great." Sean admires my work.

"Hey, brother," Wick greets me, then looks at Piper. "Hey there, sweetheart." His big arms incase her, kissing the top of her head. "How'd the visit with your mom go?"

"Better than I hoped," Piper tells him.

"That's good to hear," Wick says. "Listen," he faces me. "Sean plans on riding his bike out of here, so I'm gonna head back to the bar before the delivery guy arrives. They were three cases short last time, and I want to make sure some of our merchandise hasn't fallen off the truck if ya get what I mean."

I nod. "No worries, mate. You run into any problems, give me a call," I tell Wick as he heads for his truck.

"Hey, Uncle Malik, wait up," Piper calls out. "Can I catch a ride back with you?" Piper looks back at me. It feels like she's running away, and I have a sudden urge to grab her, kiss her hard, and tell her to stay. Wick watches on, his truck door hanging open as he waits to see what Piper wants to do. Piper gives me a small smile before jogging toward my brother's truck and climbing into the passenger seat.

I watch them drive away. "It's for the best," I mumble to myself. I need to stop this shit before it goes too far. I need to make myself not fall for my brother's daughter. I should prevent myself from falling for a woman I shouldn't want and can't have.

The truth is, Piper is under my skin.

Every thought I have of her is a battle—a war I struggle to win with myself. Sometimes it takes a good fall to know where you stand in life. Piper undeniably will be my downfall.

8

PIPER

It's late afternoon, and instead of heading home for the day after leaving the clinic, I decided to swing by the clubhouse and hang with my dad, Uncle Abel, and the rest of the guys. Promise is in court, so that means Jaxson is here with dad and currently playing with Payton and Josie out back. Payton and Josie have been with the club for as long as I can remember, but the truth is, I don't see them as club girls; they are family. Josie and Payton have been like sisters to me. I'm not naive; I know what they are to the men in the club, but since the guys have started settling down with women and families of their own, Payton and Josie's positions with the club have changed. They are simply a part of the family.

"Your dad tells me you're workin' at the clinic with Dr. Channing again this summer. I figured you'd want to take a break and chill while you're home," Uncle Abel says, sitting across from me with his feet kicked up on the coffee table. Uncle Malik is sitting at the bar with Tequila, and Fender is kicked back on the sofa with my dad. I look at Uncle Abel and shrug. "It doesn't really feel like work when you're doing something you love."

"Shit," Uncle Malik shakes his head. "When the hell did you

grow up? Most kids your age are off partying it up at the beach and gettin' lit with their friends. Fuck, that's what I'd be doin'."

"Don't fuckin' encourage her, asshole," dad flicks his bottle cap across the room, hitting Uncle Malik in the chest, and I chuckle. That's also the same time the door to the clubhouse opens, and Tai strolls in. I have been avoiding him since I fled his house the other day. I was done hearing his I want you but can't have you speech. Looking up, I take in his black t-shirt stretched tight across his broad chest, and the way his faded blue jeans sit low on his waist and hug his ass in the most drool-worthy way. *Stop it, Piper. Get a grip.*

Tearing my eyes away from Tai, I pretend to be engrossed with the movie playing on the muted tv screen while listening to the conversation between him and the guys.

"I thought you were supposed to meet with the realtor this afternoon," Uncle Abel asks Tai.

"I'm meetin' with her in an hour to go over some extra paperwork and tie up some loose ends that were holdin' us up with the previous owner. I saw the bikes out front and figured I'd come to have a beer before I do. What was you all goin' on about when I came in?" Tai takes a seat at the bar beside Tequila, who answers his question. "Not much, just kickin' it with Piper. What about you? I hear congratulations are in order. The club is opening another Kings Custom, and Jake has asked you to head it up."

"I'm fuckin' stoked for you, brother," Fender adds.

Over the next several minutes, the guys sit around and discuss all the details about opening the garage. And while they are going on about that, my phone chimes with an incoming text.

Colton: Hi.

Me: Hey.

Colton: I heard you were home for the summer.

Me: How did you hear that?

Colton was my high school boyfriend. We dated for about a year but ended things after graduation. He knew he was going off to college in Florida, and neither of us wanted to attempt a long-distance relationship. Besides, I was never as serious about Colton as he was about me. Sure, he's great looking and treated me well, but our relationship lacked something. There were no butterflies, no spark.

Colton: I'd like to see you. How about dinner?

I ponder his invitation for a moment then decide what the hell. It would be nice to catch up.

Me: Sure, dinner sounds fun. When?

Colton: How about Leon's in an hour?

Me: Perfect. I'll see you there in an hour.

Colton: Great! Can't wait to see you.

I smile and tuck my phone away in my purse. When I look up, my dad's eyes are on me. "Everything okay, Bean?"

"Yeah. That was Colton. He heard I was home for the summer and asked if I wanted to have dinner with him."

"For what? Please don't tell me that little prick wants you back."

I roll my eyes. "Colton is not a prick. And no, we are not getting back together. He goes to school in Florida now. He just wants to catch up."

"Catch up my arse," Tai mutters underneath his breath, but I pretend I didn't hear him.

"I met the guy a couple of times," Tequila jumps in to defend. "And he seemed pretty cool. Does he still play baseball?" she asks.

"Yeah, he got a full-ride playing for Florida."

"I don't care how nice or how talented the kid is, nobody is good enough for my baby girl," dad declares vehemently.

"Come on now, brother," Fender chuckles. "Some asshat is bound to catch Piper's attention eventually or vice versa. Face it, man, your daughter is a knockout. And I mean that in the most respectful way. Just puttin' that out there before you decide to kick my ass. Piper is like a sister to me."

"You're lucky, cause that's the only thing keepin' me from puttin' my foot up to your ass, brother."

"Dad," I groan. "Please stop," I plead, my cheeks heating from embarrassment. "There is no way I am discussing my current love life or future one with you or any of the guys."

"Fuck me," my dad growls, placing his head in his hands. "Jesus Christ, please tell me my little girl did not just say the words love life."

"Alright, then." I stand abruptly and swing my purse over my shoulder. "This conversation is officially over. I have a dinner date to get to." I walk over to my dad, lean down, and kiss his cheek. "I'll see you at home later."

"Yeah, yeah. Love you, Bean."

"Love you too, dad."

As I go to leave the clubhouse, I chance a glance at Tai, who is still perched on a stool at the bar and notice the intense grip he has on the beer bottle in his hand and the way he's grinding his teeth as he watches me walk away. I also don't miss the way Tequila takes in the weird tension ping-ponging between us just before she elbows him in the side, gives him a strange look, then says something to him. And though I'm curious about what she said, I look away and walk out of the clubhouse.

When I arrive at Leon's, Colton is standing outside on the sidewalk in front of the dinner. Leon's was a staple during my high school days. All the kids came here to hang out after school to grab a burger and fries.

As I'm climbing out of my car, Colton gives me a huge grin. "Damn, look at you. What's with the new look? Not that I am complaining because it's hot."

"I just felt like a change," I smile, giving him a side hug.

"Blonde suits you. Really, Piper, you look great."

"Thank you."

"Shall we." Colton pulls open the door to the dinner and motions for me to step inside in front of him? As soon as the bell alerts our arrival, Betty, a waitress who has worked at Leon's for as long as I can remember, walks out from the back. "Well, look at what the cat dragged in. How ya doin' girly?"

"I'm good, Betty. How about you?"

"Oh, you know how it is. Nothing ever changes around here. Same shit, different day. You two want to sit at the counter, or do you want a booth?"

"Booth," Colton answers.

Betty shows us to a booth. I sit on one side while Colton slides into the seat across from me.

"You two need a menu, or do you already know what you want?" Betty asks.

"I'll have a cheeseburger with fries, and water."

"You got it darlin'. How about you, Colton?"

"I'll have the same as Piper but add a slice of apple pie to my order."

"Okay. Give me a few minutes, and I'll have that out to you."

"So," Colton starts once we are alone, "how have you been? Texas treating you okay?"

I look across the table and take in my ex-boyfriend. With his brown hair and blue eyes, he really is a handsome guy. "Things are good, and I like Texas. It's not like being home, but I like it well enough. What about you? How's Florida? Baseball going okay?"

"Baseball is great. The guys on the team have been welcoming. All in all, I can't complain. I miss New Orleans, though, and my friends. Moving away has been weird, you know?"

I nod. "Yeah, I get it."

Colton and I continue to make idle chit chat, and before I know it, Betty returns with our food. A moment later, movement over my shoulder catches Colton's attention. "Isn't that one of the guys from your dad's club?"

I turn in my seat just as Tai steps into the dinner. Quickly, I turn back around in hopes that he will not see me sitting here. I have no such luck because about five seconds later, a pair of black boots come into view, stopping right next to the booth I'm sitting in. Slowly my eyes travel up, landing on Tai's face as he towers above me.

"Is there something you needed, Kiwi?" A look of irritation briefly flashes across his face when I use his road name. Ever since the rally incident, I started calling him Tai, but I only do that when we are alone. If I began saying Tai instead of Kiwi in front of the guys, I'm afraid it would raise speculation.

I wait for Tai to answer me, but Betty interrupts. "Hey Kiwi, you joinin' Piper and her friend for lunch? Want me to bring your usual?"

"Yeah, doll. The usual sounds great."

Without another word, Tai drops down into the booth beside me, giving me no choice but to scoot over and make room for him. What the hell is he playing at here?

"Uh, you know, Kiwi, I'm kind of in the middle of something here," I jerk my head toward Colton.

Draping his arm over the back of the booth behind my head, Tai looks at me long and hard. "You don't mind if I join you two, do you, Curtis?" he asks, not bothering to take his eyes off me.

"Uh, sure. No problem, man. And the name is Colton."

"You see, babe. Curtis here doesn't mind at all," Kiwi says purposely calling my ex by the wrong name and it's pissing me off.

A few beats of uncomfortable silence pass before Colton speaks again. I know he doesn't know what to think of Tai imposing on our non-date, but he's also not dumb enough to say anything.

"So, I'm going to be in town for another two weeks, and I'd like to spend more time with you. Some of the old gang is getting together next Saturday and spending the weekend in Biloxi. Do you want to go? I can pick you up..."

"No," Tai grinds out, cutting Colton off mid-sentence, shocking me.

What the hell is he doing?

"Since when do you speak for me, Kiwi? Is there a memo I missed stating that you're suddenly my keeper?"

"No memo, babe. That's just the way it is."

I can feel my blood start to boil. "Have you lost your mind?" I hold up my hand. "You know what, don't answer that." Turning my attention back to Colton, whose eyes dart between Tai and me, I tell him, "I'd love to go. What time..."

This time I'm the one who is cut off when I'm abruptly pulled from the booth by Tai, then dragged across the dinner and down the hallway that leads to the back. Pulling me into the woman's bathroom, Tai flips the lock and presses my back against the door, caging me in. His nostrils flare. "You're fuckin' playin' with fire, Piper."

I narrow my eyes on him. "I don't know what you're talking about, Kiwi."

He slams his palm against the door above my head. "Stop callin' me that. To you, I am Tai, and you fuckin' know it."

"What the hell does it matter what I call you?" I hold my breath, thinking Tai will finally pursue this spark between us, but when he doesn't answer, I shake my head. I try to step away from him. Only his next question causes me to freeze.

"You fuck him?"

Shocked by his intrusive question, I gasp. "What?"

"Last year, when you two were together, did you fuck him?"

"That's none of your goddamn business."

"Answer the fuckin' question. Did. You. Fuck. Him?" Tai growls out each word.

If Tai thinks he can bully me into answering his question, he has another thing coming. "Do you really want me to tell you about all the things Colton and I did with each other? How about I tell you about the times I sucked his cock. Hmm? Oh, I know. You want me to describe in detail how he used to go down on me?" I smirk. "Wait, that wasn't what you asked, was it? Well, to answer your question, no, we haven't fucked."

By the time I finish my rant, my heart feels like it is about to beat out of my chest. It's not like me to be so crass or even this blunt. But the way Tai came into the dinner, took over my date, then went full-on caveman here in the woman's bathroom, brought it out of me. I'm sick of the mixed signals and tired of the back and forth. And by the set line in Tai's jaw and the murderous look in his eyes, I might have made a mistake with my little confession. Even I can admit I probably went a bit too far.

"Are we done? I want to get back out there before Colton starts to worry I ditched him."

"No, babe. We are far from fuckin' done. In fact, we are just gettin' started."

Before I have time to process his words, Tai's mouth comes crashing down on mine. His lips are soft but demanding as his tongue traces the seam of my mouth. I open, granting him access. Tai doesn't hold back, and neither do I as I take what I have wanted for so long. His kiss is everything I imagined it would be, stealing my breath away, yet breathing life back into me, all at the same time. Tai pulls away and rests his forehead against mine. His chest rises and falls with his rapid breathing, and my body starts to tremble. I wait with bated breath for him to say something, anything. And just as he is about to, there is a knock on the bathroom door followed by Colton's voice.

"Piper, are you in there? Is everything okay?"

Tai growls deep in his chest.

On shaky legs, I turn and flip the lock on the bathroom door.

Tai takes a step back, allowing me to pull it open. Colton is standing there with a concerned look on his face. He takes in my appearance then flicks his gaze to the man standing behind me, then back to my face. I watch a light bulb go off in his head, and the situation once again turns awkward. Luckily, Colton handles it well. "I, uh, just wanted to tell you that something came up and I have to go. I paid the check already."

"Thank you, Colton. It was nice catching up."

"It was good to see you too, Piper." Colton gives me a warm smile then looks over my shoulder to Tai, giving him a nod before walking away.

Turning back to Tai, I open and close my mouth several times, but no words come out. Taking a deep breath, I go to speak the same moment his cell rings. Pulling it from the inside of his cut, he answers, "Yeah?" I watch as Tai listens to whoever speaks on the other end. "Alright, brother. I'll be there in ten."

Pocketing his phone, Tai takes a step forward, invading my space once again. Placing his finger beneath my chin, he brings my eyes to his. "This isn't over." Then lightly brushes his lips against mine before disappearing out the door, leaving me to wonder what the hell just happened.

9

KIWI

I storm out of the fucking dinner ready to murder someone and to kick my own arse for yet again losing control. I may have crossed a line just a little, but right now, I don't give a shit. The moment Piper mentioned seeing her ex, I saw red. The instant I stepped into the dinner and saw her smiling at him, it further infuriated my already agitated state of mind. Jealousy is an emotion I'm not used to feeling, and I'm not too fond of it. It makes me want to mark Piper, tell the world, and every fucking swinging dick within a one-hundred-mile radius, she is mine. Especially, after that shit she hurled at me about her and that fucking tool. It's my own damn fault for asking if she had fucked him. I have no right being jealous. Yet here I am, fighting a losing battle.

Standing beside my bike, I pull my phone from my pocket and shoot a text to Fender.

Me: Give me a hand at the garage

While waiting for his reply, Piper exits the building. I drink her in as she moves across the lot to her car. She spots me looking her way as she opens her door. If looks could kill, I would be a dead man. Damn, she is fighting mad, and it's sexy as hell. I have a hard-on for that hot sassy mouth of hers. I saw a side of her I have never seen before today. She was fierce—a force to be reckoned with. To be truthful, Piper had every right to chew me out the way she did. Despite my actions and the fact I was a complete arse, I don't regret it. The taste of her kiss is burned on my lips forever. No way in hell would I take it back. I'm hooked, and like an addict, I want more—so much more. In those few brief seconds, I felt so fucking high no one could touch me. Then I had to get a fucking phone call. One I couldn't ignore. A shipment the club was expecting three days ago just arrived. The new shop opens tomorrow, and the items on that delivery are crucial to running the hydraulic lifts in the garage.

My phone vibrates in my hand.

Fender: Now?

Me: Yeah

Fender: You got it.

Mounting my bike, I peel out of the parking lot, putting distance between Piper and me. As hard as I try, my self-control is damn near nonexistent when I'm near her. I need to rein in my emotions. If Piper's ex-boyfriend notices something between her and me, I'm doing a piss ass job of hiding my feelings for her. There's a lot of shit the club and my brothers will overlook, but pursuing Piper isn't one of them. The club means a lot to me. Riggs and the others have given me a home away from home. Much of who I am lies with being a Kings of Retribution member. Like my parents and siblings back in New Zealand, Riggs, Nova, Wick, Fender, and Everest are family. As much as I know I mean the same to them, I don't think Nova would look the other way when it comes to his daughter. In his eyes, not a single man could ever be good enough for Piper. If she were to get involved with a biker, he would be livid. Let that biker be me—his brother, he will flip his shit.

Piper is right. I can't keep giving her mixed signals. One minute I'm pushing her away, keeping my distance. The next, I'm pressing my lips against hers to make sure some dipshit kid knows she belongs to me. I've fallen so fucking hard for that woman. The struggle to do what is right for the club's sake has me all fucked in the head.

Before I realize how fast I'm going, I fly past a cop car. He lights me up, and I slow, pulling the bike to the side of the road. *Great.* In my side mirror, I watch the cop's driver door swing open. Jesus. Officer Roberts strolls his smirking ass my way. His partner, who I recognize right away as officer Andrews, steps out of the passenger door but hangs back a couple of yards. We have a good relationship with several of New Orleans's finest, and usually don't have any issues dealing with them. But this one? He's fresh out of the academy, and a cocky arse son of a bitch. Roberts stops a good three feet at my right side.

I slide my shades to the top of my head and look at him, waiting for him to speak first. You can tell the man works out. Probably all he does in his spare time, but his stature doesn't intimate me. "You bikers seem to think you own this city and don't need to heed the speed limits or any laws for that matter." Roberts rests his hand on top of his weapon attached to his side and taps his finger against it. "Clocked you doing sixty in a forty-five."

I don't have time for his shit.

"Just give me the damn ticket, Roberts." My words are sharp with irritation.

"Watch the attitude," Roberts pops off, and it hits a nerve.

"Look," I say in the most polite even tone I can muster, "You're still relatively new around here, so I'm going to overlook the fact that you feel the need to compare dick sizes with that arrogant act you have goin' on at the moment, but let me assure you, mine's bigger."

"Are you trying to intimidate me?" Officer Roberts takes a slight step forward.

"Roberts," his patrol partner, finally steps in.

Gritting his teeth, Roberts moves past his hurt ego. "License and insurance," he asks, and I lean forward to retrieve my wallet out of my back pocket. He takes my credentials and walks to his car. The asshole proceeds to sit in his car for several minutes, while Andrews leans against the side of their patrol car, his head ducked in the window, looking as if he's giving his rookie a stern talking. Finally, Roberts returns, handing me my license, insurance card, and a ticket.

"We done here?" I shove everything into my wallet.

Roberts looks pained when he says, "You're free to go."

I wait until both officers are safely in the patrol car before merging into traffic.

Ten minutes later, I'm pulling up to the garage, where Fender already has the bay door open. "Hey, brother."

"Sorry for the holdup." I walk over to the fridge toward the back of the garage, open the door, and snatch a cold beer from inside. I down damn near the entire bottle while I stand there.

"What has you fired up?" Fender asks, eyeing me as I stride toward him.

"Nothin'." My short answer leaves him staring at me a little too long. "What?" I ask.

Fender leans back against the shop wall, folding his arms across his chest. "This wouldn't have anything to do with a woman, would it?" My eyes cut back at him, and I scoff. Downing what little is still in the bottle, I toss it into the trash.

"No."

"Lie to someone else, brother." Ignoring him, I stare out into the empty street, as he continues. "Ever since Piper has been back, you haven't been your usual laid back, I don't give two shits self."

My jaw clenches, but I remain quiet. "I've caught the way you look at each other."

"It's nothing," I tell him.

"I don't think it's nothin', brother. I think you two have caught feelings for one another." When he gets no response, he adds, "Now, I'm not one to dish out lectures and shit, or tell someone how to live their life, but this is Piper we're talkin' about here."

"Don't you think I know that?"

Out the corner of my eye, I see Fender nod. "You need to figure this shit out and fast. It's only a matter of time before Nova finds out. When he does..."

Before he can finish his sentence and continue to dig the knife any deeper, I cut him off. "Either way, I'm screwed." My tone almost sounds defeated.

The delivery truck finally arrives and starts backing up to the bay door. Fender's hand clasps my shoulder. "Listen, man. I know you're strugglin'. I'm speaking to you as your friend, and from experience when I say love makes you do crazy shit. I wish I had the answers for you or some meaningful words of wisdom to help you, brother. Just know, my mouth is shut. This conversation stays and dies here between us."

The sky is clear, and the sun is hot over Crescent City today. It's nearly noon, and the parking lot is alive with music and people in the community coming out to show their support for the grand opening of Kings Custom. The smell of smoked B.B.Q. and spicy Cajun crawfish permeates the air. Near the shop entrance, Riggs has a canopy set up with misting fans, tables, and chairs for those seeking refuge from the heat of summer. Inside, the women are selling Kings Custom merchandise.

"I'd say things are getting off to a good start." Everest stops beside me, then takes a bite off the burger in his hand. Off to my right, I briefly let my eyes settle on Piper, who's scooping ice cream onto cones for several kids waiting for a cold treat. I quickly divert my attention as my brothers, Wick, Nova, and Riggs, make their way over.

"The turnout is amazing," I face Everest. "I appreciate you gettin' the kids down at the youth center involved."

"They're a good group of kids," Everest states, just as a BMW pulls into the parking lot. Promise's friend, London, climbs out of the car. Everest hones in on her as she sashays in our direction.

"Wow. You got yourselves a little block party going." She blatantly lets her eyes roam over Everest, who stands there wordless. London turns toward me. Digging in the large bag she has draped over her shoulder, she pulls out a whiskey bottle. "Congratulations." She hands me the bottle.

Above the music and people, a guttural rumble echoes through the city streets, reverberating off the nearby buildings. It's the sound only a Harley can make. The ground beneath our feet vibrates the closer it gets. "Fuck yeah!" Riggs booms with excitement. "They made it."

"They?" I ask.

"Our Montana brothers." Riggs slaps my back.

"No, shit?" All The Kings of Retribution in one place?" My brothers begin to holler, their voices booming as they welcome the Montana Chapter to our city, and I join them. Faces in the crowd turn to see what the commotion is all about as the roar of straight pipes closes in. Onlookers part, as all the men, along with their old ladies, ride their bikes into the parking lot.

Luna, Promise, and Tequila have joined us. "Looks like there's gonna be one hell of a party tonight," Tequila cheers.

"Holy shit. Whatever is in the Montana water is magical. Those men are F.I.N.E, fine." London fans herself. "Damn, and they're all taken. Figures." Her statement causes us to laugh—all except Everest. London notices and smirks.

One by one, our brothers dismount their bikes. Greetings are passed around amongst the men, and the women introduce themselves to one another. "Laisses le bon temps rouler," Riggs calls out. He and Jake shake hands. "Fuckin' glad you're here, brother."

"Wouldn't have missed it."

Once the crowd is gone, and the shop is locked up, we ride out toward the clubhouse. The feeling of riding alongside all my brothers helps to distract me from my thoughts of Piper. The smell of exhaust fumes mixed with smoke pits cooking meat from the restaurants as we pass them by fill the air as it whips at my face. Faces in the crowds along the sidewalks all blur together as we ride. I lose myself in the white noise as twelve Harleys make their way through the streets of New Orleans. The closer we get to the clubhouse, the air changes. It's the smell of the mighty Mississippi River that flows nearby. The gate opens, and we roll onto the compound, parking the bikes in a row.

Hours later, the clubhouse smells of smoke and whiskey. Music and laughter fill the air as I sit toward the back of the room, on a black leather sofa, alone, watching everyone have a good time.

"What are you over here sulking about?" Josie plops down beside me as I nurse the beer in my hand.

"I'm not sulking," I lie. I am sitting here, brooding. I was a dick earlier ignoring Piper, and I'm feeling like an arse for it. But what choices do I have? I need to stick to my guns and steer clear of her.

"Come on. Enjoy yourself. Look at the place." She spreads her arms, and as she continues to talk, my eyes follow Piper as she moves across the room. "When will this, all The Kings of Retribution being under the same roof, happen again?"

Before I even choose to respond, Fender waves me over, shouting above the noise. "Kiwi, bring your ass over here."

Standing, I join Fender, who is sitting with the guys, and I pull a chair over to the large round table. "What were ya doing way over there, alone?" Everest asks.

"I was takin' a breather." A pack of smokes sits in the center of the table, next to a half-empty bottle of Jamison. Reaching out, I pluck one from the box. Striking the lighter, I light the cigarette and breathe in the nicotine until it burns before expelling it from my lungs.

"It's been one hell of a day," Logan, Montana's VP, says as he pours himself a shot of whiskey. "The shop looks damn good, congratulations again, Kiwi." Logan stands, taking one of the bottles sitting in the middle of the table. "I hate to run out on my brothers, but I'm buzzed and hungry for my woman. I'll catch you guys later." Our heads move as we watch Logan stroll across the room, pull Bella, his woman, from among the other old ladies, and toss her over his shoulder.

"How was the ride? There's a lot of road between here and Polson." I strike up a meaningless conversation to keep from thinking about Piper.

"Not too bad," Jake answers. "I can't speak for the rest of my men, but my body is stiff as hell. I haven't ridden a stretch of highway like that in a long time."

Quinn's shot glass clinks against the wood table as he sets it down. "You don't stop ridin' once you're old. You only get old when you stop ridin'." A few of the brothers from Montana look at Quinn like he's grown a second head.

"First smart thing I've heard fall out of your mouth all night," Gabriel grunts.

"At least I can form a sentence instead of someone trying to decode a sequence of man grunts as if they're Morse code," Quinn smirks, and I can tell right away he likes poking the bear.

"I'm gonna shove a pool stick up your ass. How's that for a complete sentence, dickhead." Gabriel downs a shot, and we all burst out in laughter.

I look around the room, searching for Piper, but she's nowhere within sight. Suddenly, I feel tired, or maybe I just want to drag my arse far away from the clubhouse, temptation, and the need to find her.

10

PIPER

Night has fallen, and the clubhouse is booming with conversation and laughter for the second day in a row. Yesterday was the grand opening of Kings Custom, and it went off without a hitch. Dozens of people from our community showed up to offer their support for New Orleans' latest business. The entire club is proud to have a chain bike shop, and I'm even more proud the club offered Tai the position to run the place. For as long as I can remember, Tai has spent a lot of his time rebuilding bikes, using the small shop located out back here at the clubhouse. Tai can take almost anything apart and put it back together by memory. It doesn't matter what it is, a motorcycle, a truck engine, a lawnmower. You name it; he can disassemble and put it back together, making it like new again. Hell, when I was ten, I was playing with my Easy Bake Oven at the clubhouse when it suddenly quit working. Tai witnessed my upset and wasted no time getting to work on fixing it for me. I remember sitting at the bar watching as he took it apart, located the problem, fixed it, and put it back together. It took him three hours. In the end, my tears had dried, and Tai was my hero.

"Hey, Bean," my dad calls out to me, snapping me out of my

wandering thoughts. "I'm goin' on a beer and ice run, want to tag along with your old man?"

I smile. "Sure."

Following dad out to his truck, I jump into the passenger side while he climbs in behind the wheel.

"This turned out to be a wild weekend. With the Montana Chapter showing up and all."

"Hell, yeah. I'm fuckin' stoked. Jake and the boys have been promisin' to come down for over two years. None of us knew it would be now. And I know it means a lot to your uncle, and especially to Kiwi, they showed up to support the opening of Kings Custom."

"I'm happy for Kiwi. Running the garage will be perfect for him. And having a proper place to build his custom bikes and show them off to the public."

"I'm happy for him too. This business will be good for him and the club."

I nod. "The community coming out to support the club made it special too. I heard one guy say he was going to start bringing his business to the garage because the place he normally goes has been jerking him around."

"Oh, yeah?" dad asks.

"Yup. He was talking about Mr. Dennis's place."

"Makes sense," dad remarks. "Old man Dennis retired last year, and his nephew took over the shop. Service hasn't been the same since."

We spend the remainder of the ride to the store in comfortable silence. It's not until we are strolling through the beer aisle with me, pushing the cart that dad speaks again. "How's everything going down at the clinic?"

"It's great. I know I've told you before but being back has made me realize how much I miss home; how much I miss my family and the clinic. It's crazy that just a year and a half ago, I had no clue what I wanted to do with my life, and now I have never been so sure."

Dad puts his arm around my shoulders. "Remember, when I told you it would come to you, that everything would eventually fall into place?"

I look up at him, "I remember. Always so wise," I chuckle.

"Always a smartass." Dad pokes me in the ribs.

Sighing, I begin to nibble on my bottom lip.

"Spit it out, Bean. You're chewin' on your lip and that means you got somethin' on your mind."

"I was just wondering what your thoughts would be on me moving back home and finishing school here?"

"Are you that homesick?"

"It's not only that. I'm also working on building a relationship with Madison. We're taking things slow but being back home would make our progression easier." I let out another sigh. "I'll admit I only went to Texas because running away seemed easier than staying. Not that I regret my year in Texas because I feel like I have grown a lot. Being away from home has helped me put things into perspective. I now know more than anything what I want."

"And what is it that you want?" Dad asks.

"I want to be with my family, I want to see my brother grow up, I want to continue working for Dr. Channing, and I want to keep building a relationship with my mom. I can't do any of those things in Texas."

"You know I will support any decision you make, Piper. As long as you're doing it for you and not because we all miss the hell out of ya." Dad squeezes my shoulders. "I'm fuckin' proud of ya, Bean. I have your back no matter what road you choose."

"Thanks, dad. That means a lot."

After loading up on beer, we hit the produce section because Payton called saying they needed more steaks to grill and some charcoal. I also spotted one of those small kiddie pools and suggested dad get one for Jaxson along with some cute little Spider-Man arm floats for him and some pink princess ones for Uncle Abel and Luna's little girl Aria. I have agreed to help look after the little nuggets since Payton and Josie will be busy in the kitchen cooking.

"I appreciate you offerin' to help with the kids today, Piper."

"No problem, dad. Spending time with my brother and cousin is no hardship. I adore them and want to soak up as much time with them as I can. Plus, you guys haven't seen your brothers in a while. Keeping the kids entertained is the least I can do."

Once we make it back to the clubhouse, the smell of food cooking on the grill and the sound of music assaults us when we step out of the truck. Tai spots us and immediately comes over to help carry the bags inside. When I reach into the bed of the truck for a bag of ice, my arm brushes his, and the connection causes me to shiver. Tai, however, refuses to even look at me. I tamp down my disappointment and try to brush it off as he does not want my dad to notice anything. But an ugly feeling swarming in my gut says he is pulling away again. He also hasn't made good on his promise since our kiss in the bathroom at Leon's. At first, I figured it was him being busy with the opening of Kings Custom, and now I'm not so sure.

"Hey," I murmur. He grunts in return as I walk alongside him into the clubhouse. "Everything, okay?" I ask.

"Fine. Just busy, Piper." Tai sets the bags of groceries down on the counter in the kitchen, then leaves without sparing me another glance, further hurting my feelings. Plastering a fake smile on my face, I turn to Payton and Josie, who are busy preparing the food. "Need any help here?"

Josie shakes her head. "Nope. We have it covered. Why don't you head out back and enjoy yourself?"

"Yeah, okay. I'm going to set up the pool for the kids. Holler if you need anything."

Before heading outside, I go upstairs to my old room to change. Walking in, I see it is clean, and just as I left it. Knowing I have clothes here, I pull open the top dresser drawer searching for my bathing suit. Stripping out of my clothes, I put on a two-piece purple swimsuit then slide on a pair of denim shorts over the bottoms. Next, I tie my hair up into a ponytail and slide on a pair of flip flops I found in the closet. Grabbing the quilt off the bed, I make my way back downstairs and outside where I spot Promise and Luna over by the kid's pool with Sydney, Tequila's niece. "Hi," I sign when I approach them. With Luna being deaf, I made it a point to learn sign language. Even though she sometimes likes to use her voice and can read lips, I still sign when talking to her.

"Hey, Piper," they say in unison, and Sydney waves.

"Piper, these arm floaties you got the kids are too cute," Promise tells me as she puts them on Jaxson.

"I know they don't need them with this pool since it's not deep enough, I just couldn't pass up buying them."

"Aria loves hers," Luna signs, pointing to her daughter, who is already in the water.

"Are you sure you don't mind watching them?" Promise asks.

"Of course not. Besides, I have Sydney to keep me company too." I smile and Sydney nods her head vigorously. "The four of us are going to have a good time, aren't we?" I say, taking Jaxson from Promise as he reaches out for me. I nuzzle my face against his cheek, causing him to squeal. "You two go hang with dad and Uncle Abel." I look at Luna who hands her daughter off to Sydney. "Go catch up with the girls. I promise we'll be fine."

After some extra assurance that I can handle these two munchkins, Luna and Promise take their leave across the yard to where all the men and their women congregate. Bringing my attention back to my brother, I tickle his belly. "Ready to play?"

A few hours later, as the sun begins to set, painting the New Orleans sky in a beautiful shade of orange, I lay on the quilt with

Jaxson and Aria sleeping next to me. The two wore themselves out and crashed about thirty minutes ago. And Sydney took off when Josie brought out the ice cream. As I gently stroke Jaxson's hair and watch him sleep, a feeling of being watched washes through me. Looking over my shoulder, my eyes connect with Tai's. I don't know how long we hold each other's gaze, but the moment is soon interrupted by Promise and Luna. "We're going to take them inside and get them settled." They both reach down and carefully pick up the sleeping pair. "Thanks again for watching them," Luna signs.

"Anytime," I tell her.

Standing, I brush a few pieces of grass off my legs and again take a peek to my right to where Tai is. He's talking with Logan and Gabriel, but as if he can feel my eyes on him, he looks my way. This time a pained look crosses his face before he turns back to the guys, says something, then turns and walks away into the clubhouse. My heart sinks a little more with each slap of what feels like rejection. Doing my best to brush it off, I head over to the buffet table where the food is, start fixing myself a plate, and then take it over to the picnic table at the far corner of the yard.

"Mind if we join you?" a soft voice asks, and I look up to find Alba, Bella, Mila, Grace, Emerson and Sofia standing there with their plates.

"Sure, I'd love some company."

The six old ladies of the Montana Chapter take a seat. I recognize each of them from pictures and the guys talking about them, but today is the first time I'm meeting them all in person. "Are you all having a good time?"

"We're having a great time," Grace, who is Jake's woman, says. "I've never taken such a long trip on the bike, but I loved it."

"Me too," Mila adds. "The scenery was beautiful. I can't wait for Reid to show me around New Orleans."

"I think you'll love it. There is so much to do here, and the food alone is worth the long drive."

By the time 2:00 am rolls around, the party has died down, and everyone is starting to settle in for the night. I'm in the kitchen helping to put food away and clean when my dad comes in. "Hey, baby girl."

I turn away from the sink. "Hey. You and Promise heading home?"

"Naw, she's upstairs with Jaxson. The three of us are crashing here tonight."

"Oh, well, I let Sam and Sophia take my room, so I'm going to go home."

"You sure? You can bunk with Promise and Jaxson, while I take one of the couches down here."

"Thanks, Dad, but I'd rather go home."

"Alright, Bean. Are you okay to drive? I can have Everest take you home or at least follow you back."

I shake my head. "I'm good."

Pulling me in for a hug, he kisses the top of my head. "Thanks for helpin' out today. Don't know what I'd do without ya."

"You're welcome, dad."

Tossing the dish towel on the counter, I grab my purse that's hanging on the back of the kitchen chair and swing it over my shoulder. "I'll see you in the morning."

"See ya, baby girl."

As I'm stepping outside the clubhouse, I run into Everest, who has his back against the wall while smoking a cigarette. "Hey, Piper. Figured you'd crash here with everyone else."

"No, I feel like going home. Besides, you guys have a full house."

"That we do. Kiwi just took off for the night too. You're the last one out. Want me to follow you home?"

"No." I shake my head. "Thanks, though."

Giving me a chin lift, Everest flicks his cigarette to the ground and makes his way over to the gate. Once I climb in my car and roll through, I watch in my rearview mirror as he secures the gate then begins walking the perimeter of the compound. Once I arrive home, I pull out my phone and shoot off a quick text to my dad. I know he will have waited up for me to let him know I made it.

Me: I'm home.

Dad: Night, Bean. See ya tomorrow. Love you.

Me: Goodnight. Love you too.

Tossing my phone onto the passenger seat, I lean my head back against the headrest and close my eyes when out of nowhere, I get a spur of the moment idea. I briefly contemplate if what I am considering is crazy. "Fuck it," I mutter to myself.

Shifting my car into gear, I back out of the garage. Twenty minutes later, I'm pulling up in front of Tai's house. Taking a deep breath to calm my nerves, I cut the engine and climb out. The front porch light clicks on the moment my feet touch the first step. Knocking on the door three times, I wait for Tai to answer. A few seconds later, the door swings open, and his large frame fills the space. I take in his shirtless chest, the large colorful tattoos covering his left rib cage, and the way his jeans sit low on his hips with the button undone.

"What are you doing here, Piper?" Tai asks, resting his forearm above his head against the door frame.

"I wanted to see you. I thought maybe we could talk."

"About what?"

Fidgeting with the strap of my purse, I'm suddenly getting the feeling coming here was a mistake. "I want to talk about us, and what happened the other day?"

"There's nothin' to talk about."

"Seriously, Tai? Are you going to stand there and tell me we don't have anything to talk about after YOU kissed ME? I swear to God, if you open your mouth to throw some cliché bullshit excuse like the kiss was a mistake, I will not be held responsible for my actions."

"Dammit, Piper!" Tai slams his fist against the door. "You're my brother's daughter. That means you are off-limits."

"So, you're pulling away again because you're scared of my dad?"

"No. I'm ending this," he gestures between us, "before it gets started because I respect Nova."

"Maybe if we just talk to him..."

"No," Tai cuts me off.

"So that's it? Just like that?" I throw my hands in the air. "You are the one who has been giving mixed signals."

A regretful look crosses his face, but I don't give him time to respond. I have officially had enough. "Forget it. I hear you loud and clear," I walk away but stop and turn back. "I was prepared to go head to head with my father for you. That's how much you mean to me."

"Babe," Tai calls out, his voice laced with pain.

Ignoring him, I climb into my car, and without a backward glance, I drive away.

<hr>

The next morning, the blare of the doorbell rouses me from sleep. After last night's events, I came home and cried until sleep finally claimed me. Through bleary eyes, I peer over at the clock on the fireplace mantel to see it's barely eight o'clock. The doorbell goes off again, followed by a knock. "Hold on. I'm coming," I grumble, throwing the blanket off me and sitting up on the edge of the couch. Just as I make it to the front door, the pounding starts again. "I said, hold on!" I shout as I swing it open. My mouth falls open when I see who's standing on the porch.

"Took your ass long enough."

"Jia! Oh my god, what are you doing here?" I pull my friend in for a hug.

"Good to see you too, Piper. Now, are you going to invite me in? My tired ass needs caffeine, pronto."

Moving aside, I let Jia in. "Why didn't you call to tell me you were coming? I thought you were spending the summer with your parents?"

"My dad was called away for business, and there was no way I was spending two months alone with my mother. So, I hopped on a plane last night, and here I am."

"Oh, man. That sucks, Jia. I know you were looking forward to spending some time with your dad."

Jia waves her hand at me. "He promised his trip was only for a week. And to make it up to me, he's sending me to Vegas. He got me tickets to all the shows I've been wanting to see. I told him the only way I'd go is if I got to take my best friend with me. So, what do you say? Our flight leaves in three hours."

"Are you serious? A week in Vegas and you want to take me?"

"Yup, all expenses paid by dear old dad. Come on, Piper, don't make me go alone."

I mull over Jia's proposal then decide the trip couldn't have come at a better time. After last night, I could use the time to clear my head. "Okay, I'm in."

"Yes! I knew you wouldn't let me down. Vegas, here we come," Jia cheers, throwing her hands in the air.

"Follow me upstairs and help me pack. I need to call my dad to let him know what's up and call my boss. I have lots to do in only three hours."

11

KIWI

I wake to Chance lapping at my hand dangling over the edge of the mattress. "I guess it's time to roll my arse out of bed, huh?" I scratch behind his ear. Cracking my eyes open, I peer at the window and notice it's still dark outside. "Shit, Chance. The sun isn't even up yet." Lifting my head slightly, I look at the alarm clock sitting on top of the nightstand and sigh. 5:00 am. "Alright, I'm getting up."

Shifting, I sit on the edge and scrub my palm down my face. I was fucking sleeping like shit anyway. Things couldn't have gone any better with the grand opening of Kings Custom. Having the entire club and town coming together to celebrate was epic. By the end of the day, we had more than a dozen potential clients interested in our services. The only problem was, I couldn't let myself thoroughly enjoy the weekend celebration. I tried, but all I could focus on was Piper, and try like hell to keep my distance.

A heaviness settles on my chest, replaying the moments I watched Piper with her sibling and the other kids yesterday. Watching her painted a picture of what our future could look like.

Envisioning her holding a child of our own came so easy to me. I saw my future sitting yards away but so far out of reach. I trust Fender when he said it's not his place to say shit, but he's right. It won't be long before Nova notices that something has shifted between Piper and me, which is why, for the first time, I didn't interact with her. I was purposefully cold and distant. Driving a wedge between us is the only way I know how to keep things from going any further.

Then she goes and shows up at my door last night. My words were harsh. Even though she tried to mask it with venomous words of her own, I hurt her. And it fucking killed me inside. I have all these feelings bottled up inside to give her, and I can't show them without exposing it to the club. If I do, the ripple effect could destroy everything we care for.

Throwing my head back, I sigh heavily. I took an oath when I was given a permanent position with The Kings of Retribution, to put my club and brothers above myself and others. Piper is part of that oath because she is my brother's daughter.

I rise from the bed. The hard part is knowing I am willing to risk damn near everything I've worked so hard for to be with Piper. What I am not ready to risk is Piper's happiness. She loves her family. Her dad is everything to her, and so is the club she grew up in. It would be selfish of me to ask her to sacrifice it all to be with me.

After taking care of Chance's bladder, I load him onto his specialized canine wheelchair, and he follows me through to the kitchen. After filling his food bowl with kibble, I head to the bathroom and take a quick shower.

A short time later, the goats and cat are fed, and I'm on my bike, with Chance in tow, heading for the clubhouse. It's still early. The sun is just starting to rise. I travel down the road, with nothing but the sound of tires hitting the pavement and the roar of my

Harley. Feeling a bit shitty for cutting out on my brothers last night, I stop by the pastry shop several blocks from the clubhouse.

As I walk through the door of the bakery, the bell chimes overhead. Mr. Guidory walks out, wiping his palms down the front of his white apron. "Hey, there, Kiwi." His smile grows when he sees my mate strapped to my back. "Well, I'll be. Don't think I have ever seen such a sight before." He rounds the counter, stopping for a second to snatch a freshly baked cookie from a tray beside the cash register. "Hey, there, boy." He breaks off pieces of the cookie and feeds them to Chance. I feel crumbs hitting the back of my neck as he munches on his treat.

"I hated leavin' him alone so much during the day, so I started searching for ways to travel with him. I found this company that makes custom carriers for pets." I reach my hand over my shoulder and give Chance a pet. "He doesn't seem to mind it, and I get to have him with me throughout the day."

"You got a heart of gold taking care of a special needs animal," Mr. Guidory says. "So, what can I do for you today?"

"I'll take three dozen doughnuts."

He smiles and grabs three boxes from beneath the counter and fills them with a variety. The bell chimes above the door and I spin to see Edith, his wife, walk in. "Frank, you forgot your lunch. You know what the doctor said." Finally, noticing me standing there, she stops talking. "Kiwi." Her eyes light up. "How are you?" She touches my arm. "I'm good, Mrs. Guidory." She peers past my shoulder, and I hear Chance panting in my ear. "Oh my, would you look at this." She scratches Chance behind the ear. "I bet you get a lot of attention from the females with this cute face," she refers to the dog, not me. "When's that sweet momma of yours gonna visit again? I finally found that cake recipe I was telling her about during her last visit. What was that—a year ago?"

"Yes, ma'am. And I'm not sure when they will visit again. I may fly home next time," I tell her.

"You have a good family, Kiwi. All of them." She waves her hand. "Look at me, running my mouth." Mrs. Guidory turns to her husband of fifty years and hands him a lunch bag. "It's a turkey sandwich on whole wheat. No mayo. Some cut up watermelon and carrot sticks."

Mr. Guidory opens the bag, looking inside. "No tater salad or chips?" he grumps.

"The doctor has you on a low sodium low-fat diet, Frank."

"You're starvin' me, woman." He exaggerates his words, and I hold in my laughter. They've been married for years. Several months ago, Frank had a mild heart attack. They are a massive part of this community. Everyone loves them. When they had to close their doors for a few weeks, the club donated money to help them get by until Frank was back on his feet again. "I'm gonna waste away to nothin'," he continues.

"Oh, hush." She swats his chest as he wraps his arm around her waist. She kisses his cheek. "You old fart. You know I love you."

"And as I'm eating my rabbit food, I'll remind myself how much I love you too," he kisses her forehead. Mrs. Guidory gives him another playful swat, walks behind the counter, and grabs an apron from a hook on the wall.

"You take care, Kiwi," Mrs. Guidory calls out before disappearing into the kitchen. Mr. Guidory rings up my order.

"God gave me a good woman," he declares, taking the cash I hand to him.

I smile, then my thoughts shift to Piper. "Have a good day, Mr. Guidory."

"You too," he calls out as I exit the bakery.

The clubhouse is quiet when I roll in. From the looks of it, most of the men slept in. Not wanting to disturb anyone, I cut my engine at the gate and coast the rest of the way. Untying the three boxes strapped to the backseat and Chance's wheels, I carry them inside. As I suspected, no one is awake, so I head for the kitchen to start some coffee. The moment I push open the kitchen door, I'm greeted by a man's naked arse, bent over in the fridge. "For fuck's sake, I can see your fartbox."

Quinn stands, holding a can of whip cream and a container of strawberries. But that's not what throws me off. He's wearing a fucking Mardi Gras mask. The kind with the long-ass feathers fluting out above the head, reminding me of a Carnival headdress. "Hey, brother. I didn't realize anyone was awake." He closes the refrigerator door, then sniffs the air. "I smell sugar. Those donuts you got there?" He waltzes my way with no care in the world that his balls and hammer are swinging free. I sit the boxes down, and Quinn adjusts what he's holding to free up one hand. He flops a box lid open, plucks a couple of chocolate glazed rings from the inside. He grins. "Catch ya later," then strides out of the kitchen.

So, that just happened. Shaking my head, I laugh to myself. I've heard of Quinn and his uniqueness but experiencing it firsthand was interesting. Chance barks. He's probably just as confused as I am. "This stays between us, boy," I say to my dog and take him off my back. I get him situated in his wheelchair, then cut him loose. As I go about making coffee, Payton, one of the club girls, strolls into the kitchen.

"Kiwi," her voice sounds as if she just woke up. "I wasn't expecting to see anyone awake yet." She shuffles to the table where the donut boxes sit. "Oh my god. Carbs." Payton plucks one out. "I thought you went home last night?" she questions as she takes a bite.

"I did." I lean against the counter as Payton moves about the kitchen, gathering breakfast items from the cabinets and refrigerator.

"Well, you missed all the shenanigans." She laughs.

"Trust me. I got a good dose of it this mornin'." I shiver.

A few hours later, I'm at the bike shop. It's Monday, we don't officially open the doors until Wednesday, but I thought I would get a head start on a bike I'm hoping to have finished by the end of the day. The rumble of bikes draws my attention as I stroll across the shop. Nova, Riggs, and Logan pull up to the bay door and shut off their engines. The bike I'm working on is on the lift. Continuing with the task at hand, I begin working on the clutch line. "Fender said we'd find you here," Riggs says as my brothers stroll inside. Logan removes his shades to check out my other work in progress, a custom hardtail chopper I've been working on in between jobs.

"Goin' old school, huh?" he runs his hand along the unfinished frame. "You fabricate these z-bars yourself?" He's really taking in every detail.

I stop what I'm doing and wipe my hands with a shop towel. "I did."

"Damn, nice work, brother." Logan admires my craftsmanship.

"My dad taught me everything I know. He could take apart and rebuild just about anything you set in front of him." I pause as fond memories of working in my dad's shop back home enter my thoughts. Damn, I miss those days. Back when life was less stressful. "Can I offer you mates a beer?" I stride to the far end of the shop, where a refrigerator is found, and pull open the door. Retrieving the six-pack inside, I turn and hand each of the guys a longneck. "What's the plan for today?" I ask Riggs, knowing since the other chapter is in town, we'll most likely party the entire time.

"Everyone is gonna do their own thing for most of the day, then we'll show our brothers a good time hanging out at Twisted Throttle," Riggs says.

Nova's phone rings. Pulling it from his pocket, he swipes the screen. "Hey, Bean." He nods a few times. "Call me when you get to the hotel."

Hotel?

"I love you too," Nova says, then shoves his phone away. "Every damn grey hair I have is from worryin' about that daughter of mine." Nova lifts his beer to his lips.

"Did Piper decide to go back to Texas?" I ask, worried that pushing her away caused her to leave.

"Her girlfriend, Jia, talked her into a girl's trip. The two of them jumped on a plane for Vegas early this morning." Nova continues to speak, but I have no clue what he is saying because I tune him out. When I think of Vegas, only one name comes to mind. My stomach tightens as a knot forms, and my thoughts run wild with all the awful things that could happen. It doesn't take long for my worry to turn to anger.

"Vegas isn't a safe place for two young women to be on their own." I work hard at checking my attitude, but the tone of my voice gives me away.

Nova narrows his eyes. "She's safe."

"What's got you on edge?" Riggs asks, and I look at him. He's good at reading people. "Does this have to do with Donovan?" My fists clench at my sides, and Riggs takes notice. "He hasn't been seen or heard from in years."

"As long as we don't have a body to count for, I still consider him a threat," I tell him. Nova eyes me but says nothing. He knows the sorted details, but it's not my brothers who remain haunted by the fact Donovan Black is out there somewhere. And it doesn't change the fact that bad men prey on beautiful young women like Piper and her friend. My thoughts go to a dark place. Depression sucks, but I've been dealing with it for a long time now. I think about the young girls I met throughout the year I was in Vegas. Their faces burned into my memory, guilt eating at me daily. I helped the motherfucker. Even though I was unaware, I caused several women's disappearance, some of whom were never found. I feel like I'm choking on the thoughts swirling in my head.

"Tai," Nova calls me by my first name, and it jerks me from

going any deeper. I look at him and try to shake the uneasy feeling I have. "You are not like him." His hand clasps my shoulder. "Piper is safe. I wouldn't let her go if I weren't convinced she would be okay. She's staying in an upscale high-security hotel and checks in regularly. We have nothing to worry about," he says, fully believing every word, but nothing he says is sinking in.

12

PIPER

"Oh, wow!" I exclaim as I peer out the floor to ceiling window of the hotel suite Jia and I will be staying for the next few days. "This view is amazing."

"It really is," Jia says, coming up behind me. "Dad reserves the same room every time he comes here on business or when he brings me to see a show."

"It must happen often. The receptionist downstairs recognized you the moment we walked into the hotel."

"Oh, yeah. Dad comes to Vegas at least five times a year. We also come together during spring break and for one week out of the summer. He doesn't stay anywhere but here."

"What about your mom? Does she come with you guys?"

Jia snorts. "My mother thinks it's beneath her to mingle with tourists or do anything I consider fun. If it doesn't involve lunch with her friends, a trip to her plastic surgeon, or laying out by some pool, she won't do it. But that's okay, dad and I have more fun without her. He's nothing like my mom."

Jia says all this like it's no big deal, but her eyes tell a different story.

"So," she says, changing the subject. "What do you want to do first? I'm a little beat considering I jumped on a flight from Florida to New Orleans, and three hours later, I was on another plane to here."

"Well, I didn't get but two hours of sleep before you showed up at my house. I spent the entire day and night at the clubhouse. We had a party to celebrate the grand opening of Kings Custom with the Montana Chapter, who surprised us with a visit. I say we go to the restaurant downstairs for a bite to eat, then come back up here and rest up for tomorrow."

"Sounds good to me."

When Jia and I arrive at the Italian restaurant, we don't have to wait and are shown to a table right away.

"What's good here?" I ask, looking over the menu.

"Everything. Seriously, order anything on the menu, it's all good."

A minute later, the waiter arrives with our drink order. "Have you ladies decided?"

Jia doesn't bother looking at the menu. "I'll have the Lobster Ravioli."

"And you, Miss?" the waiter peers over at me.

"I'll have the same, but I'll have some of the Calamari to start."

"Very well. I'll have your order out to you soon."

Just as I pick up my glass to take a sip of water, my phone chimes with an incoming text, Jia rolls her eyes. "Let me guess, your dad?"

"Shut up," I laugh. "He's just protective. Sure, he's a little much, but I'm used to it."

Tapping on the phone screen, I expect to see a text from my dad, but I see one from Tai instead.

Tai: Are you ok?

Tai: Talk to me

Tai: I'm sorry

Letting out a frustrated sigh, I ignore the last text and toss my phone back into my purse.

"You okay?" Jia questions.

"Not really," I sigh.

"Is this about that guy you were telling me about? The one in your dads' club? The sexy one with the accent?"

I nod. "A few days ago, he kissed me."

Jia gasps and claps her hands. "Tell me everything."

"I wouldn't get too excited, and there is nothing to tell. He kissed me. I thought it would lead to something more, but it didn't. He chose to end it before it started."

"What the hell for?"

"It's complicated."

"Complicated how?"

"You'd have to understand how club life works to understand why things between Tai and me could be a disaster. I'm the daughter of The Kings of Retribution Enforcer. That makes me off-limits to any other members. It's like an unwritten rule."

"Oh," Jia's shoulders slump. "So, would he like, be kicked out of the club or something?"

I shrug. "Honestly, I don't know. But I went to Tai's house last night and told him I was all in. I told him I was willing to face my dad and the club for any chance that we could be together, but he made it clear he didn't feel the same way."

"Damn, Piper. I'm sorry."

I wave Jia off and try to fight back the tears that threaten to spill. "It is what it is. No sense in dwelling."

Luckily, our food arrives, and our conversation about Tai ends. Minutes later, Jia and I are enjoying the comfortable silence along with some delicious food when out of the corner of my eye, I notice a few patrons whispering and pointing toward the entrance of the restaurant. My eyes travel to where they're attention is to see a familiar face striding in with his bandmates in tow.

"Holy shit! That's Easton Evans and some of his band mates from East of Addiction," Jia whispers.

I watch as Easton speaks to the hostess, and she not so subtly bats her eyelashes while she shows him to a table. As he follows behind the woman, Easton's gaze drifts across the room, stopping on me. He looks shocked for a moment. Then his lips lift into a smirk. I give him a smile of my own, and wave.

"Fuck, he's coming this way." Jia begins to fidget in her seat. "Act normal."

Easton stops beside our table, and I almost laugh at the shocked look on my friend's face.

Easton plops down in the seat next to me and rests his arm on the back of my chair. "Fancy seeing you here."

"How's it going, Easton?"

"Can't complain. What about you? What brings you to Sin City, Piper?"

"Just a girl's trip with my friend," I point to Jia. "Easton, this is my friend, Jia."

Easton reaches his arm across the table. "Good to meet you, Jia."

Though still star-struck, Jia does manage to shake Easton's hand.

"What about you? Are you in Vegas on business or pleasure?"

Easton gives me a panty-melting grin. "Both."

I shake my head. "You know, I just saw your sister yesterday. The Montana Chapter is in New Orleans."

"Oh, yeah? I haven't talked to Em in about a week. How is everyone?"

"They're good." I give him a warm smile.

"So." Easton helps himself to a breadstick, taking a big bite and talking around a mouthful. "What are your plans while in town?"

"Jia and I are going to hit up a few shows, maybe check out the club scene."

"Does one of the shows on your itinerary involve yours truly?"

"I wish," Jia cuts in. "Tickets have been sold out for months."

Easton beams his signature smile at Jia then gives me a wink. "Lucky for you, I have connections."

"Seriously!" my friend shrieks.

Easton laughs. "Piper is family, and families also get VIP backstage passes." Pulling out his phone, Easton starts firing off a text. "Are you two staying in this hotel?"

I nod.

"The tickets and passes will be at the front desk by tomorrow morning. The show is Thursday at eight o'clock." Then he writes his phone number down on a napkin and hands it to me. "Here's my cell. I already informed my manager you were coming but call me if you run into any trouble getting in."

I take the napkin from him as he stands. "This is great, Easton. Thank you."

"Anytime." He raps his knuckles on the table. "It was good seeing you again, Piper." He gives Jia a chin lift. "You, too, beautiful."

Once Easton has returned to his table, and out of earshot, Jia loses her shit. "You, wench. You never told me you know Easton Evans. He's like the sexiest man on the planet. Not only is your family made up of badass, alpha bikers, but you know the frontman of East of Addiction. How exactly do you know him?"

I chuckle and shake my head. "His sister is Emerson, the wife of Quinn, who is the Sergeant At Arms for The Kings Montana Chapter."

Lifting her hand, Jia signals the waiter over. "Change of plans. We're going shopping. I need a kick-ass outfit to wear to the concert."

It's dark by the time we step out of the boutique a few blocks from the hotel. Jia and I are exhausted with the day's events, but we both found something to wear for Thursday night.

The next day Jia and I return to the hotel after seeing Cirque du Soleil. I had never seen one of their shows, and have to admit it was amazing. Now we are getting ready to hit one of the clubs. Tonight, I have on a red V-neck dress with long sleeves and an open back. The hem lands about three inches above my knees, and I have paired the dress with some red and gold three-inch strappy heels. My makeup is done in a smokey eye, along with my flaming red lipstick. Lastly, I tie half of my long hair up into a ponytail, leaving the rest to hang on my back in waves.

"Damn, Piper. You look hot," Jia compliments when she steps into the bathroom.

"Thanks. You don't look so bad yourself."

Jia runs her hands down the length of her black satin dress then does a little twirl. "Thank you."

"Ready?" I ask, tossing my lipstick tube, cell phone, ID, and cash, and most importantly, my pepper spray into my clutch.

"Ready." Jia beams.

Three hours later, I'm sitting at a table, taking a break while sipping on some water while watching Jia out on the dance floor with a random guy she has been grinding against for the past forty-five minutes. The guy's friend tried dancing with me earlier, but I was able to give him the brush off. Before we came, I told Jia I was only interested in having a good time, not hooking up.

"What are you doing sitting over here by yourself?"

Peering over my shoulder, I take in the same guy from before. Does this dude not know how to take a hint? "Just taking a break," I hold up my water bottle then turn back to the dance floor, ignoring him.

"My name is Chris."

I let out a frustrated sigh when Chris sits in the vacant seat across from me.

"Are you going to tell me your name?"

Still trying to ignore him, I don't make eye contact when I answer, "Piper."

"Piper. A pretty name for a pretty girl."

I struggle not to roll my eyes at his corny pick-up line. Finally, I give him my full attention. "Look, I'm not trying to be rude, but I just came here to dance and hang with my friend."

"Well, it looks like your friend has other plans," Chris tips his head in the direction of the dance floor where Jia is hanging all over his buddy. And luckily, she happens to catch my eyes at the same time. I cock my head to the side and give her a look, one that says I am ready to get out of here. I watch as Jia leans in close and says something to her dance partner then starts making her way through the crowd toward me.

"Hey, you ready to go?" she asks when she makes it to my table.

I stand. "More than ready."

"Hey, you ladies aren't leaving yet, are you?" Chris asks.

"Yeah, we're pretty beat. But it was nice meeting you and your friend," Jia tells him, thumbing over her shoulder at Chris' friend who has now joined us.

"That's too bad. But listen, there is a party happening tomorrow night at a friend's house. He's a big-time music executive. The guest list is VIP only." Chris pulls out his wallet and hands Jia a card. "The address is on the back. Tell whoever is at the door you're with Chris and Mike."

"Sounds like fun." Jia takes the card from Chris, then he hands one to me.

I don't share the same enthusiasm as my friend. These two clowns give me a bad vibe. Plus, my dad's voice is ringing inside my head. He may be overprotective, but he's never steered me wrong. Call me daddy's girl if you want, but I always listen to him.

Back at the hotel room, I confront Jia on my concerns about this so-called VIP party, mostly since she hasn't shut up about it since leaving the club.

"Jia, I'm not going to that party, and I don't think you should either."

Kicking her heels off and tugging her dress off over her head, she asks, "Why not? Chris and Mike seem cool. And you never know who we might meet at the party."

"Chris gave me the creeps, and how do we know they were not lying about who is throwing the party? It sounds a little fishy to me. I mean, why ask a girl you just met to come to an exclusive VIP party where there will supposedly be celebrities in attendance?"

"Come on, Piper. You never know. Live a little."

I shake my head. "I live plenty. I'm not going, and I'm asking you as a friend to trust me. I don't want you going either." I give Jia a pleading look. "Please."

She sighs. "Fine. I won't go."

***

The next day was just as fun as the day before. Jia and I indulged in some retail therapy, had lunch, then ended the day by pampering ourselves at the hotel spa. The plan for the night was to hit up the strip and sightsee, but a headache kept me in. While I went to lie down, Jia said she would order some room service and watch a movie. By the time I wake from my nap, the room is dark. Looking at the clock beside the bed, I see it's 10:00 pm. I can't believe I slept for four hours.

Climbing out of bed, I pad out of the room I'm staying in and down the hall to Jia's room. I knock on the door. "Jia. You up?"

When I don't get an answer, I crack the door open to find the room empty. Pushing in the rest of the way, I notice several articles of clothing scattered across the bed. Next, I make my way out of the room and into the dining area to find a sheet of hotel stationary on the table. Picking it up, I read the note Jia left for me.

Piper,

I was bored and didn't want to wake you. I decided to go to the party after all. Don't be mad. I'll check in soon.

Jia.

"Shit," I mutter to myself. Jogging back into my room, I go straight to my phone to see if Jia has called or texted. Swiping my finger across the screen, I see I have a message from her. It was sent at seven fifty-eight, letting me know she had arrived at the house. After quickly shooting off a reply, I go to my suitcase and pull out a pair of jeans and a t-shirt. Once dressed, I slip on my tennis shoes and tie my hair back in a ponytail. When I'm done, I check my phone to see I haven't gotten a reply back from Jia. It's only been an hour, but I have a nagging feeling in the pit of my stomach. She promised she wouldn't go, but I can't sit here and wait for her to come back. I wait another fifteen minutes and send another text. When Jia still fails to respond, I call. Dialing her number, I wait for her to answer. Her phone goes straight to voicemail instead. Frustrated with my friend, I go into the bathroom and grab the clutch I was using the night before. Opening it, I fish out the card Chris gave me. I slide the card along with my phone in my back pocket. I also grab the tube of pepper spray and stick it into the waistband of my jeans. Quickly, I make my way out of the hotel and to the elevator, riding it down to the lobby. As soon as I step out of the hotel, I grab a cab.

"Where to sweetheart?" the driver asks. I reach into my back pocket for the card but it's not there. *Shit.* I must have dropped it.

Luckily, I remember the address on the card and recite it to the driver.

Peering out the window as the car stops in front of a large house, my first thought is I have mistakenly given the wrong address. There is no party happening here. There are a few lights on in the large two-story mansion, but no vehicles are parked out front.

"You coming or going, lady?" the driver asks.

"Um...I..." Just as I am about to tell him I've made a mistake, the front door to the house opens. Chris, the guy from the club who invited us here, steps out the same time three cars pull into the circular driveway beside the taxi, and several people start spilling out. The men are dressed casually, and the women dressed much like they would if going to the club. And when I step out of the cab, I can hear music coming from inside the house. Turning back to the driver, I give him some cash. "Do you mind waiting? I'll only be a few minutes."

"No problem."

Making my way toward the front door of the house, Chris spots me and smiles. "I see you changed your mind."

"I haven't changed my mind. I just came to pick up my friend."

"Oh. Well. She's inside. I can take you to her if you want."

Nodding, I follow Chris inside the house. He shuts the door behind me and nods toward his left. "She and Mike are this way."

I take in my surroundings and notice there does seem to be a party going on. To my right is a large living room with a few people mingling. And as I follow Chris, we pass through the kitchen, which leads to a backyard. In the yard there has to be at least fifty people. Some are in the pool, and some are simply standing around and dancing. When we pass a few men and women standing in the open doorway of the kitchen that leads to the back patio, one of the women gives me a curious glance, and a tall man with dark hair and a neck tattoo wearing a suit leers at me briefly then turns his attention back to his date. By the time we reach the back of the house, the unease I was feeling before intensifies but I keep a handle on my nerves because I need to find Jia and make sure she is okay.

"Your friend is just through here," Chris gestures to the closed door at the end of the hall. When he opens it, he steps aside to let me through. In front of me is a pool table and to the right of the pool table is a brown leather sofa. My hand flies to my mouth when I see Jia passed out on it. "What the hell. What did you do?" I rush to her side and drop to my knees on the floor next to the sofa. I touch my hand to Jia's forehead to find her skin covered in sweat and clammy. When I don't hear Chris' response, I look over my shoulder to find the dark haired man with the neck tattoo looming behind me. The look on his face sends a chill down my spine, and I force my mouth to move. "What the hell is going on?" A sharp pain radiates from the back of my head. My vision blurs at the edges, and I reach out, trying to grab hold of something. Voices around me sound muffled as I feel my body sway, just before everything goes black.

13

KIWI

I rode all fucking night—just me, the road, and persistent thoughts of Piper. My brothers all know about Donovan Black, and every sorted detail of the operation he was running years ago. That knowledge alone has made me edgy for the past forty-eight hours and my stomach in knots. No matter how Nova feels, Vegas is not the place for two young women. Vultures lurk around every damn corner in search of their next victim. The assurance that Donovan possesses no active threat since he hasn't been seen or heard from since he went into hiding eleven years ago does nothing to shake the uneasy feeling in my gut.

I thought my bike and the highway would bring me some peace like so many times before. Instead, I'm home, standing under the spray of water, hot enough to cause some pain, but I'm too distracted to care. I smack my palm against the wet tile. "Goddammit," I growl. I should have pushed the issue further. Then again, if I did, would my worry have raised flags of suspicion? Would my brothers wonder why my concerns are so strong? Would they have seen right through me?

The tension in my neck and shoulders grows, and I feel a

headache developing near the base of my skull. Closing my eyes, I try to relax and clear my mind, but visions of Piper are all I see. I think back to the night she returned home and walked through the door of the bar like it was the first time she walked into my life. Then my mind takes me back to Leon's and the kiss we shared.

My cock grows heavy as I replay the feel of her lips against mine. I wrap my hand around my cock, like I've done every night for the past year, and give it a few strokes. Then she throws it in my face that her lips have been wrapped around another man's dick before, and someone else has tasted her sweet pussy—and it wasn't me. Fueled by jealousy, anger, and need, my strokes become aggressive and fast. My hands ache to explore Piper's curves—to squeeze her full tits, rolling her nipples between my thumb and forefinger, before sucking them one at a time into my mouth. I throw my head back and squeeze my cock harder. I want to run my tongue through her center and suck her clit until she comes in my mouth. The pressure of my impending release builds, along with my breathing. The moment I visualize my cock sliding into her pussy for the first time, I explode, coming so fucking hard my vision blurs. My thigh muscles quiver as I ride out the rest of my release. Bringing my heavy breathing under control, I relax my body as the water cascading over me begins to turn cold.

Suddenly my mind is clear, and it hits me. Why haven't I thought about this before? Turning the water off, I step out of the shower, snatch a towel from the rack, and wrap it around my waist. With water dripping from my hair, down my back, I walk out to the living room. Sitting on the couch, I open my laptop. As a safety precaution, the club has trackers on every family member's phones, and I'm the one who makes sure every device is running as it should. Knowing the code, I sign into the app and tap on Piper's cell number. Leaning back on the couch, I sigh. Piper looks to be at the hotel. A small sense of relief washes over me, but it's still not enough affirmation to put my mind at ease.

She's fine. Piper knows how to take care of herself. At least, that's what I continue to tell myself as I close my laptop and make my way back to the bedroom. Drying off, I toss the damp towel into the clothes basket. Laying in his dog bed, Chance slightly raises his head. I give him a head scratch before turning off the lamp, then sliding into bed.

Closing my eyes, I will my brain to shut down, but I can't help thinking about Piper. I've texted her many times since she left, but everyone was ignored.

After lying in bed for what feels like an hour, mental and physical exhaustion finally help me succumb to sleep.

<hr>

The following morning, Chance's barking wakes me from a deep sleep. Looking at the time, I notice it's nearly 9:00 am. "Shit." I throw my blanket to the side. I never sleep this late. Rubbing the sleep from my eyes, I rise from the bed. "Sorry, boy. Come on. Let's take care of your bladder, and then I'll get you fed."

Because Chance's hindquarter is paralyzed, he can't empty his bladder himself, so I need to help him. Retrieving a piddle pad, I sit on the floor beside him. Laying Chance on his side, I express his bladder by squeezing it the way Dr. Channing taught me.

Once we've finished, I discard everything and wash my hands. Chance and I make our way through the house to the kitchen. He eagerly awaits next to his bowl for his meal. While he eats, I brew a cup of strong coffee. Ready for his morning exercise, Chance then maneuvers his way to the backdoor. Grabbing his wheelchair, I get him securely strapped in, then pull open the door. Taking my coffee with me, I step out on the porch as Chance zooms down his doggy ramp I built the day he came home to make his access to the yard as easy on him as possible. The first thing he does is to run toward the goats, barking. I chuckle, watching him.

I take in a deep breath of fresh air. It's peaceful out here. No neighbors. A strong breeze sweeps across the back porch, causing the old wind chimes to clink. I look off in the distance and notice storm clouds rolling in. Then, what I think is thunder, morphs into the distinct rumble of Harleys. Stepping off the porch, I stroll around the corner of the house and see my brothers barreling down my driveway. My gut clenches, and I'm on high alert. Something isn't right.

They roll up and quickly cut their engines. Chance rolls around, sniffing at the bike tires as I approach. Nova is the first to look at me, his face tight with worry. Looking at all my brothers, they wear similar expressions. "What's goin' on?" I sound desperate for an answer and don't give a damn.

"I haven't heard from Piper in nearly twelve hours. It's not like her not to check-in," Nova states.

"I checked on her location late last night, and from what I saw, she was at the hotel." The guys eyeball me. "Look, I don't trust anything to do with Las Vegas. All of you know that. For my sanity, I checked on her whereabouts around ten," I admit, and the only questionable look I get comes from Fender.

Nova scrubs his palm down his face. "I need you to open your computer and pull up all her recent activity." Nova and Fender follow me to the back of the house, then inside to my living room. Removing Chance from his wheelchair, he stretches out on the cold wood floor. My brothers wait as I open my computer and tap into Piper's phone. I retrace her activity from the time she left Louisiana, pinpointing every stop she and her friend made once they landed in Nevada.

"Her phone hasn't moved since last night. The battery life is good," I state. "And you've called her?" I then ask.

"Several times," Nova says. "Promise too. Even called the room directly, and still nothing."

It's not normal for Piper to ignore contact with her family.

Something doesn't feel right. Everything about the situation is wrong. I look up at Nova from my computer screen. "What does your gut say?"

"Something isn't right," Nova states and I couldn't agree more. Nova retrieves his phone and calls Riggs.

Forty minutes later, after planning for one of the club girls to drive out to my place and pick up Chance, Nova, Fender, and I are pulling up to the clubhouse. The place is dead silent as we enter.

"They guys are in Church," Bella, Logan's woman says, and several of the other old ladies look up from where they sit. Giving her a nod, Nova, Fender, and I cross the room and walk into church finding every member seated at the table.

"What's the word, Prez?" I ask, sitting beside Nova after he pulls out a chair.

"We don't know much yet. I'm still waiting to hear back from Cowboy. He is supposed to contact the commander and authorize the use of one of the team's aircrafts. The fastest way to find out what is goin' on is to for some of us to fly out to Las Vegas, and ASAP," Riggs addresses us all before his eyes settle on Nova. "I know you're worried, brother, we all are." Riggs lights a cigarette. "It's not like Piper to avoid contact with anyone in the club."

My jaw clenches. Anger is an understatement for what I'm feeling at the moment. No matter how hard I try, Donovan haunts every aspect of Piper's lack of communication. What if her and Jia fell victim to the same scenario as all those women did years ago. It doesn't take much for my thoughts to darken, and the fear of never finding Piper hits me like a Mack truck.

"Get out of your head, Kiwi. We have no idea what is going on at the moment," Riggs singles me out.

"She should have never been allowed to go to Vegas," I grind my teeth. It takes all my strength to keep from coming undone. I voiced my concerns, and now Piper could be in trouble.

"There have been no signs of Donovan since he gave us the slip years ago," Riggs tries to convince me, but his words fall on deaf ears.

"I can't explain it, Prez, but nothin' I do shakes the feeling that he's about to crawl out from under the rock he's been hidin' under," I admit.

"Who's Donovan?" Quinn questions. Jake and Riggs share a look. Before interrupting and overstepping my Prez, I give Riggs a look, and a nod gives me his approval to explain.

"Donovan Black is my birth father. He helped organize and sell women, in one of the country's largest sex trafficking rings, eleven years ago." What I don't care to share is the fact that I played a part.

"Hey," Wick's voice booms, earning everyone's attention, yet he is looking directly at me from across the table. "You need to let that shit swirling around in your head go, brother. That sorry excuse for a human used you. One day, you will get retribution—he will pay for his sins." Wick holds my attention for a beat. "We'll find out soon enough if your premonition will become our reality."

"Until then, we all need to keep level headed," Jake interjects, and he's right.

Riggs' phone buzzes, vibrating against the table. Palming it, he answers. His words are short, giving no clue to who is on the other end. The moment he lays his phone down, he locks eyes with Nova. "That was Cowboy. His connection at Lakefront will fly us to Vegas." Pausing, Riggs looks at his watch. "We have less than an hour to get our shit and leave." Riggs faces Jake. "Brother, I know ya'll are due to hit the road today..."

Jake throws up his hand. "Say no more. My crew will remain here until further notice." He faces Logan. "Have our women call our family back home to let them know we will be extending our stay."

Riggs stands, clasping Jake on his shoulder. "Thanks, brother."

"No thanks necessary. We take care of our own," Jake says.

"My men go sort out your shit. Kiss your women and children if you have them, then get your asses outside. We hit the road in twenty," Riggs orders, then he slams the gavel, ending church.

As everyone is filing out, Riggs stops me. "You sure you can handle going back? I know you swore you would never return to Vegas."

Letting my defenses down for a moment, I tell him, "Nothing is going to stop me from making sure Piper is safe." The conviction in my voice is firm. Riggs eyes me for a beat and, for a split second, I think I just fucked up.

Riggs levels me with a hard stare. "We'll get answers soon enough. Just keep your head on straight. Got it?"

14

PIPER

Waking up, the first thing I notice is I have a blinding headache. The second is I'm surrounded by darkness. I blink a few times to make sure my eyes are open, and my head is not playing tricks on me. Wherever I am, it is pitch black. Not being able to see what's around me causes my breathing to pick up and echo off the walls that surround me, and I start to panic.

"Hey," a small voice calls out, and I try desperately to see where it's coming from.

"You need to calm down before you pass out."

"Who are you? Where am I? Where is Jia?" my questions come out in a strangled cry.

"My name is Lelani, and if your friend is the girl who was put in here with you, she is right beside you. She must still be passed out. Those guys probably gave her something."

Sticking my hands out in front of me, I feel around on the floor until I connect with a body. Whoever this person is, they are not moving. I hold my breath as I move my hands up until I touch her hair. It's long and soft. I feel around her face, and like before, it's cool to the touch and sweaty. "Jia?" I nudge. "Jia?" I call out again.

This time she lets out a moan. "Piper?"

I breathe a sigh of relief when I recognize her voice.

"Piper, I don't feel so good. And how come we're in the dark? Where are we? I can't see you." Jia begins to panic as she tries to sit up. "Piper, what's going on?"

Suddenly Jia lurches forward and begins to vomit all over the front of my jeans. It reeks of alcohol, and I try not to gag. Without being able to see, I do my best to hold her hair away from her face. Once she is done, I help hold her up with one hand while sticking the other out in front of me, looking for a place to let her lay down away from where she just vomited. "Come on, Jia. Lay down."

"Your friend will probably start feeling better now that she has thrown up whatever was in her system," Lelani tells me.

"Do you know where we are, Lelani?"

"No. But the walls and the floor are metal, so I'm almost certain we are not in the house. And you said it was dark and that you couldn't see anything. Also, when you were brought here with your friend, the door that was closed sounded heavy. It also sounded like it was locked with one of those levers. My guess is we are in a metal shed or some sort of storage building."

Just as I am about to respond to Lelani, a loud clicking noise followed by a burst of light floods the room as the door opens, revealing the man with the neck tattoo and beside him is another guy pulling on the arm of a struggling woman.

"Let me go!" she screeches as she claws at his face. The guy snarls just before he rears back and punches the woman across her left cheek.

"Shut the fuck up, bitch." Then hauls her up and tosses her inside what I can now see is one of those mobile storage units. There's a company logo and a telephone number on the inside of the door. The woman lands with a thud and crab crawls away from her assailant until her back hits the solid wall. She has tears and mascara running down her face and a noticeable bruise forming on her cheekbone.

Three more men step into view; each of them has a woman clutched in their grasps—all three-look like the one who is currently huddled in a corner sobbing. The three women look to be in their early/mid-twenties, and all three are dressed as if they were going to a club or party. The man points his gun and motions for the women to climb in. With terrified looks, they do without protest.

With a nod, the men leave at the same time another guy with thinning hair and a round stomach walks up joining the group. "Time to roll out. What are we going to do about the blind bitch?" he asks, nodding toward a woman sitting six feet to my right. She has fiery red hair, a long blue flowy dress on, and looks to be in her mid-twenties...Lelani. Is she blind?

Neck tattoo shrugs. "That asshole Derrick said he was going to bring us a prize, he failed to mention the girl is blind. We'll let the boss decide what he wants to do with her. In the meantime, I want you to find Derrick. If the fucker thinks this makes us square, he better think again. One body doesn't wipe away his debt."

It's pretty clear what's going on here. Growing up in an MC, I am not immune to the bad shit that happens in the world. My dad shielded a lot from me, but he taught me a lot too. And the way these assholes are talking about Lelani or any woman like they are pieces of expendable property has me seeing red. My hands ball up into fists. I also remember the pepper spray I have tucked into the band of my jeans. I contemplate making a move but decide now is not the time. Especially when I see that neck tattoo has a gun in his hand. My eyes cut to his weapon then up to his face. He's looking at me with a smirk on his face.

Returning a smirk of my own, I tell him, "You have no idea what you've done."

"Oh, yeah. And what are you going to do about it?"

"I won't have to do anything, asshole."

Jia, who has her head laying in my lap, whimpers when she notices neck tattoo guy becoming irritated with me.

"What the fuck does that mean, bitch?"

I hold the guy's gaze and keep my smirk firmly planted on my face even though I'm terrified on the inside. "You'll find out soon enough."

The man stares me down, his knuckles turning white around the gun in his hand.

His friend nudges him. "Leave it alone, Boz. The bitch is just running her trap. We need to get on the road."

Before slamming the door, enclosing us in darkness yet again, Boz, as his buddy called him, delivers one last bone-chilling look with his dark eyes. A look that leaves me with chills.

"Piper?" Jia rasps.

"Yeah?"

"What do you think is going to happen to us?"

Her question causes the new girls to whimper. Lelani has yet to say another word, and I briefly wonder who that Derrick guy is to Lelani and how Lelani fell into the same trap as the rest of us.

I continue to stroke Jia's hair in hopes to keep her calm. "My family will come for me," I say with conviction.

The moment the words leave my mouth, a truck engine roars to life, and the walls begin to vibrate. A few seconds later, we're moving.

Minutes tick by and I don't know how long we have been on the road, but it feels like it takes an eternity for the sobs of the four other women in here with myself, Jia, and Lelani to turn into light whimpers. Jia is awake, but like me, she hasn't said a word. As for Lelani, she too, hasn't made a sound.

"Lelani?" I call out.

"Yeah?" she croaks.

"The guy, those men were talking about, Derrick. Who is he?" I don't know why I ask her such a random question.

I hear Lelani's deep exhaled breath, almost like it pains her to answer.

"Derrick is my brother."

My stomach knots. "Your brother did this to you?"

"Yes."

"Well, don't worry, Lelani. We'll be getting out of here soon."

"What makes you so sure?" one of the other girls asks.

Jia is the one to answer her. "Because Piper's badass biker family will find us. Won't they Piper?"

"They will. I know they will."

"How will they know where to find you?" This question comes from Lelani.

"They just will. Trust me."

"I pray you're right."

Me too. I just don't say that out loud.

I wake with a jolt at the sound of tires squealing and the truck coming to a stop. The tin box we are in has become almost unbearable. It's so hot my shirt is drenched in sweat and sticking to my body. The sweltering heat makes me feel like I am suffocating.

Jia sits up beside me and clutches my hand. "We stopped. What do you think is happening?"

I shake my head even though I know she can't see me. The sound of two truck doors slamming shut has my nerves picking up. The other women begin to whimper at the sound of the lock disengaging. The door opens, and sunlight filters inside. The balding guy from earlier appears. "Rise and shine," he sing songs as he tosses a five-gallon bucket inside. "You have five minutes."

"For what?" I eye the bucket then him.

"To piss," he gestures toward the bucket.

I turn my lip up in disgust. "We're not peeing in a bucket."

"Suit yourself," he shrugs. "What about you?" The prick puts his hand on Lelani's thigh. "Since you can't see, I'd be willing to make an exception for you and lend a hand."

Lelani swats at the creeps' hand and shrinks away. I have had enough.

I move fast as I get up and lunge for him, knocking his hand away from Lelani. "Keep your disgusting hands off her."

The pig sneers and grabs hold of my arm, jerking me toward him until he's in my face. The smell of his rancid breath makes me want to gag.

"Listen here, you little whore!" he yells, spittle flying from his mouth.

"I'm not a whore," I seethe, gritting my teeth.

A sinister smile takes over his ugly face. "You will be. In fact, maybe I should be the one to break you in." He grabs at his crotch.

He doesn't see me reach into the band of my jeans for my pepper spray. Too bad for him. "Over my dead body, asshole." Bringing the tube up in front of his face, I make the douchebag regret ever putting his hands on me or Lelani.

"Ahh! You fucking bitch!" he squeals like a pig as he tumbles backward, falling in a heap to the gravel below. Out of nowhere, a fist comes flying at my face, connecting with my eye, knocking me backward onto Lelani, who takes me into her arms. I lose my grip on the pepper spray, and it falls to the ground, landing at the feet of the man who just hit me, Boz. He looks at me then at the pathetic excuse of a man lying on the ground. "Get your ass up," Boz kicks him.

The creep climbs to his feet, and I take satisfaction at the look of the tears and snot running down his red face, and I smirk. That only further pisses him off, causing him to lunge for me.

Boz stops him. "No. Go get cleaned up so we can get back on the road."

Boz turns his attention back to me. "The next time you pull a stunt like that, I'm going to kill your friend." Boz makes a show of pointing his gun at Jia.

With his parting threat, the door slams shut, and the world around me becomes dark once again.

15

KIWI

The entire flight to Vegas was done in silence, hearing nothing but the plane's engines. What more could we say? The six of us know we are walking into the situation completely blind. Cowboy also arranged for us to have an SUV on standby as soon as we land.

The moment the tires hit the tarmac, my blood is pumping from a sudden rush of adrenaline. We are all on our feet before the plane comes to a stop. As soon as the door opens, we file out, sprinting to the nearby hanger where our vehicle is waiting. We traveled light, meaning nothing but the clothes on our back and weapons concealed beneath our cuts.

"I'll drive," I call out, and jump behind the steering wheel.

As anxious as I am—as we all are, I keep to the speed limit. We don't want to draw unwanted attention. I weave the SUV in and out of traffic. "Come on." My grip tightens on the steering wheel every time we hit a red light. I'd forgotten how bad traffic is here in Vegas.

Finally, I see the hotel Piper is staying at up ahead. I also scope out a few guards milling about outside. I pull into the parking lot and bring the SUV to a halt right beside the valet parking stand.

Riggs turns in his seat, addressing us. "The last thing we want is trouble with hotel security. Let's get information without causing a scene. Everest, stay with the vehicle, and keep it runnin' in case we happen to run into any trouble." Wasting no time, my brothers and I exit the vehicle, brushing past the valet attendee.

Onlookers' judgmental stares fall on us as we stroll into the luxury hotel and make our way to the front desk. With wide eyes, the woman behind the counter greets us. "Welcome. How can I help you, gentlemen, today?"

"I need the room number for Jia Kook," Nova steps up.

Her eyes dart between us men. Not sure what to make of a bunch of bikers. "Um, I'm sorry, sir, but I'm not allowed to give you that information." Nova stiffens, and I can tell he is hanging on by a thread. He looks down at her nametag. "Callie, listen. I need to check on my daughter." He keeps his voice calm.

Callie blinks several times. "I could lose my job." She appears conflicted on what to do, but nervous to refuse our demand. She clears her throat and starts typing at her keyboard, her eyes lifting briefly to see if a coworker is nearby. She steps away, only to return, holding a key card in her hand. "I hope you enjoy your stay." She hands the card to Nova. Slightly leaning forward, she whispers, "I hope your daughter is okay."

A short ride up the elevator to the fifth floor, we rush down the hallway, stopping at the end, where suite 150 is located. The first thing we notice is the do not disturb sign hanging on the door handle. Nova bangs on the door first, getting no answer before slipping the key card into the slot. The lock disengages, and he slowly pushes the door open.One by one, we cautiously enter the room. The luxury suite is a decent size. Riggs gives the signal for us to spread out and investigate. I walk across the living room, take in the half-eaten takeout sitting on the coffee table, before striding into one of the bedrooms. The smell of honey and jasmine hits me the moment I step into the room and immediately realize it's Piper's suite. In a chair, near the bed, is her open suitcase, and draped across the back of the chair a red dress. Finding nothing to suggest foul play, I turn on my heels, heading back to the living room, where I find my brothers. "Anyone find anything?" I ask as I continue to make a sweep of the suite.

"Not a damn thing. This uneaten food has been sitting there for more than a day," Wick observes. His eyes scan the room as he walks to the floor to ceiling window, with a view overlooking the famous Vegas strip. He whistles. "Damn. Her friend must be loaded to score a room like this."

"Let's sweep the entire hotel. I want each floor searched. The bar, swimming pool—everything," Riggs orders, then he faces me. "Find a way to get access to the hotel security camera feed. Comb through it. If you find anything suspicious, I want to know."

"You got it." As we are about to leave, something on the floor catches my eye. Just beneath the table in the small foyer lays a black business card. My heart begins to beat rapidly, and my palms become clammy. Bending, I pluck it from the floor. Righting myself, I flip the card over. My jaw clenches as I stare at the gold embossed VIP lettering and an address. All the blood drains from my face, and my gut plummets to my feet. Suddenly I'm back in Donovan's penthouse, holding a stack of cards, getting ready to hit all the local hotspots.

"Kiwi, what the hell is the hold-up?" I hear Riggs through the haze. Pulling myself together, I look at my brother and give him the card. Pushing all other feelings aside, I allow rage to fill the void. He looks at it, then back at me. His face falls. "Change of plans." He calls over his shoulder to those already in the hallway, and they rush back inside. Riggs hands the card to Wick, and he too understands what it might mean.

"Let's roll."

"Someone needs to tell me what the fuck is going on," Nova

demands once the elevator door closes, and we descend. Wick hands the business card to him, and Nova reads it.

"That card looks identical to the ones Donovan would have me hand out when he hosted his parties." Nova and I lock eyes. He knows all about Donovan Black, so there is no need for me to explain. I would only be rehashing the same worries I had when I found out Piper was coming to Vegas a few days ago.

"Keep it together, brother," Riggs tells Nova. "It's not lookin' good, but, for Piper's sake, we need to keep calm. Let's get our asses to the address on that card and find answers."

Not one of us says a word as we exit the hotel. We find Everest right where we left him, next to the SUV.

It takes us nearly thirty minutes to get through traffic until we are traveling a winding road. When we left the hotel, Riggs placed a call to Cowboy, explaining our current situation. "They haven't gotten any red flags in this area for some time, but the commander is getting us the intel he has," Riggs states, as I roll to a stop in front of a million-dollar mansion. The front door swings open, and a young man, who looks to be in his twenties, steps out.

"This is private property."

Before he can take another step in our direction, I have my weapon pulled and aimed at his head. "Inside." His hands rise in the air as he takes a step back. Riggs orders Everest and Fender to case the outside for any threat. The door slams shut behind us as we step inside.

"Chris, where the fuck are you. The boss called. He wants..." the man behind the voice walks into the foyer. The moment he sees the gun aimed at his friend's head, he reaches inside the suit jacket he is wearing and pulls out a gun. Nova aims, a single shot rings out, and the guy's knees buckle, sending him to the floor. The weapon in his right-hand clatters as it skids across the marble tile, and blood pools beneath his body.

"Shit, man. You fucking killed him," the scared prick I have in my crosshair's bellows.

"Who else is in the house?" I back him up against the wall and press the cold hard barrel of my gun into his eye socket."

"No one, no one. I fucking swear."

Wick moves forward, with his weapon drawn to check out the rest of the home. Nova steps to my side and shoves the business card we found in the punk's face. "Someone gave this to a couple of girls." Then Nova takes out his phone and pulls up a recent picture of Piper. The guy tries turning his head, looking away. Grabbing a fist full of his hair, I slam the back of his head against the wall.

"Look at her face, you piece of shit," I order.

"Maybe she was here last night, man. I don't know." His voice trembles a little, but there's a hint of arrogance present.

"I don't believe you." My grip tightens on his scalp. I place my gun under his chin. "Look again," I tell him, and as if he already knows he won't be breathing by the time we finish with him, he stares at the phone screen. A sinister smirk appears on his face, and gone is his innocent act.

"You're too late," he confesses. Nova lowers his phone, just as Wick reappears.

"The house is empty, Prez, but I did find a stack of cards like the one Nova is holding, along with a shitload of drugs in the other room. Some of those pills are pretty strong sedatives," Wick quickly informs. The moment he mentions drugs, my mind goes to a dark place. Some shady shit took place here last night.

"You better get to talkin'," I growl at the piece of shit in front of me. My finger twitches wanting to pull the trigger.

"That pretty piece of ass, along with some other prime pussy are on their way to the auction block. You assholes are barking up the wrong tree. When my boss gets wind of a bunch of bikers walking in here, killing one of his men, there will be hell to pay." The prick dares to toss a threat at us. What does he think we'll do? Tuck tail and run? I shove him to the floor. His hands and knees hit hard against the tile. Then Nova kicks his ribcage with the toe of his boot. Before Riggs throws his hand up, motioning for him to stop.

"Who do you work for?" Riggs demands.

"Sorry, bro. I don't have a name, and if I did, I sure as shit wouldn't give it to you." Unsatisfied with his answer, Nova kicks him again, causing the asshole to cough and spittle to fly from his mouth. He laughs. "I'll tell you what. Since I'm going to die anyway, I'll throw you a bone." His laugh becomes manic. "I'll tell you what he looks like."

"Spit it out, you sorry son of a bitch," Nova rages.

The guy raises his head. Knelt before us, he points a finger directly at me. "He looks a lot like this ugly bastard." Before anyone gets a chance to process his words, I aim my gun at the fucker's head and put a bullet in it. His words cement my worries and bring my worst nightmares to life. Piper was taken, in a sex trafficking scheme, to be sold to the highest bidder. And Donovan, my birth father, is behind it.

Fender and Everest jog up just as we walk outside, and by the look on their faces, whatever they say isn't going to be good. "We found Piper's phone." Fender hand's it to Nova, who swipes the cracked screen in search of anything that may help us. "We found it on the ground near the back of the property, where the garage is located."

"Piper's last outgoing texts and phone calls were sent to Jia," Nova says.

"Get me a laptop, and I'll see if we can track her phone location," I tell him.

"I saw one inside," Wick tells me, and I rush back into the house. I follow Wick to an office in the home where a computer sits on a desk. Taking a seat in the leather chair, I get to work.

Several minutes later, I have Jia's phone locations marked on the screen. "Jia was here last night," I confirm. "And her last location had her at this address." I move the cursor on the screen. Looking around, I search for something to write on. Everest leans in and takes a snapshot of the address on the screen.

"Got it," Everest says.

Riggs once again pulls out his phone, "Let's go." He barks while jogging through the home. Leaving the dead where they lay, we rush to the SUV. "Let's scope out Jia's last known location." Riggs slams the door closed.

The address takes us to what looks to be an abandoned warehouse in a seedy area. I circle the block a few times before driving onto the property. Getting out, we approach with caution. Peering through dirty windows, we notice no activity inside, it's just as barren as the outside. The five of us make our way around the building.

"There's a roll-up door back here, but it's padlocked," Wick points out.

A noise catches our attention. Riggs lifts a finger to his lips, telling us to be quiet as we move toward the sound. Rounding the corner, we find a homeless man digging through a dumpster. "Hey," Everest calls out, his gun aimed and the guy spins around.

"Shit, man. I'm sorry. Don't shoot." He drops what's in his hands.

"We're not gonna hurt you," Riggs says as we step closer. The guy twitches and mumbles something to himself. From the looks of his arms, he's a heavy needle user. "Have you seen any men around here? Maybe a big truck or anything?" Riggs is careful with how he speaks to the guy in hopes he doesn't freak him out. Everest lowers his weapon.

"I see a lot of shit in this neighborhood," the guy tells us. He turns and starts sifting through the trash again.

"Care to share what you know?" Acting casual, Riggs pulls a cigarette from his pocket and lights it.

"Sure, man. For a price." The man looks over his shoulder and flashes us a toothless grin.

Digging in his back pocket, Riggs retrieves his wallet and pulls out a few twenties. He waves them in the air. "Have you noticed anything going on around this building the past few days?" he asks, and the homeless man stops what he's doing. Wiping his dirty, leathered hands down the front of his shirt, he ventures toward us, pushing a beat-up shopping cart.

"Sure did. They had themselves a bunch of girls over here the other night. Pretty things, they were too." Riggs holds out a twenty, and the guy plucks it from his hand. "I didn't see any trucks that night, but I did overhear a couple of men talking about making a trip south, maybe they mentioned Louisiana or Florida." The guy starts looking confused as if he's lost his train of thought. Riggs snaps his fingers, gaining the homeless man's attention again. Then hands him another twenty.

"Is that all?" Riggs asks, and the homeless man thinks for a minute, then looks around. Riggs' phone rings, so he pulls it from his pocket and listens as he keeps his eyes on the guy in front of us.

"Oh yeah, wait. I remember something else." He scratches his neck and shuffles his feet. "They said women were going to make them rich." Riggs tosses the last twenty, and it flutters to the ground. Having heard enough, we turn and walk away.

"Get back to the plane." Riggs shoves his phone into his cut. "Cowboy just confirmed his insiders contacted him less than an hour ago, informing him of cell movement within a sector here in Vegas, that is well known to be involved in the sex trade. I'll know more soon."

The vehicle's cab falls silent, and my rampant thoughts become so loud that it feels as if others can hear them.

Riggs shifts in his seat, and I feel his eyes on me. "Don't go there."

"You heard what he said back at the house." I keep my eyes on the road.

"His boss could be anyone, Kiwi. For all we know, the bastard was fuckin' with us," Riggs tells me, but his words fall on deaf ears.

"You lost your shit back there." He points out.

"He was dead either way," I say through clenched teeth.

Nova punches the roof of the vehicle numerous times. "Prez, Goddammit. What is the plan? I can't take the silence and the unknown. Abel, brother, they took my baby." Hearing the agony in Nova's voice has my grip tightening on the steering wheel.

"What's the plan?" Wick echoes from the back seat.

"I'm not going to sugarcoat the situation. We have a small window of opportunity to intercept the cargo Cowboy is tracking. The shipment in question is traveling south. Right now, we don't know where their final destination is. If we don't make it within the next 24 hours..." he leaves his words unfinished.

On the way back to the private airstrip, I weave in and out of traffic, blowing through several lights along the way. We have a three-hour flight back to New Orleans, and I'm not wasting one second getting us there sooner.

Hours later, we've landed, and the wheels on our Harleys are eating pavement as we race toward the clubhouse. The yard is filled with cars and trucks belonging to the family, leading me to believe Riggs wants everyone on lockdown. Parking our bikes, we file inside. You could hear a pin drop the moment we walk through the door. Every member, along with their women, are sitting around the room.

Promise rushes toward Nova, with Jaxson in her arms. Tears fall from her face as she walks into his arms. A heaviness descends on us all, as Nova consoles his family. "I'll bring her home beautiful," he tells her.

"Church," Riggs' voice booms, and every brother stands.

With each member standing, Fender closes the door, and Riggs puts his phone on the table. He's been speaking with Cowboy and his team since we arrived a few minutes ago. Riggs speaks. "We have confirmation that a shipping container, transported by truck, is traveling 49 south. They should reach Louisiana near midnight." Riggs stops talking when there is a knock on the door. He lifts his chin at Fender to find out who is interrupting us when the women know not to disturb us while church is in session. The door swings open, and standing in the doorway is a face we haven't seen in New Orleans in some time. Cowboy walks into the room. "For those of you who haven't met him yet, this here is Cowboy. He is one of many on the Ops team, with me, Wick, Tequila," Riggs pauses a beat, then continues. "Anyway, Cowboy is joining the mission." Riggs looks at Cowboy, giving him the floor.

"Alright. The target was traveling 49 south. Approximately forty minutes ago, satellites showed they changed course traveling I10." Cowboy opens a folder that he has clutched in his hand. "They stopped along this particular stretch of roadway." He shows the first image. "They opened the back of the container. For what reason, we don't know. We believe they are heading toward a national park in this area." He points at an aerial image, then looks around the room. "It's an ideal location to transfer the women from truck to boat. The inlets around this particular area lead straight out to the Gulf of Mexico."

"So, they're not headed for Florida?" Wick asks.

"That is still undetermined. I suggest we head out as soon as possible, with no more than five or six men. Travel only with what you can conceal on your person and get there before they arrive. I drove here in a passenger van. I'll fall in behind you guys," Cowboy informs us.

"I'd like to join you," Jake cuts in.

"I wouldn't have it any other way, brother." Riggs clasps his shoulder.

Night has fallen by the time we hit the road. Eight men strong, we head south, toward our destination, which is forty-five minutes away. Judging by the last report Cowboy received an hour ago, the men who have Piper are three hours behind us. Bikes rumble behind me as we speed down the highway. We keep to backroads as much as we can to avoid drawing attention to ourselves. The ride feels longer than it should as I think about what Piper is going through. Adrenaline courses through my veins, mixed with anxiety of the unknown. Then, I think about the last words I spoke to her, and the look on her face. I will never forgive myself if I never get the chance to tell her I'm sorry.

The farther we travel into the rural areas, streets lights become fewer, and homes are spaced further apart. The darkness of night swallows the bikes, and the air feels heavy and ominous as if the Grim Reaper himself is riding with us. Riggs and Jake slow, making a right onto a dirt road, bringing the rest of us to a stop roughly ten miles down. The smell of fish tainted water and wet grass lets me know we are near water. Riggs turns off his bike and walks down the row of Harleys. "We leave the bikes here," he orders.

Cowboy, who has stayed a decent distance behind us, arrives, pulling the van further ahead. He climbs out, joining the rest of us. "Target site is situated at the end of the next road over, nestled along the inlet. We travel on foot from here. "

Riggs, Jake, Logan, Nova, Gabriel, Austin, Cowboy, and I check our weapons, then tuck them away before we start making our way through the tall grass, trudging through mud and muck that coats our boots. I have no idea how long it takes us until we notice dimly lit lights in the distance. Riggs throws a fist in the air, and we stop moving. Huddling together, we kneel. I take in the small compound several yards away. At first glance, nothing seems out of the ordinary until I spot at least four storage pods on the farthest side of the property, along with at least eight armed men milling around. "You see what I'm seeing?" I whisper to Nova, who is kneeled beside me.

"Yeah, brother."

Just as he says those words, headlights break over the hill on the road leading toward the camp. A semi hauling a similar storage container like the ones on sight slows, the air brakes hissing as it comes to a complete stop. We look on as two men climb from the cab, meeting two other men walking in their direction, before heading toward the back end of the truck. With bated breath, we watch the double doors swing open. With guns drawn, they usher several women from inside. My eyes immediately zero in on Piper the moment she comes into view. One guy shoves her, hard, and Piper stumbles, falling to her knees. My body moves instinctively, but Logan grabs hold of my arm, pulling me back. My heart sinks, and my blood boils as I watch them lead her and the other women away, placing them into another container nearby.

Facing us, Riggs fires off his command. "Logan, you and Reid keep low and head for the north end of the camp. It gives you the highest vantage point to use your sniper rifles." Shifting, Riggs looks to his left. "Nova, you and Fender make your way around the south perimeter near those two trailers over there," Riggs points, then turns to me. "Kiwi, you and Gabriel trudge through the tall grass past Logan and Reid's mark, and position yourself near the water's edge." Lastly, he speaks to us all before we disperse. "They outnumber us. Timing is everything. When you hear my signal, move in. This ambush needs to be quick. We don't stop until every man is dead, and Piper is safe."

With a precise steady movement, Gabriel and I find our way to the water's edge, where we find three rickety oyster boats situated along the bank. Unseen behind the thick marsh grass,

Gabriel and I sit and wait. Time slows to a crawl. I can see little through the darkness, but we can hear the murmurs of men talking several yards away, nearly drowned out by the droning of cicadas and croaking frogs. The warm air is thick with the smell of decaying vegetation. A harsh voice is heard not far from our position.

"Get the boats ready to transfer the women." A few seconds later, the shuffling of feet alerts us to someone moving in our direction. Gabriel pulls a long blade from the inside of his boot. He peeks over the tall grass, then ducks back. He signals that two targets are approaching, so I slide a knife carried at my side from its sheath. We haven't heard Riggs signal yet, but Gabriel and I both know these two threats need to be eliminated. They stand only a few feet away from our location, with rifles slung low at their sides. Before the men step onto one of the boats, Gabriel and I make our move. Without making a sound, we rush them from behind. My palm covers his mouth, stifling his scream as I run my blade across his neck. The man struggles against my hold, as the rush of his warm blood coats his shirt. He fights, desperately grasping for his weapon that I've gained control of before his body goes limp. I lower his dead weight to the ground and look at Gabriel just as he pulls his blade from his target's chest. Blood gushes from the chest wound and the jagged puncture site on his neck.

Gabriel and I drag the bodies to the bank and quietly roll them into the water for the gators to find. Two shots ring out, giving us the signal, it's go time. Men shouting and rapid gunfire breakout as we draw our weapons and head toward the fight. Bullets whiz by my head as I rush toward the container pods. Popping off shots, I take down three men along the way. A couple of men now stand between me and the container we watched Piper be loaded into. Aiming, I pull the trigger. My bullets hit their mark, and one-person stumbles backward, his body slamming against the container door, and the other dropping to the ground with a shot in his head.

Running up to the container, I notice the chain and padlock. "Dammit," I slam my fist against the thick steel. "Piper. Baby, if you're in there, answer me."

"Oh my God, Tai!" Piper's terrified voice slices through the chaos surrounding me. "Tai." She begins banging on the wall from the inside.

I frantically look around, searching for anything to bust the lock, then I spot a crowbar lying beside a toolbox. As I reach for it, a searing pain rips across the top of my left shoulder. "Motherfucker," I hiss at the pain. Suddenly, I'm tackled to the ground, landing on my back. I lose my grip, and my gun lands on the dirt out of my reach. Meaty hands wrap around my neck as I grab for the knife at my side.

"It's going to feel good to kill one of you pieces of shit with my bare hands," the fucker on top of me heaves as spittle flies from his mouth.

As he chokes me, pressure builds behind my eyes. I thrust the blade upward, beneath his rib cage, then twist it. His eyes grow wide, and his hands lax. I shove him off and get to my feet. Retrieving my gun, I stand over him as he stares blankly into the night sky, his life fading. Bending, I pull my knife from his chest, wiping the blood off on his sleeve. Walking away, I leave him to die.

It's not until I've picked the crowbar up again that I realize how quiet it has become. With my back to the container, where Piper is still screaming my name, I raise my weapon, ready to shoot when I hear footsteps approaching.

"Kiwi," Nova calls before moving closer.

One by one, each brother starts to appear, battle-worn, but alive. "Report," Riggs orders.

"Everyone is dead, besides the fucker who took off running

through the marsh. Gabriel gave chase," Logan reports with a grin. "And trust me, the son of a bitch won't get too far."

"Piper," Nova yells, as I pull at the padlock.

"Daddy?"

"I'm here, baby girl," Nova reassures his daughter just as the lock busts open. I pull the chain from the handle, throwing it to the ground. Jake unlocks one locked hinge as Wick unlocks the other. They take a step back as I swing open the heavy steel doors —a burst of hot musty air blasts my face. Cowboy shines a light inside, to find several women clinging to each other, huddled in the very back of the container. My eyes land on Piper. Nova rushes passed, taking his daughter into his arms, and I can't help but wish it were me instead of him holding her. The other men walk inside the steel cage, assisting the women to their feet, and ushering them outside. "Are you alright?" Nova looks her over.

"I'm fine, daddy—promise."

"Unlock those other containers," Jake orders. Logan and Riggs take off. Cowboy says something to Jake before jumping behind the truck's wheel to transport Piper and the other women she was with. Throwing it in drive, Cowboy takes off down the road.

"Who are you? Don't touch me." A frightened voice cries out, gaining Piper's attention. Pulling away from Nova, Piper goes to comfort the woman.

"Shh. It's okay. These men are my family. You can trust them," Piper consoles the woman then turns to Austin, who was trying to help her. "Her name is Lelani. She's blind."

Kneeling, Austin whispers something to the frightened woman, then scoops her frail body into his arm, cradling her against his chest. The redhead buries her face in Austin's neck as he carries her out.

I'm still standing just outside the container, watching Piper with her father. I release a breath when her eyes search for mine once more. Giving Nova one more hug, Piper rushes toward me, throwing her body against my chest. Some of the weight I've been carrying vanishes. She doesn't say a word, and neither do I. Piper clutches onto me like I'm her lifeline, and my arms engulf her. Piper sniffles. Pulling back a bit, I place my finger beneath her chin, lifting her face, and her red-rimmed eyes lock on mine, but it's the swollen black eye, along with a small laceration on her cheek lit by the moonlight that turns my blood cold. "Who hit you?" I bark.

Piper brings her hand up, brushing her fingertips along her skin. "A guy with a neck tattoo," is the only information she can offer.

Movement in the distance catches my attention, and I notice an incredibly angry Gabriel stomping across the yard, with a mud-covered man in tow. Nova meets Gabriel before he gets closer to the women. Piper peers in the direction I'm looking, but I make her look away. "I need you to help Austin with the women. Can you do that for me?" I look down at her battered but beautiful face. The need to kiss her is strong, so much so that I find it hard to walk away. I continue to stare at her for a beat, waiting for a response.

"Yeah. I need to check on Jia and Lelani anyway." Piper starts to walk away, then stops and looks over her shoulder. "Hey, Tai."

"Yeah?"

"I knew you would find me."

"Lucifer himself couldn't have stopped me," I confess, and I hope she feels the weight of my words.

Crossing the yard, I join Nova, Gabriel, and Riggs. On his knees between them is the man who ran like a fucking coward. "Fuck you, asshole," his dead eyes look at Gabriel before spitting blood at his feet. Nova shines a flashlight in his eyes, causing him to squint. I take notice of the blood dripping from his severely broken nose. Gabriel gives him a boot to the kidney area, and the guy yells in pain.

"Gag the motherfucker," Riggs orders and Gabriel produces a bandana, along with a small roll of duct tape. Who the fuck carries duct tape around?

As he's stifling the fuckers noise, I catch a glimpse of the ink on his neck. Grabbing the dirtbag's hair, I jerk his head to one side. "Give me some light, will ya?" I ask, and Nova aims the beam. Without thought, my fists connect with his face several times before I release the man. Heaving, I lift my eyes, looking at my brothers, who stare back, waiting for an answer to my sudden rage. "He's the dirty bastard who gave Piper the black eye she's sportin'."

Nova's nostrils flare, and he looks to Riggs. "He's not talkin' anyway. He's all yours, brother," Riggs tells him, then motions for me and Gabriel to walk with him, leaving Nova to do as he wishes with the piece of shit.

Several minutes pass after making our way back to where Jake, Logan, and Austin have eighteen scared, battered and dehydrated women loaded into the passenger van Cowboy had returned with, before hearing a single shot pierce through the silence that has fallen around us. My eyes never leave Piper, who stands beside her friend Jia, and Lelani, who will be riding back to the clubhouse with us by Piper's request.

We wait a few more minutes for Nova to join us. Walking up to Piper, he kisses her forehead.

Cowboy tosses a set of keys to Logan. "Here. Get yourselves back to your bikes. I have a timer set for this place to blow within thirty minutes. That should give you plenty of time." He looks back at the van, filled with women. "I need to transport them to a secure location, where they will get medical treatment before helping them get back home to their loved ones." He finds Riggs amongst us men. "Brother," he salutes him. "Stay alive."

Wasting no time, Logan jumps into the driver seat, and the rest of us, including Piper, Jia, and Lelani, load up on the back of the flatbed truck, taking us to the location we left our bikes. With Piper's help, Lelani settles behind Austin, her arms wrapping around his waist. Jia climbs on behind Jake, gripping onto his cut for dear life. Without hesitating, Piper settles in behind me. "Need you to hold on tight, babe. We'll be ridin' out hard and fast." Our engines rumble, and I fall in line with the others, my speed increases when my tires hit the blacktop. Piper slides forward, pressing her body against mine, her legs hugging my thighs, and her hands clutching my waist. Like thunder, I hear the explosion behind us as my bike eats the asphalt, putting as much distance between us and the destruction we left behind. In my side mirrors, the night sky glows orange from the fire's flames. Flicking my wrist, I twist the throttle hauling arse alongside my brothers.

Less than an hour later, we're rolling through the gates of the compound. Barely able to stand, I pull Piper to my side. Pop is sitting outside alone, smoking a cigar, with his shotgun resting on his lap. He stands, and I stop before entering the clubhouse. "My granddaughter, okay?" he asks, his forehead wrinkles more pronounced as he looks at her with worry.

"I'm okay, Gampy, just exhausted." Piper lifts her hand, touching his arm.

Pop's eyes cut to me. "Go on and take care of my grandbaby." I can't help but feel that his words carry a deeper meaning.

Walking through the door, we find most of the members, waiting for our return. Amongst the old ladies, I spot Teagan, our unofficial club doctor. Knowing the women need to be looked after, my hands fall from Piper's waist, and hand her over to Bella, who helps her up the stairs. The other women gather Jia and

Lelani into their comforting arms, leading them in the same direction.

"Church in the mornin', men. It's been one hell of a day. Piper and those women are safe. We'll deal with the aftermath tomorrow. Mission accomplished. Get some sleep," Riggs announces.

Too wound up to sleep, I grab a bottle of whiskey from the bar and head outside. Strolling across the yard, I sit on a picnic table situated near the water. The smell of the Mississippi River fills my nostrils as I breathe in deep. Twisting off the bottle cap, I take a shot. It burns as it coats my throat. Enjoying the warmth, I take another. It's not long before I hear boots crunch against the loose gravel at my back. Then Fender is sitting down beside me. "You alright?" Reaching into his cut, he pulls out a joint.

I sigh heavily. "I'm good."

Fender takes a hit, then passes the joint to me, and I take it between my fingers, trading it for the bottle in my hand. I take a hit, inhale, and close my eyes. I pass the joint back to Fender.

"Think we'll get blowback for this shit?" Fender asks.

"We didn't leave any evidence behind," I tell him even though there is a bit of uncertainty in the back of my mind.

"What's up with the blind girl?" he asks, and I take the joint back.

"Don't know her story yet. Piper was adamant she stays with us. At that moment, Prez agreed to bring her back."

I hold the joint out, and Fender takes it. He inhales deeply, then says as he blows out the smoke, "Austin seems to have taken an interest in her." I nod, having the same thoughts watching him earlier.

We sit quietly, staring out at the slow-moving water. Adrenaline is wearing off, and my body starts to feel the effects of the past twenty-four hours. My shoulders slump. I'm fucking exhausted. My brother and I sit for a few minutes longer, not speaking a word before I decide to carry my arse inside. "Appreciate the company, brother. I'm beat." I stand.

"I'll catch ya later," Fender says, and I leave him, making my way inside the clubhouse, knowing I won't be going to my bed.

Several minutes later, I'm sitting in a chair beside Piper's bed, watching her sleep, her hair still a little damp from her shower. There's a prescription bottle on the nightstand. As peaceful as Piper looks, I'm assuming Teagan gave her something to help her rest. My heart races as I continue to stare at her. Piper blinks, her long lashes flutter against her cheeks before her eyes open. Her hazel eyes stare at me.

Piper has managed to turn my whole world upside down.

"Hi," she says in a soft, lazy whisper.

"Hey," I say. "I just came by to check on you." I go to stand, but her hands shoot out, linking her fingertips with mine.

"Don't go." Those two little words are my complete undoing, and the last few bricks in the wall I tried to build between us crumbles. Leaning down, I claim her soft lips.

"Go back to sleep," I tell her and sink back into the chair. Piper's eyes quickly flutter closed, and her fingers go lax against mine. I never thought I'd fall for Piper LeBlanc. She was the last thing my heart expected. At this moment, I decide that I'm all in. I will fight whatever battle comes my way to make Piper mine. Consequences be damned.

16

PIPER

The sunlight filtering in through the window blankets my body in warmth, rousing me from sleep. My eyes flutter open, and I blink away the nightmare that was my existence not twenty-four hours ago. Suddenly, my memories come flooding back, replacing my sweet dreams and filling me with dread. Peering over at the clock on the bedside table, I note it's nearly noon. I woke up earlier to say goodbye to my friend then took another one of those pain pills Teagan gave me to help me sleep. Jia's father jumped on a plane and made it to New Orleans around two o'clock this morning to take her home. It was a tearful goodbye. I also saw dad and Uncle Abel coming out of Uncle Abel's office before he and Jia left. I'm assuming it was to make sure Jia's dad was on the same page regarding the authorities. The club prefers to handle business themselves. Sometimes they work with the police. They will not be bringing the cops in on what went down this time, though. Not that I care. All I care about is those men who pay for what they have done. And there is no doubt in my mind the club did just that.

Stretching my arms above my head, I work out the kinks in my back and wince at the pain in my face. I have a nasty looking black eye and some bruising across my cheek from being punched by that creepy son of a bitch.

I roll to my side, then sit on the edge of the bed. I freeze at the sight of an empty beer bottle sitting on the floor beside the chair. *Tai.* I thought I had dreamt he was here in my room last night, watching me sleep and kissing my lips. Shaking my head, I push those thoughts away and pad over to the bathroom. I cringe when I catch a glimpse of myself in the mirror. My eye looks worse than it did hours ago. Ignoring the fact that I look like shit, I go about my business and brush my teeth. Once I'm finished, I change into a pair of leggings and an oversized t-shirt, then tie my hair up into a loose bun.

When I arrive downstairs, I find my dad and Promise in the kitchen with Jaxson. Tai is sitting at the table across from my dad. He looks straight at me. Dad and Promise both stand when I walk in. I tear my eyes away from Tai and look at my dad. "Bean," dad murmurs, pressing his lips against my temple.

"Morning, dad."

Promise squeezes her way between my dad and engulfs me in a bear hug. "How are you doing this morning? Were you able to get some rest?"

I return her embrace. "Yeah. I got a few hours. I feel much better. My face is a little sore, though." I reach up and lightly touch my bruised eye. At the mention of my eye, dad grinds his jaw, and I'm reasonably sure I just heard Tai growl.

Dad's phone chimes, and he pulls it out from the inside of his cut and looks at it before giving me another hug. "I'll be back to check on you in a bit." He jerks his chin toward Tai. "Come on, brother. Prez wants to see us."

Dad kisses Promise and ruffles the top of Jaxson's head. "Be good for your momma, boy."

Jaxson beams up at dad and lets out a string of babble. I can't help but close my eyes and soak up this precious moment with the four people I care about the most in my life. The moment seems so simple, but for me it's everything. I could have lost all of this. Things could have ended differently for me yesterday. It takes all I have to choke back the sob that threatens to break free. And when I open my eyes, Tai is standing in front of me. His gaze is intense. It is as if he can read my thoughts and see the pain I am trying to hide.

Reaching up, he brushes his knuckles against my bruised cheek. His touch causes my body to shiver. No words are spoken between us, and I look over Tai's shoulder to my dad, who has his back turned. But before I can open my mouth, my dad turns, and Tai is gone.

Once I am left alone with Promise, she lifts her brow as if to say I saw that. Ignoring her silent question, I stroll over to the counter and fix myself a cup of coffee. How do I explain Tai and me to her when I don't even know myself what is going on between us? First, last night and now whatever that was that just happened. My head is a jumbled mess. Luckily, Promise leads us in a different conversation. "The girls are out back having lunch; you want to go join them?" she asks as she pulls Jaxson from his highchair.

I smile. "Sure."

Outside, the women from the Montana Chapter are huddled together with Luna and Tequila. With them is Lelani. Standing off to the left is Gabriel and Austin. Gabriel looks bored by all the girl chatter and, as usual, has his eyes glued to Alba. Then there is Austin, who is standing directly behind the sofa where Lelani sits with his arms crossed, and his eyes burning a hole into the back of her head. *Interesting.*

"Hi," I offer a little wave when I approach the group.

"How are you doing, Piper?" Luna signs.

I sign back. "I'm good." Continuing to sign so that Luna is kept in the conversation, I ask Lelani, "How are you today? I hope you were able to get some rest."

Lelani, who is sitting between Bella and Grace, offers me a warm smile. "I'm hanging in there, Piper. I did manage to get some sleep. Everyone here has been so nice and welcoming."

Just then, Uncle Abel, my dad, and several of the Montana guys, including Jake, emerge from the clubhouse and head in our direction.

Jake addresses me first. "How ya doin' sweetheart?"

Jake is a big guy with an air of authority about him, but he has the kindest eyes. "Doing better. Thank you."

Uncle Abel is the next to speak. "We came out here to talk to Lelani."

"What's going on?" I ask, feeling protective.

"We need to ask her some questions. Can you do that for us, darlin'?" he addresses Lelani. When Lelani gets a worried look, I go over and sit beside her. Bella gives her a reassuring pat on the arm as she makes room for me on the sofa.

I take Lelani's hand. "It's okay, Lelani. You can trust us. My uncle only wants to help. I promise."

Lelani wrings her hands together while chewing on her bottom lip. She's clearly unsure of who she can trust, and I don't blame her one bit.

Uncle Abel continues. "Is it true your brother is to blame for you ending up in the back of that storage pod?"

A flash of pain takes over Lelani's face when she answers. "Yes."

Everyone around me shares the same pissed off look on their faces. Lelani's brother, her own flesh and blood, gave her up to be sold.

"Alright, sweetheart." Uncle Able sits in the chair across from Lelani, getting on her level. "You have a couple of options. Just know that whatever you choose, my club is willing to help. Option one is we help you get back home."

Lelani visibly swallows, and I squeeze her hand for support. "Go back to Vegas?"

"Yeah. If you choose to go back, I'll have one of my men escort you there. Do you have any family back home? Anyone besides your piece of shit, brother?"

"No. I don't have anyone. No family. I don't think I can go back."

Uncle Abel nods. "No, I don't suppose you do. That leaves us with option two. And that is you stay here in New Orleans. We help you get settled here. Whatever you need, we'll help you get it."

"I...I don't know. I've always depended on my brother. I wouldn't know where to begin on starting over."

I cut in. "You have us, Lelani. Like my uncle said, everyone here will be happy to help you."

Behind Lelani, Austin leans over and grips the back of the sofa, his knuckles turning white. As if she can sense a presence behind her, Lelani sits up straighter and turns her head slightly toward Austin. Bella looks between Austin and Lelani then over at Alba. A second later, they share a look with Grace, Mila, Emerson and Sofia. Something passes between them, and I have a feeling I know what it is. Bella speaks up. "What are your feelings on Montana?"

Lelani scrunches her face in confusion. "Montana?"

"Yeah. Would you consider coming back to Montana with me, Alba, Mila, Grace, Em and Sofia?"

"It's perfect!" Alba adds. "Sofia has a place, New Hope House. It's a place for women who are looking to start over."

Mila and Sofia nod in agreeance. Grace looks over at her husband, giving him a cheeky smile. The corner of Jake's mouth lifts into a smirk. He regards Lelani. "My brothers' invitation is extended to my club should you choose to move to Montana."

We all wait with bated breath for Lelani to make her decision. We don't have to wait long. And with a sudden burst of courage,

Lelani takes a deep breath and juts out her chin. "I think Montana sounds lovely. That is if you are sure about your offer. I refuse to be anyone's burden ever again."

"You're not a burden," Austin growls from over my shoulder, causing Lelani to jump. All eyes are now on Austin.

A faint blush creeps up Lelani's neck as she ducks her head. She can't see, but no doubt, her other senses are hyper-aware of the man standing behind her.

Jake clears his throat. "It's settled then. You'll be coming back to Polson with us." Jake stands. "Try to get some rest tonight. We ride out first thing in the mornin'." Jake regards Blake. "You cool with Lelani riding with you tomorrow?"

"Lelani will be on the back of my bike," Austin cuts in.

Jake studies Austin for a beat, then nods. "Alright, brother." With that, the men retreat inside, leaving us women alone. Lelani is the first to speak. "That Austin guy is a little intense."

"Oh, Lelani," Bella smiles. "You have no idea."

"Your dad says you're going to school to be a veterinarian. That's pretty fuckin' cool."

I smile at Grey. It's late, and almost everyone has turned in for the night since the Montana Chapter will be leaving early in the morning. I tossed and turned in my bed for the better part of an hour then decided to come downstairs and make myself some hot tea, hoping it would help settle me enough to get some sleep. Grey was in the kitchen with a bottle of whiskey when I walked in.

"I am. I just finished my first year in Texas."

"Did you always want to be a vet?"

I shake my head. "No. The decision was last minute. I started working for the local clinic in my last year of high school and fell in love with everything about it." I shrug. "I guess you can say I didn't have any direction, then one day," I snap my finger, "it just clicked."

"I get that." Grey takes a sip from the tumbler in his hand. "It was like that for the club and me."

Grey and I are interrupted when the kitchen door opens and Tai walks in. He stops dead in his tracks, his eyes passing back and forth between Grey and me. His face goes hard. I'm confused for a moment as to why he looks pissed. Then I realize how close I am sitting next to Grey. Our midnight conversation is entirely innocent, but by the way my body is leaning into Grey's, I can see why Tai would think differently.

"Brother," Grey tips his head at Tai.

Tai levels Grey with a stern look while remaining silent for several beats. "Grey."

Grey must read something on Tai's face because a second later, he stands. "I'm turnin' in." Turning his back to Tai, Grey addresses me. "It was nice talkin' to ya, Piper."

"You too, Grey. I'm glad I finally got to meet you." Grey strides past Tai, giving him a nod. Sighing, I push away from the table and take my now empty cup to the sink. "You know, we were only talking. There was no need to come in here and piss all over me. Especially when I'm not yours."

I don't wait for Tai's reply before walking out of the kitchen.

Something wakes me from sleep and when I open my eyes, I'm greeted by the moonlight peeking through the curtains in my room. My body becomes hyper-aware of a presence beside me, and I don't have to turn my head to see who it is because I can smell him. Hell, my brain and my body recognized Tai when he is near. Squeezing my eyes shut, I tell myself to stay strong. I can't let him continue to do this. To act like I mean something to him one minute, then pull away from me the next. It hurts too much. *Why is he doing this to me?*

"Why are you here, Tai?" I keep my voice steady and low.

"I'm here because I'm fuckin' done with fighting the pull between us and done with staying away from what's mine."

My heart rate speeds up, and the way Tai's husky voice says the word mine sends chills down my spine.

Throwing caution to the wind, I decide to be brave and take what I want too. Turning on my side, I look at Tai sitting in the chair beside the bed, shirtless. I drink in the sight of his well-defined six-pack abs, and the trail of dark hair that starts just below his navel and disappears into the waistband of his jeans. Taking a shuttered breath, I slowly peel the blanket off my body, exposing my bare legs as I sit up on the edge of the bed. I'm wearing a pair of black lace panties and a white mid-drift t-shirt. Mine and Tai's eyes connect. His nostrils flare, and my skin prickles. Swallowing past the lump in my throat, I stand, taking two nervous steps toward Tai, stopping between his spread legs. He leans forward, and my body shudders at the first touch of his hands against the back of my thighs. A moan escapes past my lips when he buries his face against my lace-covered pussy.

"Tai," I gasp when suddenly the material covering my center is pushed aside, and Tai takes his first taste, flicking my clit with his tongue. Deciding that is not enough, he rips the panties from my body and hooks an arm under my knee, hiking it up further, allowing himself better access.

Threading my fingers through his hair, I arch my back and buck my hips, seeking more. Too soon, he pulls away and I whimper from the loss of his mouth. Leaning back in the chair, Tai grips my waist and pulls me down, straddling him. He wastes no time covering my lips with his. I eagerly open for him. A growl vibrates in his chest as my hunger for him takes over, and I suck on his tongue.

Breaking the kiss, Tai orders, "Arms up."

Doing as he says, I raise my arms above my head, allowing him to pull my shirt off.

"Fuck," he hisses, then takes my nipple into his hot mouth. My eyes roll into the back of my head, and I shamelessly grind down against his hard cock. I silently curse the denim barrier between us. Tai must be thinking the same thing because the next thing I know, he's unbuckling his belt, then unzips his jeans, releasing his cock. I look down at the space between us and watch as he takes it in his hand and begins to stroke. Tai's cock is long and thick. I'm desperate to know what it will feel like inside me. My eyes trail the bead of pre-cum that leaks from the tip. I watch as Tai uses his middle finger, swipes the cum from the head of his cock, then rubs that same finger against my swollen clit, marking me.

"I want to feel you," I admit.

"Come here, baby." Tai palms my ass, moving me further up his thighs until my pussy connects with his cock. I shiver and let my body take over as I move my hips back and forth. With his hands on my waist, Tai helps guide my movements. Bracing my palms against his chest, I look down between us and watch with every thrust forward, as the head of his cock brushes against my clit, bringing me closer to the release I desperately seek. With my nails digging into his pecks, we fall into a steady pace. Closing my eyes, I get lost in a world that exists only to us.

17

KIWI

Watching my cock, slick with Piper's arousal, as she rubs her pussy against me has to be the hottest fucking thing I have ever seen. "Fuck," I hiss when she grinds down harder. Reaching up, I sweep my hands across her breasts, cupping them, rubbing the pads of my thumbs over her hard nipples. Piper's nails dig into my flesh.

"Tai," she moans.

"That's it, babe. Come for me." I pinch her nipples, giving them a slight tug. Piper's eyes flutter shut. Her body shudders so hard with her climax that her clit pulses against my cock. "Jesus, Piper. You are so fuckin' beautiful it hurts to look at you," I growl. I barely let her catch her breath before I'm out of the chair, carrying her over to the bed in two strides then laying her down on her back. I swiftly rid myself of my jeans before I'm back on her. Settling between her thighs, I grip her knees and push them apart. My mouth waters at the sight of her exposed, wet pussy. Reaching out, I brush the pad of my thumb against her swollen clit, causing her to gasp and her skin to prickle. Unable to waste another second without being inside her, I line myself up at her entrance. Piper grips the back of my neck, tangling her fingers in my hair the moment the head of my cock kisses her entrance. She nibbles her bottom lip, letting her eyes roam over my body as I hover above her. Both panting, we lock eyes as I slowly slide my cock into her, taking something that will only belong to me."Christ," I grind out. Beads of sweat slide down my temple. She's tight. I groan with pleasure. Lowering my head, I cover her moans with my lips, kissing her as I push in a little further. I still, and give Piper a moment to adjust. The heels of her feet hook into the back of my thighs, pulling me closer.

"Tai, please." Her voice is raspy with need.

I pull out, then slowly slide into her again. My lips leave hers, only to whisper in her ear. "You're mine, Piper." My body burns with a fire it's never felt before. It's all because of her. She makes me feel things. I need Piper like a flame needs oxygen to burn.

"I'm yours." Piper pants and I thrust inside her. Rocking her hips, Piper begins to match my rhythm. Not wanting to hurt her, I hold back. "Harder, Tai," Piper urges.

"I don't want to hurt you." I suck her neck.

"Fuck me, Tai." The dirty talk coming from her pretty little mouth releases an animalistic need to claim her without abandon. Reaching down, I lift her leg and bring it to rest on top of my shoulder. The position allows me to go deeper. Biting her lip, Piper stifles a scream as my thrusts become rougher.

I look down between us, watching my cock sliding in and out of her. "Touch yourself, babe," I command, my breaths ragged. Piper's hand drifts down her flat stomach, across her soft skin, and begins working her bundle of nerves with her fingertips. Her breathing tells me she's getting close and her pussy strangles my cock. It's never felt this good. Piper's body fits mine like she was made for me.

"Tai," Piper whispers, her breathing becoming erratic. Her walls flutter as her climax builds, and it sends electricity shooting down my spine as my body begs for release.

"You gonna come again for me?" My fingers dig into her thigh as I fuck her hard and deep.

"Oh my god," she groans as her pussy contracts. Leaning down, I cover her mouth with mine, swallowing her screams while she comes undone. Her pussy pulsates on my cock, and I explode, my release so strong lights flash behind my closed lids. Piper holds my weight as I bury my face in her neck. Not wanting to lose her warmth, I stay inside her a minute longer. Once I have my bearings, I rock inside her a few more times before gently pulling out. Falling to the bed beside her, I pull Piper close. I've never had such an intense orgasm. Piper rests her head on my chest. We lay there unmoving until our breaths even out.

I run my fingers through her long hair. "You okay?"

I feel her warm breaths skirt across my skin. Her fingertip traces the outline of one of my tattoos. "Better than I have been in a long time." A moment of silence hangs between us. The room is so quiet I hear my own heart beating wildly against my chest. "This changes everything," Piper whispers.

"Babe. Everything changed the moment my lips touched yours. You're it for me, Piper. Mine." I shift, and Piper lifts her head to look at me.

"I think I love you, Tai."

I cradle her face in the palm of my hand. "I'm completely consumed by you. Everything you say or do. The woman you are and will be. You're my first thought when I wake in the morning, the last thought before I close my eyes to sleep." I stare at her beautiful face, getting lost in her. "Falling in love with you was something I had no control over," I confess. Piper presses her soft lips against mine, leading us in a slowly heated kiss. This time she's claiming me, and I give in to her willing.

The next morning, I wake to Piper's arm draped across my chest and her leg hooked around one of mine. Laying still, I listen for any signs of activity in the clubhouse, but it's quiet. Almost too quiet. "Babe," I try to wake Piper. She only grunts her disapproval at being disturbed, then snuggles in closer. I chuckle. She's never been a morning person. I try to move, and she groans. "Babe. Come on. It's time to get out of bed," I tell her, and her eyes pop open. "Mornin'," I kiss the tip of her nose, then slide out of bed.

"What time is it?" Piper sits up in bed, pressing her back against the headboard. The bedsheet pools around her waist, giving me an excellent view of her perfect full tits.

I pluck my jeans from the floor and pull my phone from the pocket. "Shit. It's almost 9:00 am," I tell her. Piper slides out of bed and pads across the floor. My eyes roam her naked body. Her eyes dip. Piper bites her lip as she stares hungrily at my cock. Her eyes lift to mine, and I raise my brow. "Hungry?"

"Maybe," she saunters right up to me, pressing her body against mine.

"Torture. That's what this is." I look down and run my thumb across her rosy lips. "As much as I want these pretty lips wrapped around my cock this morning, it will have to wait." Piper pouts, and I almost cave. "Sorry, babe."

She huffs. "Fine." Finding the panties I removed from her body last night, she eyes the ripped scrap of material before walking into the bathroom and tosses them in the trash. She then walks to the dresser, and snatches a pair of cutoffs sitting on top. Next, Piper rummages through the drawer and pulls out a t-shirt I recognize as one of my own. She slips it over her head, then ties a knot in the front. I briefly wonder where she would have gotten one of my shirts. Brushing past me, she enters the bathroom.

Ten minutes later I'm dressed, and she steps out, her hair brushed, piled on top of her head in a messy bun, fresh-faced, and flip flops on her feet.

"Come here." I shrug on my cut, then reach out, snaking my arm around her waist. I look at her. In the sun, her bruises look deeper in color. I pepper a few light kisses on her injuries. "I'm so fuckin' sorry."

"I'm here—with you," her arms go around my neck. "That's all that matters now." Piper presses her lips against my neck. "So, what's the plan for today?" My cock swells as her breath skims my skin.

"I need to find Nova."

Piper pulls away. "My dad?"

"Yeah, babe. It's time to face the music."

"I'm a little nervous," she confesses.

"Not gonna lie, babe. I'm a bit nervous myself, but I'm not hidin' from what I want. My brother and the club deserve the right to know about us and to hear it from me." I grab her hand in mine and kiss her one more time. "Let's go."

Opening the bedroom door, we step out into the hallway and run right into Fender. His eyes go to our joined hands, then he looks at me. "Hey, brother. You disappeared last night. I thought you'd gone home." He smiles at Piper. "Hey, sweetheart. How are ya, feelin'?" he asks her.

"My face still hurts a little," she touches her bruises. "Other than that, I'm okay."

"If it's any consolation, the guy who did that looks worse than you." Fender makes light of the situation. Damn right, the fucker looks worse. I would say he looks like death itself.

"Nova around?" I ask Fender.

"Nope. Him and the other guys took off. The women wanted to get some fresh air and let the kids play outside. Prez decided the safest place to do that is Pop's place, just until the smoke clears, and we hear back from Cowboy. So, everyone is headed there for awhile." Fender shoves his hands into his pants pockets and rocks back on his heels. He eyes Piper and I for a beat. "I'm not surprised at you two catchin' feelings for one another." Fender sighs and shakes his head. "Anyway, I've gotta grab somethin' from my room, then hit the road. I'll catch the two of you later."

Piper and I finish making our way downstairs to an almost empty clubhouse. Payton and Josie are sitting at one of the tables chatting. Their chatter stops the moment they notice Piper holding my hand. "Holy shit." Josie grins, smacking the top of the table with her hand. "I called it."

"How are you feeling today, Piper?" Payton smiles sweetly at my woman.

"I'm good, and thanks for asking," Piper says.

Payton grins. As we turn to walk away, she adds, "You two look good together."

The bright sun and southern heat hit us the moment the door swings open and we step out of the clubhouse. It's days like this I'm thankful for the canopy Riggs put up months ago. Parking our bikes in the shade at least saves us from burning our arses on the leather seats of our bikes. I help Piper climb on, then slip a helmet over her pretty head. Straddling my bike, I fire her up and the two of us head out to Pop's.

The sweet smoky aroma of hickory hangs on a breeze as my bike rolls onto Pop's property, and my stomach grumbles. I notice Pop in the yard operating the grill, while Riggs along with Luna and their daughter are standing close by deep in conversation. My Harley's rumble draws Nova's attention, along with Wick's, where they are sitting with their women, and Jaxson in the shade on the front porch. Piper's hands clench at my sides, gripping me a bit harder. Nova keeps his attention on us as I maneuver my bike around the others parked in the driveway, then bring it to a stop.

Piper already has her helmet removed by the time I climb off the bike, and I hang it from the handlebar. My woman gives me a small smile. I've warned her how this could and most likely will go, but her being the optimist sees it differently. Helping her dismount the bike, I take her hand in mine. I already feel several sets of eyes burning at my back. I squeeze her hand. "Ready?" I ask her, and at the same time, I'm asking myself.

"Rip it off like a band-aid," her use of terminology is fitting, although I may need more than that soon.

We turn and walk toward the porch. I hold my head high as we approach Nova, whose eyes are narrowed slits as they drop to mine and Piper's joined hands. He stands, handing Jaxson to Promise. "What the fuck?" I hear those three pissed off words leave his mouth and mentally prepare myself for what's about to go down.

"Oh shit," Wick mumbles, followed by Tequila, nudging his side and telling him so.

"Dad," Piper opens her mouth to talk, but Nova cuts her off without taking his eyes from me.

"Zip it, Piper." Nova comes toe to toe with me. The cords in his neck tighten.

"Babe," I regard Piper, and keep my attention on my brother. Nova's nostrils flare. Things are about to go from zero to sixty fast. "Go."

"Tai, no." She squeezes my hand, wanting to stand her ground beside me.

"Go," I order again, letting loose of her hand. The moment she takes a step back, Nova's tight fist connects with my gut, knocking the wind from my lungs. Not giving me a chance to recover, I receive another shot to the ribs.

"That's my baby girl!" Nova rages, and I right myself, then look at his face. "She's off-limits!" he bellows.

"I tried to fight it, brother. I swear to God, I did." My words enrage him further. I see the punch coming, but I don't attempt to dodge it. His fist connects with my face, and an explosion of pain radiates across my jaw. From the corner of my eye, I see Piper trying to move toward me, but Wick grabs her by the arm. "I lo..." I open my mouth to profess my love for his daughter, but the words are cut short when he comes at me with a right hook. I stomp my foot, and my hand covers my eye. Fucking hell that one hurt.

"Don't you fuckin' say it!" Nova yells hovering above me.

I rise. "I love Piper." I defy his warning and wait for him to strike me again. Before he gets the chance, Piper pulls free of Wick's grip and rushes to my side. She tries stepping between me and her father, but instinct has me shoving her behind me.

"You think I'd strike my daughter?" Nova's chest heaves.

"I'm protecting what's mine," I state the truth.

"She is not yours," Nova fumes.

"Stop it, Dad," Piper screams over my shoulder.

"Piper. This is between Kiwi and me," Nova tells her.

"Daddy, I love him," she confesses, and Nova physically flinches as if she punched him. His shoulders slump, and a little of the fight he has leaves his body. "I trusted you," he spits and those three words hurt more than any physical blow he could deliver. Nova's eyes narrow, darting between Piper and me, his fists clenched at his sides. Without speaking another word, or giving me another glance, he walks away. We watch his retreating back as he crosses the yard, gets on his bike, and peels down the driveway.

Spinning, I take Piper into my arms and see tears pooling in her eyes. "I'm so fuckin' sorry, baby."

She sniffles, holding the tears at bay. Her hands caress my throbbing face. "Are you okay?"

"Don't worry about me, babe."

"Why didn't you fight back?" she sighs.

I rub my palms up and down her arms. "He's my brother—my family, Piper. I respect him too damn much to hit back. He's angry with me, and I owe him that much." I allow Piper to guide me to the porch, and I take a seat on the steps.

I watch as Promise hands Jaxson to Tequila's niece, who takes him to the small playset in the yard. Promise moves in our direction. "Come on, Piper. Let's get some ice for Kiwi's face." Reluctant to leave my side, Piper disappears inside Pop's house, and Tequila isn't far behind them. Resting my elbows on my knees, I hang my head.

"You've got balls. I'll give you that." Wick's deep voice hangs above me, and I lift my head. Wick tosses a pack of smokes that land on the porch beside me. I grab the box and slide a cigarette out. Wick hands me a lighter.

Once lit, I pull the smoke deep into my lungs, and Riggs appears. Luna gives me a small sympathetic smile as she brushes by to join the other women. "I would have done worse," Riggs states as he looks down on me. "Not gonna lie. I kind of saw this comin'," Riggs admits, and I look up at him. "I've got eyes." He stares hard at me. "I don't particularly like it myself, but it doesn't matter. My niece matters, and so does the club."

I have no regrets loving Piper, but the fact that my love for her is having an impact on the club feels like an elephant sitting on my shoulders.

"Women," Wick grunts. "They make us do stupid shit."

"Stupid, but worth it," I mumble.

"You sure about that?" Riggs asks, and I don't hesitate to reply.

"I'll risk everything because I love her, and she loves me."

He nods. "I can see that." Then he looks across the yard in the direction Nova took off. "I suspect my brother wasn't as blindsided by this as he acts. He's too fuckin' smart for that. Some part of him, like the rest of us, knew this was comin'."

The screen door behind me creaks, and the women step onto the porch. Piper lowers herself to sit beside me, holding an ice pack in her hand. I look at her face as she presses the cold compress to my chin. Her red-rimmed eyes tell me she's been crying, and I fucking hate it.

"Come on," Riggs bellows. "Let's give these lovebirds some space and try to make what's left of this beautiful day as peaceful as possible." Riggs tucks Luna into his side, and they leave us, as do Tequila and Wick.

"Everything okay?" Piper asks once we are alone. I wince when she presses the ice pack against my swollen eye. "Shit—sorry," she hisses.

"Does it look as bad as it feels?" I ask her.

"We're a matching set now," she smiles, and my chest tightens with emotion. Fuck I am so in love with this woman.

Several hours later, the dust settled. Piper and I are sitting on the porch, where I've spent most of the day. Pop strolls out of the house, with a cigar in one hand and a mason jar in the other. He settles in his favorite rocking chair. "You youngins come over here and give an old man some company." He snips the end off his cigar, then strikes a match.

Piper smiles at her granddad, who happens to be one of her favorite people. Rising from our seats on the opposite end of the porch, we join him. I pull Piper onto my lap as I take the rocking chair beside him. Pop tokes on his tobacco then he lifts the mason jar in his hand to his lips, sipping on the clear liquid inside.

"Gampy, is that moonshine?" Piper raises her brow. "You know you shouldn't be drinking something so strong. It's not good for your ulcer."

Pop smacks his lips. "After the week this family has had, I'd say a little white lightnin' is well deserved." His chair creaks as he rocks. I rub Piper's bare thigh as we sit looking out over the water. Pop sure does have a nice piece of property out here—his own little slice of heaven. As we watch the sun get swallowed by the bayou, the horizon is painted in beautiful hues of red and orange that slowly fades into deep indigo where the night sky is kissing the day goodbye.

"Gampy."

"Hmm?" Pop hums, as a puff of grey smoke billows in front of him.

"Are you upset with me too?" she asks him, and I hear the worry in her voice.

"Child, I'm not upset at all." He continues to rock and takes another sip of his liquor. "You and Kiwi go together like moonshine in a mason jar. Anyone who actually pays attention can see that."

"I wish dad could see it that way." Piper's shoulders slump. I rest my hand on top of hers tucked between her knees.

"Give it time," I try to reassure my woman even when I don't have full confidence in what I tell her. "My choices haven't always been the best-made ones in my life, but making Piper mine is one decision I'll never regret. Even if losin' Nova or the club is the price I have to pay."

At my confession, Pop twists in his chair. His weathered hands pass me the mason jar. Eyes, much like Nova's, look at me. "Son, every day, we're all just one choice away from changing our lives. Good or bad, we have to live with them." He releases his hold, and I bring the jar to my lips. The spicy burn of the alcohol runs down my throat and warms my stomach.

"However, we don't get to choose who our heart falls for." Pop looks out into the darkening sky. "My grandson will come around. Our family is strong, and you are a part of this family, Kiwi." Pop falls silent for a beat. Then, in the most casual way possible, he says, "But, if you hurt my granddaughter, make no mistakes, even though I'm slower in my old age, my aim is quick and precise."

Piper bites her lower lip, trying to hide her amusement. Grinning, I take Pop's words to heart, letting everything he said sink in before saying, "Yes, sir."

18

PIPER

Sitting with Tai, and Gampy, I watch the sun go down and listen to the tree frogs croak. It's been hours since Dad jumped on his bike, mad as hell at Tai and me. He just drove away without hearing anything I had to say, and I've been stewing on my emotions and biting my tongue on the matter all damn day. I'm so angry over the way my family handled everything. Needing to get a few things off of my chest, I stand. "I'll be right back." Leaning down, I press my lips to Tai's.

He scrunches his brow. "Everything okay?"

"No," I tell him.

Tai sighs. "Let it go, babe. What's done is done."

"I'm not a little girl anymore, and my family needs to realize that, Tai. I'm going to have my say," I answer him honestly and walk away before he talks me out of it. Spotting Uncle Abel, I step off of the porch and walk across the yard. "Why didn't you stop Dad from beating the crap out of Tai? Nobody here did a thing to stop him." I stop in front of my uncle, my arms cross over my chest.

Uncle Able shakes his head. "I'm sorry, darlin' but it wasn't my place, or anyone else's to step in." His features soften. "You know it had to go down that way. Even Kiwi knew how his brother was going to react, and rightfully so."

"Are you kidding?"

"Piper." Promise walks over and tries to calm me.

"What happened earlier today was completely unnecessary and blown out of proportion," I say.

"It's different for a father, sweetheart." My uncle tries again to get me to see reason. "There is a certain code we live by and a high level of trust along with the respect that comes with being a brother. You know that too, sweetheart." I grit my teeth to keep from arguing further because I see Uncle Abel's point. I'm aware of how the club works, but it strikes a nerve anyway.

"I need to talk to my dad," I announce. Turning, I stomp back over to the porch where Gampy and Tai are sitting. "Gampy, can I borrow your truck? I'm going to find my Dad."

"Keys are in the visor, darlin'." Gampy continues to rock in his chair, never missing a beat.

Standing from his chair, Tai walks with me over to where my gampy's truck is parked. "You going to be okay, babe? Do you think you should let your dad cool down, maybe talk with him tomorrow?"

"I won't be able to sleep until I say what I need to say. I'm so angry with him, Tai. I mean, look at your face."

Hooking his arm around my waist, Tai pulls me against his chest. "Don't be too mad at him, Piper."

I look up at Tai's battered face. His lip is split, with dried blood still on the surface of his skin. "I knew he was going to be upset, but I didn't think he would ever hit you."

"I knew what I was risking by making you mine and claimin' you in front of my brother."

"Do you regret making me yours?" I ask.

Tai takes my face between the palms of his hands. "Never.

Making you mine is the best decision I have made in my entire life." Then he kisses me.

"Go talk to your dad, and afterward, I want you to come to me."

I climb into the truck, and Tai kisses me one last time through the open window. "Are you going straight home?" I ask him.

"Yeah."

I nod. "I'll see you at your place soon."

Tai goes to walk away but abruptly stops and turns back toward me. "And Piper."

"Yes?"

"Pack a bag. You'll be stayin' the night."

When I pull up to the house, I park the truck next to my dads' bike, cut the engine and climb out. I don't bother going inside the house. I already know he's not there. Instead, I make my way around the side of the house and into the backyard toward his workshop. As expected, the large rollup door is open, light from the inside flooding out. I hear a loud, clinking sound coming from inside. When I step into the shop, my dad is standing with his back to me as he pounds on a large piece of fiery glass. I know he feels my presence but is refusing to acknowledge me.

"Dad," I call out. He ignores me. I call out again, louder this time. "Dad." Still nothing. I sigh and try again. "Dad."

When he continues to pound away at the glass instead of looking at me, I lose it. Picking up the closest thing within reach, which happens to be a beer bottle, I throw it to the floor to my right and watch as it shatters to pieces "Look at me!" I shout.

Setting his tools down, my dad finally turns toward me.

"Can we talk?" I ask.

"Now is not a good time, Piper."

"I disagree. You've had hours to stew with your feelings just like me. I think now is as good a time as any. Ignoring me is not going to change anything."

"Believe me, Piper. I'm well aware of that fact. My brother," he spits the word brother out like it leaves a bad taste in his mouth, "made me aware when he showed up at your grandfather's house with you on his arm earlier today."

"We weren't trying to be disrespectful."

"No? Because from where I was standing, it sure as shit felt like it."

"Would you rather he hide me like I'm some dirty secret?"

"You're nobody's dirty fuckin' secret, Piper," he fumes.

"Exactly! Tai and I have feelings for each other, and for some time now, but we didn't even act on them until yesterday. Tai refused to hide our relationship from you and the club, that's why he did what he did today. Believe it or not, Tai respects you."

"Respect," Dad huffs. "If he respected me, he would have stayed away from my daughter. I don't want you with him, Piper."

"I'm not asking for your permission. I'm not a child."

"You're my little girl."

"I'll always be your girl, but I'm not little anymore. Tai is my choice, Daddy."

"We'll see," he grinds out.

"What's that supposed to mean? What are you going to do, threaten Tai? Make him stay away from me? I'm sorry to say that's not going to work. Tai told me I was the best decision he's ever made, and he'd risk everything to be with me. And you know what? I believe him."

When my dad doesn't respond, I continue. "Why can't you be happy that I'm happy? You raised me around the club. You raised me around bikers, and what, now, you're all shocked when I fall in love with one? You're my dad. You should want me to be happy and find a man who treats me like I'm everything. That man is Tai."

"I do want you to be happy, Piper, but this situation is complicated. You don't understand."

"I understand. I know how things work in the club."

"Then you shouldn't have gone there," he cuts me off.

"I know you don't think anyone is good enough for me, but I'm asking you to dig deep and ask yourself, is there a better man out there to take care of me than Tai? A man you have known since he was a kid himself, a man who would die for you, for the club and me. A man who will spend his life protecting and making me happy." With those parting words, I turn and walk out of the shop. Even if my heart hurts, I've said my piece. I can only hope my dad learns to accept mine and Tai's relationship and hopefully forgive us both.

"Thanks for the ride," I tell Promise as I unbuckle my seatbelt. After my talk with dad, I went inside the house and packed an overnight bag to take to Tai's. Then I went back to Gampy's to drop off his truck. Since Promise was heading home with Jaxson, she offered to give me a lift.

"No problem, sweetie. And try not to worry about your dad. I'll talk to him. I'm sure he'll come around; he just needs some time."

"Thanks, Promise. I hope you're right."

"It'll all work out, you'll see." She smiles.

Climbing out of the car, I make my way to the trunk and grab my bag. I open the back door to say good-bye to Jaxson. Sticking my head inside, I plant a kiss on his cheek. "See ya, little man."

After waving good-bye and watching Promise disappear down the driveway, I climb the steps to Tai's porch where his cat greets me. Leaning down, I give him a scratch behind his ear. "Hey, Tom."

I hear the creak of the front door opening behind me, and before I can register what is happening, a strong arm snags me around my waist, hauling me inside. Tai kicks the door shut then pins me against it.

"What are you..." I don't get to finish my sentence before his lips come crashing down on mine, stealing the words from my mouth. Moaning, I thread my fingers through his hair.

"I need to be inside you," he declares as he pops the button on my shorts and slides them down my legs, taking my panties with them. Next, I hear the clinking sound of his belt. Once he releases his cock, Tai picks me up, and I wrap my legs around his waist. A second later, he buries himself inside me. "Oh, god!" I cry out. I'm still a little sore from last night, but the fantastic feeling of having him inside me again outweighs the discomfort.

"Fuck," he hisses through clenched teeth as he begins to thrust. His movements are brutal. I have no choice but to tighten my legs around him, bury my face in his neck and hold on. The grip Tai has on my hips is sure to leave bruises, but I don't care. Him being inside me feels too good.

"So wet for me," he rasps. "You grip my cock like you were made for me."

"Yes," I moan.

"Yes, what? Tell me, babe." Tai thrusts again, knocking the breath from my lungs.

"I was made for you. Only you."

"That's right. This pussy," Tai raises my shirt, pulls down the cups of my bra, and takes one of my nipples into his mouth, "these tits, your body, your heart, all of you is mine."

His words ignite a fire inside of me, and my pussy spasms around his cock. "I'm going to come." I claw at his back, leaving my mark.

"Fuck, I can feel it. Come all over my cock, Piper. I want to feel you."

At his demand, my orgasm hits me like a tidal wave. "Tai!" I scream out his name the same time he throws his head back and loses himself in his own release.

Once the two of us catch our breath, Tai backs away from the door. With me still wrapped around him, he walks us down the hall, to his room, and into the bathroom. He sets me down on the counter, then reaches over into the shower, turning the water on. Upon taking a closer look at Tai and his silence, I notice something different about him. He looks pained. I realize the toll today's events have taken on him emotionally. Tai hurt one of his brothers. He not only broke, but he disappointed a man he has spent years looking up to and respects. Now there's a crack in the bond between two brothers, and the wariness of that is seeping in. It also dawns on me that Tai said he needed me, not wanted but needed. He wasn't just looking for a release. Tai was looking for reassurance. Maybe he thought I would change my mind about us after talking with my dad?

"Arms up, babe." Tai's soft words zap me out of my wandering thoughts. Raising my arms above my head, I allow him to pull my t-shirt off. He reaches behind me and unclasps my bra, tossing it to the floor with my discarded shirt.

Tai steps between my legs and I wrap my arms around his neck. He holds me tight to his chest as he steps into the shower. The spray of the hot water washes over our bodies as he starts to kiss me. It doesn't take long before I feel him hard against my core. When he enters me, his movements are not rushed. This time he moves in and out of me at a lazy pace, taking his time. And this time, I give him the reassurance he needs by repeatedly whispering into his ear how much I love him.

The following morning, I wake before Tai. After what happened yesterday, I decide he needs his sleep, so while he rests I'll make us some breakfast. But first, I'm going to tend to Chance, who is happily laying in his doggy bed. Crouching down on the floor, I scoop him up and take him over to a piddle pad and express his bladder. Once finished, I strap him into his wheelchair. Chance follows me into the kitchen, where I start searching the cabinets for his kibble, locating it in the cabinet beneath the kitchen sink. "Are you hungry?" Chance gives me a little yap.

After I give Chance his breakfast, I grab the cat food bag beside the dog kibble and make my way outside to the front porch. The moment I start pouring the food, Tom darts out of the barn and across the yard toward me. "There you go, dude. Eat up." I give the cat a few strokes down his back.

"What ya doin', babe?"

I startle and scream at the sound of Tai's deep voice coming from behind me. The cat food in my hand goes flying, and poor Tom races off the porch like his tail is on fire as the bag falls at my feet, and tiny pieces of food scatter around us. "Jesus Christ! You scared the shit out of me." Tai stands at the door looking sexy with his sleep mused hair, an imprint of the pillow across one side of his face, while wearing a pair of gray sweatpants.

"My bad, babe." His lip twitches.

Tai loses his smile when we hear the rumble of a motorcycle followed by a familiar Harley driving up the driveway. Uncle Abel cuts the engine and climbs off. Tai makes a show by coming up behind me and snaking his arm around my waist.

"Kiwi," he gives Tai a chin lift.

"Prez," Tai returns, his posture guarded.

Uncle Abel makes his way up the porch. "Hey, darlin'."

"Morning, Uncle Abel."

There is a beat of awkward silence before I ask. "I was just about to make some breakfast. You want some?"

He gives me a warm smile. "I already ate, but I'll take a cup of coffee if ya got it."

"Sure." I turn to Tai. "Want a cup?"

Tai takes his eyes off Uncle Abel and grips my chin, giving me a light kiss. "Coffee sounds good, babe."

Once I take the guys their coffee, I duck inside, giving them some privacy. I sense my uncle is here because of what went down yesterday or club business. "If you two don't need anything else, I'm going to shower and change."

When I get back to Tai's bedroom, I go in search of my new phone. I want to check up on Jia and see how she's coping, and I want to text Bella and see how Lelani is settling in. Fishing my cell out of my purse, I swipe the screen. It lights up, indicating I have a missed call and a new voice message from Dr. Channing. She's probably checking on me. Promise went by the clinic the day before yesterday and told my boss I was under the weather but would be back to work soon.

Hearing the front door close, I turn just as Tai walks into the bedroom with Chance wheeling in behind him. "Where's Uncle Abel?"

"He had to get back to the clubhouse." Tai kneels and removes Chance from his wheelchair so he can lie down and rest.

"Oh. Is everything okay?"

"Yeah, babe. We're cool." When Tai doesn't offer up any more information, I change the subject.

"What are your plans for today?"

"I'm going down to the garage. I want to get there early to double-check inventory and I have a few return calls to make. I also have a client coming from Mississippi to look at a bike I've been working on. What about you?"

"I'm going to check up on Jia and Lelani. Then I'm going to call my mom and see if she wants to come to New Orleans one day this coming week for a visit, or I can go to her. She's been worried about me since getting wind of what happened. After that, I'm going to the clinic to talk to my boss. She called and left a message checking up on me. Hopefully, I still have a job."

"That woman loves you, babe. She'd never fire you."

Tai walks over to his closet, strips out of his sweats, and puts on a pair of jeans. Commando. *Yum*. Striding over to the dresser, he pulls it open and snags a black shirt.

"Yeah, you're right. My boss loves me." Picking my overnight bag up off the floor beside the bed, I dig through it for some clean clothes. "My car is still at Gampy's. Can I borrow your ride?"

"Sure." Tai slides his cut over his shoulder then reaches into the drawer of the nightstand, retrieving a set of keys and tosses them to me.

"Do you want me to come back in a couple of hours to check on Chance?"

"Naw. I'm taking him to the garage," he tells me as I follow him out of the bedroom to the front door. And that is when I watch as Tai pulls a backpack off the hook by the door. Chance goes crazy as if he knows he's about to go for a ride. Lifting Chance from the floor, Tai secures him in the pack and then slips it over his back. I wordlessly follow him outside, where he straps the wheelchair to his bike. As if I didn't think I could fall in love with this man any further, he just proved me wrong. My ovaries are literally exploding at the sight of this sexy as sin, badass biker, with a Beagle strapped to his back while riding a Harley. After giving Tai a kiss, I watch him disappear down the driveway with Chance in tow before heading back into the house to get ready.

An hour later, I have showered, dressed, and applied a coat of makeup to my face to cover the bruising around my eye so that my boss doesn't freak out and start asking questions. When I open the front door, Everest's big frame leaning up against the porch's railing, smoking a cigarette greets me. "Hey, Everest. If you're looking for Tai, he's at the garage."

"I'm not here for him. I'm your shadow today."

Realizing what he means, I give him a small smile. I'm not surprised the club is taking precautions and being extra vigilant in the wake of my kidnapping. "I only have a couple stops to make, and then I'll go to the garage and hang out until Tai gets off, so you don't have to spend your whole day with me."

Everest shakes his head. "It's cool, Piper. You do what you got to do and don't pay no mind to me."

"Well, I appreciate you looking after me."

"Anytime, darlin'." He puts his cigarette out in the receptacle on the porch. "You ready to roll?"

"Yup."

19

KIWI

It's been days since Piper, and I made our relationship known, and still, from across the table, Nova refuses to look my way. When he does, it's a murderous stare. He'll come around. I let those words play over again in my head. As for the rest of my brothers, there's a bit of tension, but that is a direct result of the negative energy whenever Nova and I are in the same proximity.

I divert my eyes. Looking out the window, I stare out at the river and watch the rain pelting against the surface of the water. I'm feeling a little edgy this morning. Riggs called church, and I can only assume he finally heard something back from Cowboy. Even though it appears the smoke has cleared and the possibility of retaliation from killing a bunch of sex traffickers and blowing up there campsite is becoming less of a threat, I haven't pushed Donovan far from my thoughts.

"Everyone is here." Riggs looks around the room. "Everest, close the door." We wait to hear what our President has to say while he takes his seat. Riggs lights a cigarette then clears his throat. "I know you men have been waiting for word on the shit that went down the other night," he pauses a beat, before his eyes land on me. "Kiwi, let me be the first to say, your intuition about Donovan was correct." The moment Riggs confirms who is to blame for all the hell Piper and the other women went through, my blood boils. I breathe in and out, calming the storm brewing inside me. All I want is the opportunity to see him one final time and put a bullet in his worthless head. I look around the table at my brothers. All but one has their eyes trained on me, and it fucking hurts, but I suck it up.

"Is he alive?" I question.

"He is," Riggs says, nodding. "He hasn't popped up on anyone's radar for eleven years because he uses several aliases. As far as the world knows, Donovan Black drowned in a boating accident off the coast of Florida seven years ago."

He faked his own death?

"Where is the bastard now?" Nova finally speaks.

Opening his cut, Riggs pulls his phone from the inside pocket. "Yesterday at 0100, in alliance with the FBI, Cowboy and the other members of the Ops team took down, and effectively apprehended Donovan, along with Marco Bianchi on their attempt to flee the country." Riggs swipes his phone screen, then slides it to his right where Wick sits. "Bianchi is already singing like a canary and beggin' for a plea deal. From what Cowboy hears, this guy was directly involved with kidnapping every woman at the party that night. He's willing to identify every single female loaded into that shipping container." The room falls silent for a beat as we absorb the information. "Anyway, Cowboy is still in the process of getting more intel to us, but he did send this image as proof." Wick looks at the phone, then slides it to Nova, who stares at the screen long and hard before sliding it across the table. Reaching out, I pull Riggs' phone closer and stare down at an image of Donovan, in a power suit, with his hands cuffed behind his back, as he is led from a private jet. His cold eyes are looking directly at the person snapping the photo, and it feels as though he is staring right at me.

He looks the same, and part of me is sickened that I look so much like him. I slide the phone to Fender, who then passes it to Everest.

"So how do they plan on making an indictment stick with only hearsay? It's one criminal's word against another," Wick asks.

"Sorry, brother. If you're askin' me for more information than what I just said, I can't give it to you because I don't have it. The Feds are tight-lipped on this case, even though they had outside help." Riggs snubs his cigarette out in the ashtray.

Donovan getting the chance to stand trial may be retribution for some, but not in my eyes. The man deserves a fate worse than his freedom being stripped from him and rotting behind bars. I know as well as everyone, there is always the possibility he could walk. There are cracks in the judicial system. It only takes one piece of evidence to go missing or one juror to throw a conviction out the window. The only thing Donovan deserves is a lengthy stay in the deepest depths of hell. I won't be satisfied until he's put six feet under. "What about our involvement?" I ask. We've been lookin' over our shoulders for days, and like me, I'm sure the rest of us would like to get back to normal and move on with our lives without havin' our family in potential danger.

Riggs' eyes train on Nova, and I can tell from the look on his face I won't like what he has to say. "They're willin' to look the other way in exchange for Piper's testimony. If they get enough surviving victims, to take the stand, and Bianchi will positively identify her as one of the women lured in that night, it will strengthen their case against Donovan."

"Piper has been through enough," Nova states.

So many thoughts are swirling around in my head, but one idea is evident amongst all the others. "I'll testify against him," I blurt out. Nova finally lifts his eyes to my face. He looks at me, not through me. He's schooling his expression well, so I can't quite read what he is thinking.

Riggs leans forward in his seat. "You sure? A decision like that not only puts your face and name out there, but it shines a light on the club as well."

"I'm willing to take that risk if my brothers are willing to do the same," I tell him. My brothers share glances, and it doesn't take but a second for all of them to answer.

Fender. "I'm in."

Everest. "I'm in."

Wick. "I've got your back, brother."

Riggs. "I'm in."

Nova is the last to answer. "I'm in."

"We stand together." Riggs looks around the table with pride. "They still may want Piper to take the stand," Riggs clarifies.

"We all know Piper. She is strong and will do whatever it takes to rid the world of a monster like Donovan and Bianchi. But, that's her choice to make, and hers alone." I look around the table before saying, "Call Cowboy and have him tell the Feds I'll take the stand against my birth father." I hold firm with the choice I have made, and remember what Pop said to us the other night about how every choice we make changes our lives. I've been through a lot of shit and fought a lot of battles beside my brothers. I'm grateful that the club is not willing to back down from yet another fight once again.

A few hours later, I'm at the shop working on a customer's bike. Our new hire Catcher is changing the oil in a lady's car on the other side of the shop. I smirk at how forward she is when she asks him if he's as good with his hands in the bedroom. He's a big tattooed guy. Hell, he's taller than Everest, and broader too. His response to her comment is a grunt. Catcher doesn't speak much and keeps to himself. I can't complain because he's excellent at his job. Before he applied, Catcher was straight forward with his background, but the club dug into his past a little further. Catcher is thirty years old. For the past five years, he's been behind bars, serving a sentence for voluntary manslaughter. The short story is that he shot and killed the man who murdered his wife and unborn child during a home invasion. Damn. I feel sorry for the guy. He lost everything that day. His wife. His kid. His freedom.

Catcher had been turned away from several job opportunities up until the day he walked into our shop. People are too fucking judgmental if you ask me. Not one person wanted to hire him based on his earlier incarceration. He wasn't looking for pity or a handout. All Catcher needs is a hand up and an opportunity to rebuild his life. And it wouldn't hurt if people showed him a little compassion either. It also turned out he had no home to go back to after they set him free. During his time in prison, he lost his house too. That's where Riggs stepped in. He gave Catcher a place to lay his head for awhile, giving him a room at the clubhouse.

The rumble of a bike pulls my attention away from my task. Looking out the open bay door, I watch Nova pull into the parking lot. He sits on his bike for a few minutes before turning off the engine. He strolls up to me. "You got a minute?" Hearing his voice, Chance, who's been strolling around the shop, makes a beeline for my brother. Nova kneels, giving Chance an ear rub before standing.

"Yeah." Placing the socket wrench into the toolbox beside me, I pull a bandana from my pocket and wipe the grease from my hands. "Catcher," I call across the shop as I'm heading inside. "Keep an eye on things, will ya?" He gives me a tight nod, then goes about his business.

Nova and Chance follow me inside, where we walk into my office. Nova closes the door and takes a seat on the black leather sofa across from my desk. Squatting, I unhook all the restraints from Chance's wheelchair and lift his backside. "There you go, boy. Go take a lay down for a spell." I pat him and set his wheelchair off to the side.

"You're really good at taking care of him," Nova mentions as I settle onto my chair.

I look over at Chance stretched out on the cold floor, his eyes closed. "Just because he's different doesn't mean he should be tossed away."

"Piper used to talk about him all the time." Nova gets a distant look in his eyes, but I know he didn't come here to talk about Chance. "I'm still pissed," Nova looks dead at me. "Let's just make that clear. My head is a little fucked with the idea of you and my daughter being together." I say nothing in response, giving him the floor to say his piece. He leans forward, placing his elbows on his knees. "I'd be a damn liar if I came in here and said I was completely blindsided by it. Hell, looking back, all the signs were there. I was just so wrapped up in having her home, then almost losing her I..." his words hang in the air for a beat as he runs his hand through his hair. "I respect the fact that you were man enough to bring it to my table and confront me head-on, but the truth is, I'm not here for you or myself. I'm here for Piper. She loves you."

"I love her too," I tell him, and he holds up a hand.

"Fuck, Kiwi," he grumbles. "As bad as I hate to admit it, I know you love my daughter. But, if you hurt her, brother, I'll kill ya." It feels good to hear him call me brother again.

There's a soft knock on the door, followed by Piper's voice on the other side. "Tai."

"Come on in, babe," I call out, and the door swings open. Piper pokes her head inside.

"I thought we could have lunch together," she smiles at me before noticing her dad sitting on the sofa, and her features turn to worry. "Is everything okay?"

"I was having a chat with Kiwi," Nova tells her, and Piper steps inside the room. She leans against the doorframe, holding a couple of takeout bags in her hand.

"Dad," Piper looks at her dad.

"Relax, Bean." Nova stands. Facing Piper, he leans in, kissing the top of her head. "I only want what's best for you."

"Tai is what's best for me, Daddy," Piper confesses.

"I know," Nova admits, and Piper's eyes widen with shock. "That's why I'm here."

"So, you're okay with this—us?" Piper glances at me, then back to her dad's face.

"I'm workin' on it. Of all the men it could have been, I'm glad it's Kiwi who loves you." My chest tightens at his words, and a lump of emotions forms in my throat. I was not expecting Nova to say what he just said. Tears pool in Piper's eyes as she looks at her dad.

"Thank you, daddy," she whispers, then wraps her arms around his waist.

"I love you, Bean. Your happiness means the world to me." He pulls away, and Piper sniffles. "Go on and feed your man." He smiles at her, before looking back at me. "Grab a beer with me tonight?" he asks.

I nod. "Sounds good."

"I'll see the two of you later." He walks out of the office, leaving his daughter shocked and staring at me.

"Does this mean...?" Piper wipes her eyes. Moving, she sits the bag on top of the desk. I grab her hand, pulling her down on my lap, and swipe away the rest of her tears.

"It's definitely a step in the right direction, babe." I tangle my finger in her hair. "Give me your mouth." I press my lips to hers.

"Aren't you hungry?" she says playfully as my hand slips beneath her shirt, cupping her breast.

"I'm always hungry for you, babe."

20

PIPER

It's been a few weeks since Tai and I officially became an us. The days that followed our coming out were tense and weighed heavily on us and the entire club. My dad and I are incredibly close, so those few days, when he was silent and keeping his distance, killed me. My dad is my rock. He has been my hero for as long as I can remember, and knowing he was disappointed enough in me to not speak to me was the worst feeling in the world. Now that the three of us have worked things out, we are back to like we were before. And I know it meant the world to Tai when dad said he couldn't imagine a better man for his daughter.

"What ya doin'?" Tai comes up behind me, where I'm sitting at the kitchen table, typing away on my laptop, and kisses my neck.

"I'm emailing the school. I want to make sure my credits get transferred and that I'm signed up for the fall semester."

"Are you sure this is what you want? Long-distance would suck, but we could make it work if you wanted to finish getting your degree in Texas."

"I already told you, I'm positive this is what I want. There was never anything for me in Texas. I belong in New Orleans with you and with my family."

"I just don't want you to feel like you have to give up anything for me. Like I told you, we'd make it work. You're mine, Piper. That means doing whatever it takes to keep you."

Twisting in my seat, I stand. Tai wraps his arms around my waist. "Tai, I'm staying in New Orleans for me, because it will make me happy. Being here with you, waking up next to you every morning, us getting to know each other more and more, being close to my dad, uncle, and grandfather. And getting to see my baby brother grow up. All those things combined are why I am staying."

"Thank fuckin' god." Tai kisses me. "Otherwise, my arse would be driving to Texas every weekend." Tai nuzzles his face in the crook of my neck and starts palming my butt.

"Tai," I breathe, closing my eyes. "I have to be at work in an hour."

"I can be fast."

I try to push him away. "Seriously, I don't want to be late like I was yesterday."

He pulls the collar of my shirt aside and bites along my shoulder, causing me to lose my resolve. "Fine. You have ten minutes."

As soon as the words leave my mouth, Tai puts his shoulder to my tummy and scoops me up into a fireman's hold. "Tai!" I squeal.

"I only need five," he declares as he races down the hall to the bedroom.

"Ten minutes, my ass," I grumble as I walk through the door of the clinic an hour and fifteen minutes later.

"Hey, Piper," Mathew greets me as I walk inside. Mathew and I switched shifts today because he had mentioned needing the afternoon off. And now I feel like shit for possibly making him late.

"How's it going, Mathew? Sorry, I'm late. I feel terrible."

"No problem. It's only a few minutes, so it's no biggie. It gave me the chance to catch up on some homework anyway."

"How's summer school been going? Are you ready to start your senior year?

"It's going good. And yeah, I'm ready. I'm looking forward to graduating." Mathew gathers his textbooks and shoves them into his backpack.

Once Mathew is out the door, I check the schedule to see who is coming in this afternoon. I also check messages and make a few return calls.

"Piper," Dr. Channing pokes her head out of her office door. "Can I see you in here for a minute, please?"

"Sure." Walking into her office, I take a seat in front of her desk. "What's up?"

"I wanted to ask what your plans are for your next semester. Are you returning to Texas?"

I shake my head. "No. I have decided to stay in New Orleans and finish my degree here. In fact, I have already transferred my credits over and will be taking fall classes."

"I assume you are going all the way with this?"

I'm suddenly curious about her line of questioning. "Yes. I have three more years before I have my bachelor's degree, then I will have four years of veterinary school, and of course, an internship, the whole nine yards." Dr. Channing smiles. "What's this about?" I ask.

"I have something important I want to propose to you."

"Okay."

"How do you feel about me becoming your mentor? When you finish with your degree, will you intern here at my clinic?"

"I would say yes!"

"I figured you would. Now, I know that is still some years away, but my asking you now goes with my next question."

"Next question?"

Dr. Channing nods. "My husband and I have been talking a lot over this last year about retirement and planning for the next chapter in our lives. My practice means the world to me and with retirement comes having to let it go. And the only way I can do that is if it's to the right person. I believe that person is you."

I sit stunned for a minute. "What are you saying?"

"I want to help with your journey by becoming your mentor and asking if taking over my practice is something you'd be interested in doing one day?"

"Oh my god!" I jump to my feet. "Are you serious?"

"I'm completely serious," Dr. Channing chuckles.

"Yes! A thousand times, yes! It would be an honor."

I spend the remainder of the day riding my high. The afternoon only got better with four adoptions. One couple even adopted two of our dogs. The pair had been here since they were brought in at the start of the summer. A man found them in a box on the side of the road. Sadly, three of the puppies in the litter were already dead, but Duke and Oliver, who are Husky and Golden Retriever mixes, had managed to survive the New Orleans heat. Unfortunately, dog dumping is not uncommon in the city. If only people spayed and neutered their pets, the stray population wouldn't be so dire. That is also why Dr. Channing works with surrounding clinics in New Orleans to offer the procedure at low cost, making little to no profit.

"Hey, Miss Piper!" The bell above the door chimes, and in walks eight-year-old Lily Jones, holding a small cage with her guinea pig in it and her mom trailing behind.

"Hi there, Lily! How are you and Mr. Lucky doing today?" Mr. Lucky is her guinea pig's name.

"Mr. Lucky is doing much better. He finished all his medicine."

"I'm so happy to hear that, Lily. How about you and your mom go back to room one, and Dr. Channing will be in to see you in a few minutes."

"Okay," she giggles and skips down the hall.

An hour later, after Lily and her mom have left with Mr. Lucky, who was given a clean bill of health, Dr. Channing and I are leaving for the day. "I'll see you Monday, Piper. Have a good evening."

"You too, Dr. Channing," I call out as I slide into my car and head for the garage. Tai doesn't close the shop for another hour, and when he does, we will hang out at Twisted Throttle.

Walking through one of the bay doors, I spot Tai working on a bike. I smile. "Hey."

Tai looks up, his eyes heat as he watches me get closer. Standing, he pulls a bandana from his back pocket and wipes his hands. "Hey, babe." He hugs me. "You have a good day?"

"I had the best day," I can't hold back my excitement. I've been chomping at the bits to tell him my news.

"Yeah? Tell me."

I fill Tai in on the offer Dr. Channing presented me with today. "Can you believe it! God, Tai. I can't believe she chose me."

"That's fuckin' great news, baby. Hell, yeah, I can believe it. You're amazing, Piper, and you're going to be a fuckin' awesome vet, babe." Tai picks me up and crushes me against his chest.

"I can't wait to tell everyone."

"Let's not wait. Come on. I'm going to close down so we can head over to the bar and celebrate." Tai jogs over to the bay door and starts closing the garage down. He then goes to the back and cuts out all the lights. When he returns, he pulls his keys from his pocket and grabs my hand. "Let's go, babe." Stopping at the front entrance, Tai locks the door, pulls out his phone and taps on the screen, setting the alarm. With me still firmly in his grasp, he leads me over to his bike. After Tai swings his leg over and starts the engine, I climb on behind him.

"Ready, babe?"

Wrapping my arms around his waist, I kiss his cheek and nod. "Ready."

When we arrive at the bar, I notice a couple of extra bikes parked out front; bikes I don't recognize. And when Tai leads me inside, I am surprised at who I see here. My mom. Even more surprisingly, she is sitting at the back of the bar with my dad, Uncle Abel, and her old man, Crow. I can't hold back my smile when I approach the table. My mother catches sight of me and stands.

"Why didn't you tell me you were coming? I would have taken off work early."

My mom came down for a visit two weeks ago, and I am happy to say our relationship is getting stronger by the day.

"Crow had some business to handle two towns over, and we decided at the last minute to swing by. I hope that's okay."

"Of course. I'm happy you guys decided to visit." I hug her while Crow stands and offers Tai his hand. The two men shake and do that manly chin lift thing, then the four of us take a seat. I sit between my dad and Tai.

"How was your day, Bean?" My dad leans over and kisses my temple.

"It was great," I beam.

"Tell them your news, baby." Tai rests his arm on the back of my chair.

"What news?" dad asks.

"Umm...Dr. Channing has offered to be my mentor. And she asked if when I finish with my degree, would I be interested in taking over her practice when she retires."

"You're fuckin' kiddin' me?" Dad booms.

I shake my head. "No. Dr. Channing said that she and her husband talked about retirement, and the subject of her practice and what she was going to do came up. Dr. Channing said she wanted it to be me who took over. That she believes in me." I smile.

"Hell yeah, she does. We all believe in you, Bean." I blush at my dad's compliment.

"Wow, Piper. This is wonderful news," my mom boasts.

All the guys tip their bottles and express their congratulations.

"Thanks, guys. I mean, I know it's not for several years, and I have a long way to go, but I am thrilled at the thought of someday owning my own practice. I will have to work out the kinks, like how I am going to afford it. I'm sure I can apply for a loan at the bank or something. I have time to figure all that out later," I wave my hand.

"You know the club will help you out, Piper," Uncle Abel offers. My dad nods, agreeing with his brother.

"We got you, baby girl."

"That won't be necessary, Prez," Tai cuts in. "When the time comes, I'll take care of it." Tai looks at Uncle Abel, then at my dad. There is a brief unspoken conversation between the three. Both my dad and uncle tip their bottles and nod like the decision has been made.

"I appreciate you guys offering, but I can figure out how to pay on my own." I don't look at Tai when I say that, but he knows my comment was direct at him as well. I can feel his gaze burning a hole in the side of my head.

"I said when the time comes, I'll take care of it. End of story."

What?

Dad shakes his head, and Uncle Abel chuckles. My mom looks amused, and Crow sits silently, but I don't miss the smirk on his face.

Turning in my seat, I face Tai. "Excuse me?"

"You heard me, Piper." Tai stands his ground.

"I heard you, but you obviously didn't listen to me when I said I would figure it out."

Leaning in close, bringing his face an inch from mine, Tai gently but firmly grips the back of my neck. "You're my woman, Piper. Part of being my woman means I am going to take care of you. It's not because I don't think you have the ability to take care of yourself. I know you can. It means that I have the pleasure of providing for you—for us. Piper, you will be spending the next four years working on your bachelor's degree, then the next four years after in vet school. You will be working hard every day to make a life for you, for me, and our future children. While you are working hard to make your dreams come true, and mine by simply breathing; the least I can do is the same while supporting you in any way I can. Now, do you have a problem with that?"

I sit stunned with my mouth gaped open at the beautiful words that just came out of Tai's mouth.

"Fuckin' A, brother. Best goddamn man for my baby girl," my dad grunts. "Now, close your mouth and answer the man, Bean."

Doing as I'm told, I answer my man. "No, Tai. I don't have a problem with that."

"Didn't think so." He kisses me.

A couple of hours later, the bar is packed, booze is flowing, and Fender has taken the stage. Twisted Throttle always draws a massive crowd on the nights he sings.

"He's good," my mom boasts, clapping her hands when Fender finishes his first set and steps past his usual harem of women who come to listen to him sing as he makes his way toward the bar where the guys are sitting.

"With a voice like his, I'm surprised his name isn't in neon lights and his songs on the radio."

"Dad said some big wig offered him a contract some years ago, but Fender turned him down. He said that kind of life wasn't for him."

My mom nods. "I get it. It's like that with all these men who are a part of the club. Men like Fender are a different breed. Their club and their brothers are what's important to them. And there is nothing wrong with that," she pauses, becoming quiet for a second before saying, "So..."

I turn my attention away from the guys and face my mom when she begins to speak again. "Crow is throwing a party next weekend at the clubhouse for my birthday, and I was wondering if you'd want to come up for the day." She throws her hand up and adds, "You don't have to. I just thought..."

"I'd love to," I cut her off and smile.

"It means a lot to me that you'd want to be there, Piper." She places her hand over the top of mine.

"It means a lot that you invited me."

A grating cackle interrupts mine and my mom's conversation. I look over my shoulder to see that the object of my annoyance is none other than one of the women from Fender's fan club. Only it's my man she has her sight set on. I watch as the brunette tries desperately to get Tai's attention. You would think with the way he's ignoring her, the bitch would give up. *Desperate much*. I roll my eyes and sigh.

"Unfortunately, that is something you never get used to." My mom gestures toward the bar.

"No, but that doesn't mean I'm not going to put the woman in her place."

Standing, I make my way toward the bar. As if he can sense my presence, Tai turns on his stool, meeting my eyes. Coming up behind him, I slide my hand up his back while maneuvering my body directly between him and the desperate woman beside him, effectively nudging her out of the way. I don't bother looking at her.

That is until she scoffs, "Rude."

Slowly, I turn and confront her. "No, what's rude is a lady so desperate for a man's attention that she can't even take a hint when he flat out ignores her, leaving me, his woman, to handle her myself. Now, if you would kindly move along," I make a shooting motion with my hand, "and cackle somewhere else, me and my eardrums would greatly appreciate it."

With an offended huff, the woman hops off her stool and makes her way to the opposite end of the bar to where her friends are.

When I turn back around, Tai has an amused look on his face.

"What?" I narrow my eyes. "Don't act like you wouldn't do the same thing if the tables were turned. Hell, you get pissed when any man so much as looks in my direction," I sass.

"She's right, brother." My dad walks up and slaps Tai on the back. "And just so you know, your woman is always right."

"Welcome to the fuckin' club," Uncle Abel says, raising his beer bottle. My dad and Crow do the same, making me and my mom burst out laughing.

Later that night, I lay draped over Tai's chest while he rubs lazy circles across my back, feeling sated from the two orgasms he gave me.

"What ya thinkin' about?" Tai's deep sleep filled voice asks.

"I'm thinking about how happy I am at this moment and how perfect today was. And I'm thinking about how much I love you."

We both fall silent for a moment when I ask, "What about you? What are you thinking about?"

"I'm thinkin' if I died tonight, I would die the happiest fuckin' man alive."

21

KIWI

Waking early, I slide from the bed, then look back at Piper sound asleep, her long hair falling across her face. Reaching over, I brush my knuckles across her cheek, pushing her hair to the side. I watch her sleep, her lips slightly parted. How the fuck did I get so lucky? I peer over to where Chance is curled in his bed, snuggled beneath that damn old shirt. His head rises at the sound of one of the old wood floor panels creaking as I stroll across the room, stepping into the bathroom.

Reaching into the shower, I turn on the water. While the water warms, I brush my teeth. I start thinking about the past weeks since Piper and I became us and can't think of a time in my life I was happier than I am now. Nova and I are good too. The club is also back to normal. With Donovan sitting behind bars, and his bond denied due to him being a flight risk, we've gone back to our typical day to day without much worry. Of course, our guard can never go down completely. His involvement in the sex ring was part of a massive underground operation that ripped a gigantic hole in a much larger organization.

I rinse and spit, then place my toothbrush into a white ceramic cup, and smile. Usually, I would have tossed it back into the drawer, but a few days ago, Piper decided the bathroom needed a makeover, making it the only renovated room in the house. We painted the walls a dark grey, which I have to admit looks great with the white shower tiles. I hung one of those frameless shower doors for her too because she felt it would help open the small space, and admittedly it does. To save money, we painted the old vanity black and left the old wood flooring because it gives the home character.

I step into the shower and close my eyes, letting the hot water soak into my skin. I hear the glass door slide open, then shut, before slender arms embrace me from behind. Piper's palms rest on my chest, and I cover her hands with mine. "Good morning," she says, her voice husky from sleep.

Twisting, I face my woman, my cock already hard for her. She presses her wet body against mine. I brush her hair over her shoulder, exposing her neck. Leaning down, I run my lips across her skin, causing it to prickle, and she moans. I palm her breast. Dipping my head, I suck her taut nipple into my mouth, and her sharp gasp has my cock throbbing. Needing to taste her first, I sink to my knees. I groan at the sight of her pussy, then run my tongue through her center. Piper's fingers slide through my hair, her nails scraping against my scalp as she pulls me closer. My tongue swirls her swollen clit. "Tai," she moans. I slip two fingers inside her and feast on her delicious pussy until her slick walls contract, and Piper comes in my mouth. She shudders as I taste her pussy one last time. Standing, I pull back and look at my woman. Piper's eyes roam my body. Fisting my cock, she watches me stroke myself. She bites her lower lip. As much as I'd like to see those pink lips of hers wrapped around my cock, I need to be inside her. "Turn around."

Turning, Piper presses her palms against the shower wall. Teasing, she wiggles her ass, then spreads her legs and arches her back.

My fingertips trail her spine, and then my palm skims over her soft skin as I grip her hips. "God, you're beautiful. Fuckin' perfect." I sink into her. "Who do you belong to?" I pull out, then thrust, burying myself inside her once more.

"You, Tai. Only you." She breathes erratically.

I press my chest against her back, covering one of her hands with mine, anchoring myself and slipping my other hand between her thighs. Piper's head falls back against my shoulder as I rub her clit. Her hips rock back as I thrust forward. In tune with each other, we find our rhythm.

"I'm close," she moans.

"Come for me, babe." I feel her walls flutter before her pussy squeezes my cock. "Fuck." My body jerks with my release as Piper screams my name. It's always so fucking good. I won't ever get enough of her.

Wrapping my arm around her waist, I hold her close until our breathing levels out, then gently pull out. Spinning around, Piper faces me, wearing a lazy smile. "Good mornin'," I cover her mouth with mine.

"Is that going to be your usual way of saying good morning?" Piper's hands travel down my sides before gripping my ass. "Because I wouldn't mind this becoming a part of my daily routine," she sasses between kisses.

"Getting to taste your sweet pussy and having you come all over my cock sounds like the perfect way to start a day." I walk us back under the spray of water. I get lost in her for a bit longer before we finish our shower.

A short time later, chores are done, and I've made arrangements with Payton to drive out soon and pick Chance up to hang out at the clubhouse for a while today. Piper and I are loading up and heading north toward Hell's Punishers territory. Piper's mum invited her to the party her old man and the club are throwing for her birthday. Piper places the small gift she bought her mum the other day into a bag strapped to the back of my bike. "Do you think she'll like it?"

I kiss her forehead and place the helmet on her head. "Yeah, babe," I tell my woman and help her settle on the seat. Their relationship is still a work in progress, but Piper, being the kind person she is, didn't want to show up empty-handed. It's a handcrafted, blown glass hummingbird. It isn't extravagant in any way, but I'm sure Madison will be over the moon because her daughter gave it to her. Hell, what mother wouldn't? I remember finding shiny rocks as a kid and giving them to my mum. She would look at them as if they were diamonds and make a huge fuss over how beautiful they were. The memories make me smile. She kept every rock I ever gave her, placing them in glass jars that she still keeps on her bookshelves.

"What are you smiling about?" Piper asks.

"My mum."

"It's been a while since you've seen your family," she mentions, and it makes me miss them more.

"Maybe it's time I fly home for a visit," I tell her and slip my shades on over my eyes. "I want to take you with me."

Piper smiles at me, wide-eyed. "To New Zealand?"

I chuckle. "Yeah, babe. I want to show you where I grew up."

Her smile quickly turns into a frown. "Do you think your family will have a problem with us being together?"

"Why would they?" Piper's eyes fall to the ground, and she shrugs. It's not often I see my woman feeling unsure and worried about what others think of us. I don't like it. "Look at me," I touch her chin with my fingertip, and Piper lifts her face. Her hazel eyes lock with mine. "You've met my family before. They adore you."

"That was before, Tai."

"Trust me, babe. My Mum, Dad, and sisters will be over the

moon that I have fallen hard on my arse in love with you." Dipping my head, I kiss her mauve painted lips, and she tastes like the caramel coffee creamer she uses. The flavor lingers on my tongue as I pull away. "You good?" I ask, and Piper gives me a smile that makes my chest ache. Being loved by Piper feels like I won the fucking lottery. She is the reason I breathe. I've killed men for her and would do it again—die for her if that's what it took to keep her safe. She doesn't know it, but, in the mornings, I watch her sleep—doing so brings me peace. In those quiet moments, my future is so clear. In her, I see everything: marriage, a family, growing old together, and I want it all.

"I'm good," she replies, pulling me from my thoughts. I swing my leg over my bike, and Piper slides forward, slipping her warm hands beneath my cut. My bike rumbles as I start her up, and we pull away from the house. The sun filtering through the pecan tree branches flicker like a disco ball as I drive down the long dirt road. I increase my speed as soon as we hit the open highway. Piper presses her body into me, and her long legs move forward. Dropping my arm, I reach back and wrap my hand around her calf. The warm air kisses my face as we cruise down the road, and all I can think is how fucking perfectly happy I am.

Several hours later, I'm standing outside the Hell's Punishers clubhouse smoking a cigarette alongside Crow and a few of his officers. I look around the yard, at the Harleys scattered around. Bikers, some with their women, are hanging around a massive pile of wood where they plan to have a bonfire later tonight. Like any other MC party, men are drinking and getting loud, and music plays through indoor and outdoor speakers. This is the second time I've stepped foot on their compound, which is much different than ours. Their clubhouse is a single level building, situated smack in the middle of a large piece of flat land. It's gated, surrounded by a barbed-wire fence. Our backdrop is the Mississippi River, neighbored by abandoned industrial buildings, where theirs is in the Delta farmlands. Crow's land is open, with no obstructions as far as the eye can see. Not much of a place to hide should someone be dumb enough to roll out here and start some shit. Smoke fills my lungs, and then I blow it out. "How many acres am I lookin' at—if you don't mind me askin'?" I gaze out at the property. The grass is lush and green. My eyes lift to the sunset sky.

"Twenty acres," Crow answers, and I let out a low whistle. "It's been in my family for generations. As I'm sure you know, the Hell's Punishers have been out here for years." I nod. From what we know, his grandfather established the club. The clubhouse door swings open, and Piper steps out, followed by Madison.

"You ready to go, babe?" I flick the remains of my cigarette to the ground and snub it out with the toe of my boot.

"I'm ready." Piper smiles. Turning, she embraces her mum. "Happy birthday," she tells her, and Madison's face lights up.

"I'm beyond happy you came out today." Madison pulls back and looks at her daughter. "Best present I've ever gotten," she tells her. "You sure you have to go?" her mum asks, not ready for Piper to leave. "You're more than welcome to crash here for the night." Madison looks at Crow for agreement, and he nods his approval.

"Thanks, but we need to get back home," Piper states. "Let's get together in a week or two for lunch, and maybe a little shopping," she adds.

"I'd like that," Madison says, giving Piper one last hug.

On my bike again, we head south, back home to New Orleans. Piper waves as I pull away from Hell's Punishers clubhouse, kicking up a dust cloud as we travel down the half-mile dirt road. In all, it turned out to be a good day. My woman thoroughly enjoyed herself. I've noticed a change in Piper the more her and Madison get to know one another. They still have a way to go, and the mother-daughter bond may never be what it should have been, but it's a good start.

Turning off onto a different exit, I take a detour, taking a backway home on some old country roads—the landscape around us farmland, mostly soybean crops, and cornfields. I look at the bike's gas gauge and notice I'll need to stop and refuel. Five miles down the road, I swing into a small gas station and pulled up to one of four pumps they have. Turning off the engine, I climb off. "You need to use the restroom?" I ask Piper.

"I'm good," she says, watching me pull my bank card from my wallet. I punch my code on the keypad, then fill the tank. I still feel her eyes on me.

"What's on your mind, baby?"

Piper sighs. "Honestly?"

"Always," I tell her, replacing the gas pump nozzle and twisting the gas tank cap closed.

"My mom asked me about kids."

"She did, huh?" I grin.

"Do you want kids?" Piper asks.

An old brown Chevy turns in off the road and rolls passed, parking on the far side of the building. The engine backfires, causing Piper to jump. I give her my attention and answer her question. "I'd love to have kids."

"Yeah?" Piper smiles at me.

"Absolutely. A shit ton. I want a big family." Before mounting the bike, I ask her, "What about you—do you want kids?"

"Yeah. I mean, not right now, but someday." Leaning down, I kiss my woman.

"We've got nothin' but time to make plans for our future." I kiss her one more time. As I mount the bike, I notice clouds rolling in, and the sky turning from hues of purples to a dark grey.

"Looks like rain." Piper eyes the sky as well.

"Let's get going. Hopefully, we can keep the bad weather at our backs." The engine rumbles, and we pull back onto the road. The temperature drops a few degrees, and I can feel the extra moisture from a pending storm building in the air. A few miles down the road, I happen to glance in my side mirror. Behind us, cresting the hill is a truck. If I'm not mistaken, it looks like the same brown truck that pulled into the gas station a few miles back. I keep the bike moving, but my eyes are on my side mirror. The truck starts gaining speed, closing in on us from behind. Within minutes the fucker is riding my ass, and it's starting to piss me off.

"What is up with this guy?" Piper speaks loudly in my ear, acknowledging the jackass's reckless driving.

I continue to watch the asshole in my mirror. The truck lurches forward again, this time so damn close I swerve to avoid his front end clipping my back tire. "Motherfucker!" I growl. He does it again—this time, close enough for me to get a look at the driver's face. My grip tightens, and my gut clenches. Behind the wheel is the oldest Thibodeaux brother, and in the passenger seat, his younger brother. *Shit.* This isn't good. "Babe," I yell, and Piper leans into my back. "Get on your phone and call one of the guys. Tell them we have trouble." Piper's body tenses against mine from the urgency in my voice. Everything about the situation feels wrong. Something isn't right. "Now," I bark, knowing shit is about to get real.

"I can't find my phone," Piper yells into my ear.

Fuck.

"Hold on," I tell her, and her grip tightens on my waist. Giving the bike some gas, I accelerate, trying to put distance between me and the motherfuckers in the truck. "My phone is in the inside pocket of my cut," I yell back at her. "I need you to reach for it," I tell her and focus on maintaining control of the bike.

"What's going on?" Piper's voice trembles and I can tell she's freaking out.

"Do as I say, babe." I notice the truck gaining on us again. I keep both hands on the handlebars as she reaches around, digs into my cut, and pulls my phone from the pocket. Suddenly the truck moves into the other lane. The driver swerves into us, and I swerve to avoid getting hit. Piper screams, her hands clutching me again.

"Tai, I dropped the phone!" she yells, and I'm scrambling to figure out my next move. The truck swerves again, moving back into the other lane, and I fucking gun it. In a risky move because of my speed, I let go of one handlebar and reach for my weapon. Aiming behind us, I fire at the truck. He seems to back off for a moment, but soon I hear the unmistakable crack of a rifle shot. They're shooting at us. I return fire, my bullet hitting the front fender as they move into the oncoming traffic lane. He floors it, and the truck gains speed.

Trying to keep the bike on the road, I raise my arm and retake my aim just as the passenger window comes into view. Suddenly, I'm staring down the barrel of a gun. Taunting us, he jerks the steering wheel trying to hit my bike. His tire clips mine, and I lose control. Time seems to stop, and everything happens in slow motion. The bike leaves the road. I'm not sure how I manage it, but I have Piper in front of me, my arms wrapped around her waist, tucking her as close to me as possible to try and keep her safe. Us and the bike are skidding across the asphalt and loose gravel before going down a grassy side embankment. Our bodies roll a few times, but I hold my woman tight. What feels like forever happens within seconds before we stop moving. All parts of my body ache when I go to move. "Piper," I'm afraid to let loose of her.

She moans. "Tai."

"Babe," I get myself into a seated position and carefully ease her to do the same. "You hurt anywhere?" I'm looking her over before checking myself out.

She's still wearing her helmet, and I thank God for that. "My ankle hurts," she looks down at herself, and I take in her ripped jeans and skinned knees that are bleeding slightly. "Are you okay?" she asks.

I ignore my pain. "I'm good," I tell her and take in our current location. I notice my bike several yards away, the frame wrapped around a tree, and that we slid between two large pines. Literally three feet in either direction, we could have been in worse shape than we were.

"Are they gone?" Piper asks.

"We don't need to stick around to find out," I tell her. We're stuck out here, with no transportation, no phones, and I've lost my weapon. Before I can get to my feet and search for my gun, twigs snapping beneath heavy footsteps has me pulling Piper behind my back.

"Well, well, well. Look what we have here," a familiar face smirks as he and his brother walk toward us. The younger Thibodeaux, the one who's dick I broke, carries a rifle at his side, his dark eyes filled with hate.

"What a small world. Never thought we'd run into one of you sorry bikers again, but," the older brother spreads his arms wide, "here we are."

"It's our lucky day." The younger brother sneers, his eyes looking past me to Piper.

"Take your fuckin' eyes off my woman," I warn him.

He laughs. "You hear that, Earl?"

Piper tugs on my arm and whispers. "Look down to your right." I quickly glance down and spot my gun, lying about two feet away.

"You have no one to rescue you out here," Earl says. "I'm thinking we'll kill you first, then my brother and I will have a little fun with your girl there." He spits at the ground. "What do you think, Carl?" they continue to trudge down the hill in our direction.

"Move when I move, and stay behind me, got it?" I whisper to Piper as low as I can. Her fingers clutching my cut tells me she understands. I only have one chance at getting to my weapon, before trigger happy there takes a shot at me.

Keeping in front of Piper, using my body as a shield, I reach for my weapon, lift my arm, and take aim. The moment I squeeze the trigger, I watch the younger brother's knees buckle, just as a force propels my body backward.

22

PIPER

Tai's body jerks, the force of his weight knocks us both backward. "Tai!" My ears are ringing as I scramble from beneath him. "No. No. No." My hands are all over his body. "Tai!" a gut-wrenching scream leaves my body, and panic washes over me as I realize he has been shot. *There's so much blood.* "Tai!" I yell again, my voice sounding muffled and far away. Tai moans and struggles to move his hand over the ground, searching for his weapon again.

"Get out of here," Tai grunts, then collapses.

"You killed my brother, you son of a bitch!" the guy roars. He pulls the rifle from his dead brother's hand and rushes toward me.

Not thinking twice, I lurch over Tai's bleeding torso and grab the gun that's lying on the ground beside him. I swing around and raise my arm. My hand shakes, unable to control the fear coursing through my veins. I've shot a gun several times. My father taught me at a young age how to handle a weapon, but I never thought the day would come when I would have to use one. Right now, I don't have time to think about how scared I am. I know what I have to do. It's either him or me. Determination and the will to live takes over. My hand steadies, and I aim. My actions are quicker than his.

A breath later, I pull the trigger. The guy stumbles back a couple of steps, his free hand gripping his chest where my shot hit him. Blood begins to soak through his dirty shirt. Cold eyes lock on me, and he struggles to raise the rifle again. I fire another shot. The bullet pierces his eye socket, and he crumples to the ground.

I let the gun slip through my fingers.

I just killed a man.

I quickly focus, turning my attention back to Tai. He's struggling, and it's gut-wrenchingly clear by the amount of blood seeping from his body, the dire state he is in. *Okay. Think Piper.* My palm rests on his chest. "Fight, Tai," I cry, then notice that his breaths are becoming shallow. I press my palm over the wound in his stomach, trying desperately to slow the bleeding. His warm blood seeps between my fingers. "Oh, god! Oh, god! Tai!" I touch his face. "Open your eyes, baby. Please."

With tears running down my face, I stand. I need to get us out of here. Tai needs help and fast. Leaning down, I hook my arms under his armpits and attempt to pull him up the embankment. Grunting, I manage to pull his body about two feet, but it's a struggle. I yell with frustration. "Shit!"

My chest heaves. *You got this.* Not giving up, I tug again, but my results are the same. I quickly realize I'm not strong enough to pull Tai's weight up the embankment to the road. Out of sheer desperation, I scream. "Please! Somebody help me!" It's useless. Nobody is around to hear my pleas. I realize I have only one option. I have to leave Tai here and go for help on my own. The weight of my choice is suffocating. Pushing through the agony of my only option, I press my lips against his, my tears falling on his face.

"I love you, Tai. Do you hear me? I love you." I sniffle. "I have to go get help. I'll be back. I swear it." I tear myself away from his bloody, unconscious body and make my way up the steep embankment as fast as my shaky legs will carry me. When I reach the road, I look around, trying to sort out what to do from here. Thinking fast, I ignore the pain in my ankle and run toward the old truck's open door that the two men were driving. There's a sign of hope when I see the keys hanging in the ignition. Climbing in, I turn the key. Nothing happens. *Dammit.* I try again and still nothing. I hit the steering wheel with the palm of my hand. "Come on, you sorry piece of scrap metal!"

On the third attempt, the piece of shit truck starts. Shifting into gear, I make a U-Turn and haul ass back toward Hell's Punishers clubhouse. Every second that passes feels like hours, and my gut clenches the further I drive away from Tai.

It's not long before I turn off the main road and onto the gravel path that leads to the compound. Less than a mile in, the iron fence surrounding their clubhouse comes into view. I press my foot harder into the gas pedal. As soon as the truck begins to accelerate, it backfires. Suddenly, the truck sputters, then the engine dies—the hunk of junk rolls to a stop. "Shit!" Flinging the door open, I jump down and take off in a sprint down the dirt road, ignoring the pain in my ankle. In the distance, a shadowy figure appears to move near the gate. I start screaming. "Help! I need help!" My lungs burn, and my throat feels like it is on fire, as I wave my hands in the air. "Get my mom!" I call out. A look of recognition crosses his face, and I yell again. "Get somebody, anybody! Please! I need help!" I throw my body at the gate, and the red-headed prospect moves into action. He pulls the gate open, and I take off again, running toward the clubhouse. Seconds later, Crow bursts through the clubhouse door, my mom and several of his men come spilling out behind him. His eyes widen, taking in my bloody appearance, and his whole demeanor changes, his body becomes rigid, and he's suddenly on high alert. I don't stop running until I crash straight into Crow's arm. He catches me. "The fuck, Piper?"

I struggle to catch my breath as I find my words. "He shot Tai." My breathing is erratic.

"Who?" Crow demands.

"These guys, they ran us off the road, and one of them shot him. Please," I clutch his cut and choke on a sob. "We have to go."

My mother gasps and pushes her way past her old man. She takes me in her arms as Crow begins to bark out orders. "Doc, you ride with me in the cage. L.A., you, and Goose ride out behind us."

Crow turns to my mom and me. "Madison, I want you to go inside." I can tell my mom wants to protest, but the look on Crow's face stops her, and she does as she is told.

There is a flurry of activity as Crow leads me to a black SUV. I climb in the front seat, and Crow closes the door. Doc climbs into the backseat, as Crow sits behind the steering wheel. Shifting the SUV into gear, tires spin against the gravel as he drives away.

"How far out is he?" Crow asks.

"I don't know, maybe five miles. Please hurry," I cry. "He is losing so much blood."

"I need you to calm down, Piper, and tell me what happened. Can you tell me about these men, and where they are now?"

"It all happened so fast. We stopped for gas, and not long after, a truck came up behind us. They tried running us off the road and then started shooting. Tai tried to lose them, but they clipped his bike, and we went down an embankment. I didn't get a good look at them until they pulled over, got out of their truck, and approached us again. They were the same men I had a run-in with weeks ago on my drive home from Texas." I say everything in one breath.

"Slow down," Crow tries to calm me. "Breathe."

I try to focus on my thoughts. "Tai managed to shoot one of them, but the guy fired off a shot too." I take my eyes off the road and look at Crow. "There was so much blood. I tried to get him up the embankment, but I wasn't strong enough." I'm unable to control my tears. "I wasn't strong enough, Crow. I tried. I promise I tried. I didn't know where else to go or what else to do."

"I know ya did, sweetheart. You did real good job coming to get me."

Swiping the tears from my face, I nod and bring my attention back to the road. It's not long before we come upon the spot where I left Tai. Pieces of his bike are scattered along the pavement. Crow brings the SUV to an abrupt stop. Not waiting, I open the passenger door and take off running toward the place I left Tai. Doc and Crow follow me down the embankment. Doc reaches him before I do and immediately checks for a pulse. He looks over at Crow and nods. He then rips Tai's shirt open, exposing the bullet wound. The grim look on Doc's face says it all.

"He needs a hospital right away," Doc barks. Crow and Doc fly into action, not wasting any time lifting Tai's lifeless body off the ground. I look on helplessly as they carry him to the SUV. They place him behind the back seats, and Doc climbs in with him. I stand frozen on the side of the road, my body feeling numb.

"Piper, we have to go, sweetheart." The urgency in his tone causes my head to snap in his direction, pulling me out of my daze. Climbing into the back of the SUV, I crouch beside Tai and palm his cheek. He feels cold. Even though he is unconscious, I talk to him. "I need you to be strong. You can't leave me." I do my best to focus on his face and not the hole in his stomach that Doc is currently tending to. Out of the corner of my eye, I watch Doc rummage through a duffle bag and pull out a box. Ripping it open, he takes white gauze, presses it firmly against the bullet wound, and then rechecks Tai's pulse.

"How far away is the nearest hospital?" I ask.

"Ten minutes," Crow tells me.

"Shit. I'm going to need you to step on it, brother," Doc urges before pushing me away. I watch in horror as Doc begins to perform chest compressions. Bile rises in my throat, and my body begins to shake.

"No! Please, no!" My hand covers my mouth.

"Piper," Doc barks. "I need you to pull it together and help me. Can you do that?" he asks while continuing CPR. I nod.

"When I count out fifteen chest compressions, I want you to pinch Kiwi's nose and blow into his mouth. Do that two times".

"Okay," I tell him. *You can do this, Piper.*

Doc counts. When he stops at fifteen, I pinch Tai's nose and cover his mouth with mine, attempting to breathe life back into his body.

Doc and I work together, giving it our all. Tears run down my cheeks onto Tai's face as each one of my breaths delivers a silent prayer. *Breathe, baby. Breathe.*

Doc stops compressions and checks for a pulse. "It's weak, but it's there," he announces.

I choke on a sob and rest my forehead against Tai's. "Stay with me, baby." I run my fingers through his matted hair.

When the SUV stops, I lift my head. We've arrived at the hospital. Crow jumps out of the truck while a team of doctors and nurses rush out the emergency room doors toward us. Crow throws open the back, and Doc begins relaying information. "Gunshot wound to the abdomen. He lost pulse en-route. I performed CPR."

"Pulse rate now?" I hear a doctor ask.

"There, but weak," Doc replies.

"Let's move!" an older male doctor orders. Four nurses jump into action and swiftly transfer Tai from the back of the SUV to a gurney. I jump out of the truck and go to follow, but another nurse stops me. "I'm sorry, but you can't go with him. I can show you to a waiting room if you like," she says with a calm tone.

"Please, I need to be with him," I plead as I try to push past her.

She gives me a sympathetic look. "I know you're worried. I promise you the doctors and nurses are going to help your friend."

"He's not my friend," I cut her off. "He's my everything."

The nurse's face softens before walking away.

"Come on, sweetheart," Crow comes up behind me and places his hand on my shoulder.

I ignore the stares and hushed voices of the people staring as we walk into the waiting room. Blood covers my clothing, and I don't have it in me to care. Crow has his phone to his ear and talks in a hushed tone, but I can still hear the words he's saying. "Nova, it's Crow. You and your men need to haul ass up here. Your guy took a hit." Crow listens intently to my dad on the other line. His eyes cut to me. "Physically, she is okay. We had to bring Kiwi to the hospital." Crow listens some more, then turns his head away and steps away for a second. When he speaks again, I hear, "It's not good, man. Your brother is in a bad way."

I squeeze my eyes shut and lean back against the wall beside the vending machine. *This can't be happening.*

"Piper." I open my eyes to Crow standing in front of me, holding out his phone. I take it and place it to my ear.

"Hello," I croak.

"Bean." At the sound of my dads' voice, I break down again. "Daddy," my voice cracks as more sobs break free.

"I'm comin' baby girl. I'm comin'. Hold tight for me."

"I can't lose him, dad. I can't."

"Don't think like that. Kiwi needs you to be strong," he says over the sound of his motorcycle roaring to life.

"Someone needs to call Tai's family," I tell him.

"Your uncle is handlin' that baby girl. We'll get them here. You focus on stayin' strong, and I'll see you soon. Okay?"

"Okay." I hang up and hand Crow his phone back.

Thirty minutes later, the doctor taking care of Tai rounds the corner to the waiting room. He scans the area, his eyes landing on me, Crow and Doc. I jump to my feet and meet him halfway across the room. "How is he?"

"Mr. Cooper is on his way to the OR. The gunshot wound he received to the abdomen caused him to lose an extensive amount of blood. He's bleeding internally, and unfortunately, we won't know the extent of his injury until the surgeon gets in there to explore the damage. Mr. Cooper coded five minutes upon arrival, but we were able to bring him back. He is upstairs getting prepped for surgery as we speak. If you like, I can have a nurse take you up to the third floor to wait. Normally the surgeon likes to talk to the family and answer any question you may have before he begins, but in this circumstance, there simply wasn't time."

An hour later, I'm pacing the hallway outside the waiting room. My thoughts are scattered, and I'm struggling to keep it together.

"Piper!"

I stop pacing and turn to see my dad at the other end of the long corridor, making his way toward me. Not far behind him is Uncle Abel, Uncle Malik, Fender, and Everest. "Dad!" I run straight into his arms.

"Fuck. You scared the shit out of me, Bean. Are you alright?" I nod into the crook of his neck. Dad releases his hold on me as Crow and Doc walk up to us.

"Any news on Kiwi?" Uncle Abel asks.

I shake my head. "They took him to surgery over an hour ago. We haven't heard anything since."

Dad scrubs his palm down his face. "How the fuck did this happen?"

"Do you remember when I was driving home from Texas, and I told you about those two men who approached me? The ones I suspected of messing with my tire?" My dad's face goes hard. "It was them. It's weird, though, because they knew who Tai was. They ran us off the road, and Tai had to lay the bike down."

Dad looks at Crow. "Where are the motherfuckers now?"

"Dead. Your boy was able to take one of those fuckers out before he was shot."

"And the other?" Uncle Malik fumes.

Crow looks at me then looks at my dad and the rest of the guys. I didn't tell Crow what happened to the second guy. My stomach knots, and my body begins to shake as the memory of holding the gun in my hand and pulling the trigger takes root. "I killed him," I confess. Then out of nowhere, I have tunnel vision, and the room starts to spin. A tingling sensation washes over me, and I struggle to stay on my feet. My dad is there to catch me. He pulls me to his chest, slowly backs us against the wall, and slides down to the floor, setting me on his lap.

"Head between your knees, Piper."

I do as he says. With my back against his chest, I lean my head forward.

"Good, baby girl. Now deep breaths. In through your nose and out through your mouth. Nice and slow." He rubs my back. I take several deep cleansing breaths while concentrating on the soothing rumble of my dad's voice. "It's okay, Piper. You're okay."

"I killed someone." It's not that I feel sorry for the scum I shot. I just don't know how to process the fact I am responsible for ending a person's life.

"You did what you had to do to survive, Piper. You saved yourself, and you saved Kiwi. Don't give that piece of shit the power to turn you inside out. You'll get through this baby girl. Your family will get you through this."

Taking a shuttered breath, I lift my head and look into my dad's eyes. We don't speak. Because no matter how old I get, the little girl in me will always believe that as long as I'm in my fathers' arms, everything will be okay.

It's nearly one o'clock in the morning when a middle-aged man wearing blue scrubs and blonde hair walks into the small waiting room. Instantly, everyone is on their feet.

"Are you all here for Tai Cooper?" he asks.

"Yes," Uncle Abel is the first to answer.

"I'm doctor Carrick. I was the surgeon who operated on Mr. Cooper. Once I opened him up, I discovered the bullet's damage to his small intestine and liver, all of which I repaired. Luckily, the bullet missed any major arteries. I was also able to remove the bullet. Mr. Cooper is stable at the moment and was taken to the ICU."

You can hear the collective sigh of relief.

"I do want to warn you. Even though the surgery was a success, Mr. Cooper is not out of the woods. We are having trouble stabilizing his blood pressure."

"He's going to be okay, though. Right?" I ask.

Dr. Carrick shakes his head. "I'm sorry. I can't make you any promises. The next twenty-four hours will be critical. We will continue to monitor him, and I will give you another update in the morning."

"Can I see him?" I ask, eager to lay eyes on Tai.

"Only one visitor at a time for now." He looks down at his watch. "You have fifteen minutes. The rest of you will have to wait until regular visiting hours."

Giving my family a small hopeful smile, I follow the doctor out of the waiting room. When I walk into the ICU room, I'm not prepared to see Tai lying in a hospital bed with so many tubes sticking out of him. His skin is pale, and he looks nothing like himself. I step further into the room and stop beside the bed. Reaching out, I take his hand in mine and close my eyes. I have so many emotions running through me at the moment, but my voice is stuck in my throat. Instead of saying all the things I want him to hear, I remain quiet, and hope he feels my presence. Everything else fades away. The room is still, and the only sound that can be heard is the whooshing of the ventilator helping him to breathe.

———

The following evening, I'm sitting on a bench outside the hospital's front entrance with my dad, sipping on a cup of cafeteria coffee. I'm a bundle of nerves waiting for visiting hours to roll around so I can see Tai again. I would have camped out at the hospital, but my dad convinced me to go back to the Hells' Punishers clubhouse with him and the guys to get some rest. Crow was gracious enough to invite us to stay with his club for as long as we needed. When we arrived, my mom was beside herself with worry and fussed over me. However, I was able to get a shower and change out of my bloody clothes, but sleep did not come. All I could think about was Tai. I'm pretty sure the nurses taking care of him are sick of me by now because I've called every fifteen minutes to check on him.

Before heading out this morning, the hospital called with news that Tai's blood pressure was stabilizing, and as soon as he wakes, they will transfer him out of the ICU to a regular room.

"Any news on Mr. and Mrs. Cooper's flight?" I look at my dad, who just got off the phone, and take another sip of coffee.

"Yeah. That was Wick. They're five minutes out."

I nod. I don't even know if Tai has told his family about us, and I hate they will find out under these circumstances.

Just as the thought enters my mind, Uncle Malik enters the parking lot with Uncle Abel, Fender, and Everest trailing behind on their bikes. The SUV carrying Tai's family pulls into a parking spot. Standing, I toss my cup into the trash bin and make my way over to the truck beside my dad. My nerves kick in. *What do I say to his mom? Will she blame me for her son being in the hospital? Will she think I'm not good enough for Tai?*

The back door to the SUV opens, and Mrs. Cooper steps out. There is no mistaking the worry etched on her face or the fact she has spent the last eighteen hours crying. The moment her eyes land on me, her face softens, and a warm smile spreads across her face. Kora Cooper is a small woman, standing at about 5 feet 2 inches tall. She has shoulder-length dark blonde hair mixed with a little gray and has kind blue eyes.

"Piper," she exhales her small smile not quite reaching her bloodshot eyes.

"Hi, Mrs. Cooper." I give her a smile of my own.

"None of that Mrs. Cooper mess. Call me Kora." And she surprises me by pulling me in for a hug.

"My boy has been talking my ear off about you." She pulls back and gives me a once over. "You're even more beautiful than the last time I saw you." And just like that, all my worries about Tai's mom vanish.

Tai's dad approaches me, along with his three sisters. "How are you holding up?" His dad embraces me like I'm family.

"Hi, Mr. Cooper. I'll be better when I get to see Tai again," I tell him, then Frankie, Molly, and Poppy take turns hugging me as well. Tai's dad looks at me. "He's a fighter," Mr. Cooper assures me.

After greetings are over, and we fill Tai's family in on his condition, I take Tai's mom and stepdad up to see their son. We step off the elevator and make our way down the corridor toward the ICU wing. "They will only allow two visitors at a time. You can go sit with him for fifteen minutes and then come back out here, and the next two people can go."

Mr. Cooper looks between me and Kora. "You two go on in. I'll wait and stay out here with the girls. I'm going to make some calls and find us a hotel to stay at while we're here."

When Mr. Cooper is out of earshot Kora turns to me. "My husband is as tough as they come, but his children are his weakness. He is trying to be strong for the girls but knows once he sees Tai, his resolve will break."

"I'm sorry this happened to Tai," I tell her.

Kora places her hand on my cheek. "This is not your fault. Thank you for being strong and sticking by my son's side."

"Always." I hold back the tears, I feel stinging my eyes.

"I know you will, honey." Kora pulls me in for another hug, comforting me.

A few minutes later, I stand at Tai's bedside as his mom holds his hand. She quietly weeps as she stares down at him. I place my hand on her arm. "We should go," I mention, and she nods, then releases Tai's hand. Leaning down, I kiss his temple. "I love you," I whisper in his ear.

Suddenly, an alarm on one of the machines starts beeping. I look around, confused. "What is going on?" Two nurses rush inside the room. Kora and I take a step back as one nurse quickly lowers Tai's hospital bed.

One nurse presses a blue emergency button. "He's crashing," she yells. Then starts chest compressions. "Get the doctor in here now!"

"What's going on?" I shout.

"I'm sorry, but I have to ask you two to leave." Another nurse comes in and ushers us out of the room.

"No!" his mom shouts then starts to cry. "That's my child in there." Her pained expression rips my chest wide open, and my knees buckle.

No.

Not now.

Don't you dare take him away from me.

"What the fuck is goin' on?" I hear my dad's voice, but it sounds so far away. Strong arms lift me off the floor. "Fuck!" My dad's voice cracks. I fist his shirt as I break down.

Over the next thirty minutes, we all wait on pins and needles for any information on Tai. Mr. Cooper looks like he's barely keeping it together while he consoles his wife and daughters. Uncle Abel, Fender, Everest, and Uncle Malik all carry grim expressions, while my dad does his best to keep me from crawling out of my skin.

I close my eyes because they burn from crying so hard, and my body still trembles with anxiety, as I rock back and forth, telling myself Tai will be okay. An uneasy silence settles around me, and I open my eyes to Tai's doctor entering the room. The moment my eyes lock with his, my heart stops.

EPILOGUE

I stir as the salty smell of bacon pulls me from sleep. Instinctively my hand reaches for the other side of the bed. The sheets are cold, and for a moment, I wonder if I'm still dreaming. A wet nose nudges the tips of my fingers that dangle over the edge of the mattress, telling me it's time to get up. Throwing the cover aside, I sit up on the edge of the bed and curl my toes against the wood floor, warmed by the rays of light flooding in through the bedroom window. As if to say hello, Chance lets out a bark then scampers out the opened bedroom door. I cross the room and stand in front of the window, feeling the sun on my face.

"Hey, you." I close my eyes and let the sound of her sweet voice penetrate my soul. Six weeks ago, I came damn close to never hearing or seeing her beautiful face again. Turning, my eyes fall on my woman. I take her in. Her white summer dress flutters around her bare feet as she walks into the bedroom, and I have to remind myself to breathe.

Without saying a word, I pull her flush against me, wanting to feel the warmth of her body against my skin. Her scent engulfs me. "You always smell so good." Dipping my head, I cover her mouth with mine, stealing her breath as my own. Someone clearing their throat pulls us apart, but only slightly. Across the room, in the doorway, stands my baby sister.

"Should I just eat your share of the bacon?" Poppy smirks, and I know Mum sent her to bug me.

"Those are fightin' words," I say with a playful tone.

Piper smiles at me. "Come on. She's been at it all morning." She pulls on my hand, leading me out the door and into our small kitchen.

"Mum, you've got to stop stealin' my woman every morning."

"I'm getting to know my future daughter-in-law and teaching her how to cook some of your favorite dishes."

"Mum," I sigh. For weeks she's been talking about marriage and babies. I haven't even proposed yet.

"Kora, leave our son alone." My dad walks in from outside, and Chance rolls in behind him. He grins and shakes his head, knowing Mum won't listen. "How are you feeling, son?" he asks.

"Restless. I'm tired of sittin' on my arse all day," I tell him, then ask, "Have Frankie and Molly called?" My other two sisters had to fly back to New Zealand yesterday morning because they had to get back to their jobs. I hated for them to leave. Having my entire family around, crammed into my small house, felt like old times, and I've loved every second of it.

"They made it," my dad says.

I glance around the kitchen and notice the buffet of food covering the countertops. "Mum, what's with all the food?"

"Oh." My mum looks at me, her face beaming. "I invited the boys and their wonderful families out for brunch." She wipes her hands on a kitchen towel, then tosses it near the sink. "Let me fix you some coffee before they arrive." She reaches in the cabinet for a mug.

"I can make my own coffee, Mum." Letting go of Piper, I cross the room. I love her, but she's been running herself ragged ever since I came home from the hospital.

"No, no. You just relax and take it easy," Mum tries shooing me away.

I kiss the top of her head. "Mum, I'm good. The doctor cleared me two days ago. I think I can lift a coffee mug without killin' myself."

My mum spins. "Tai, don't joke like that. We almost lost you." Her voice sounds pained.

"Shit, Mum. I'm sorry." I hug her and look over at my dad, then at Piper, standing with my baby sister. There is nothing like a mother's love, and she has poured her heart into taking care of me without asking for anything in return. My mum sniffles and I feel like a dick for making light of everything. "I appreciate all that you and the rest of the family are doing for Piper and me. I didn't mean to sound ungrateful. I'd love a cup of coffee." My mum pulls back and smiles up at me. "Sorry for sounding like a shit," I apologize.

"I know I'm a tad overbearing, but taking care of you makes me feel better," she says, patting my cheek. "Now, then. If you're feeling up to it, your father could use help setting up the table and chairs on the back porch."

My dad walks over, pulls my mum to him. "I love you, woman." He smashes his lips to her.

"Not in front of the children," my sister says dramatically while covering her eyes, and I laugh.

"Tai, join me outside. Let the ladies get back to women's work," dad jokes, then swats my mum's arse to get a rise out of her, and it works.

"Say that when you're scrubbing the dishes later," Mum grins.

My dad chuckles. "Come on, Son. Slip some shoes on your feet. I've got something I'd like to show you," my dad announces just as we hear the rumble of Harleys approaching. "And your brothers are just in time," he adds. My dad has that look on his face, one where he's trying extremely hard to keep a secret. It's the same look he had every Christmas morning when he woke everyone in the house before sunrise because he couldn't stand waiting any longer to open presents.

Piper hugs my neck. "Why don't you get dressed? I'm going to finish helping your mom and sister." She kisses me just beneath my ear because she knows it drives me wild. I groan and pull her into me, wanting her to feel the effect she has on me. Her eyes widen. "You'd better put that away," she giggles.

"Oh, you're gettin' it tonight," I warn, and her pupils dilate.

"Promise?" Piper whispers. Her nails trail down my bare chest as she steps away.

Several minutes later, I'm dressed and walking out the door onto the back porch. I take in the new railings and fresh paint. My dad has been busy lending a hand and fixing up the place while I've been recovering from my near-death experience. My hand goes to the long scar on my stomach. When I shot the younger Thibadueux brother, he happened to get a shot at me as well. The motherfucker hit me right in the gut, and the bullet traveled around in there, ripping up my insides. I lost a shit ton of blood and had to be resuscitated three times. Fucking scary to know, my heart stopped beating. The surgeon had to slice me open and do exploratory surgery to find and repair what the bullet damaged. Then, there was a high risk of infection following the procedure. In all, I spent three weeks in the hospital.

Across the yard, near the barn, I spot my dad, Riggs, Nova, Wick, Fender, and Everest talking with one another, so I make my way over. "How's it goin'?" Riggs has a beer in his hand.

"Can't complain," I tell him. "What's goin' on?" Nova flicks his cigarette to the ground, then Fender and him pull open the heavy barn doors. Inside sits the fully restored hardtail Harley I was working on. It looks just like the image I sketched. "Who did this?"

I walk up to the bike and run my hands along the emerald green finish that makes me think of my woman and the night that changed my life.

"All of us," my dad says. "The guys here mentioned you were working on a chopper restoration. While you've been on the mend, I've been sneaking off to your shop. When I wasn't working on it, they were."

"Don't sell yourself short," Fender says to my dad, then looks at me. "Your dad here did most of the work. I see now where you got all your skills."

"Well, what are you waiting for?" my dad says. "See how she feels." His excitement is contagious, and I smile so fucking hard my face hurts. I swing my leg over the bike. It's the first time in six weeks that I've sat on one. I reach out and grip the handlebars. A wave of emotion hits me all at once, and I struggle to hold them at bay. Not trusting my voice, I stay quiet for a beat.

Riggs clears his throat, and I look at him. He looks over his shoulder toward the house, where the women and children gather on the back porch. "While it's just us men, I need to share something with you." He tosses his empty bottle into a metal trash barrel nearby and shoves his hands into his front pockets. "Got word this morning, there will be no trial for Donovan Black, and the man arrested with him."

His news feels like a punch to the gut. "The fuck?"

Riggs' hand goes up. "Hold up. I'm not finished. A man can't stand trial when he's dead. Correctional officers found him early this morning lying in a pool of his own blood; his throat sliced open from ear to ear."

"What about the other guy?" I ask as I absorb what he's saying and what this means for Piper and me.

"Dead too," Riggs states.

We're all quiet for a few minutes until my dad breaks the silence. "Well, I say we have ourselves some beer and celebrate."

Riggs laughs. "Ben. I like the way you think."

Brunch turns into an entire day of the family hanging at my place. Even though I prefer having Piper on the back of my bike, I joined my brothers for a short ride and took the new chopper for a spin. *Peace.* It's the only word to describe how I feel getting back on the road, hearing the hum of the tires against the blacktop alongside my brothers. Adrenaline surges through my veins when I brave a bit more throttle. The engine growls, and the world around me moves by a little faster. All the bullshit weighing me down about Donovan Black, and my past is stripped away by the wind. Once the sun starts to set, we turn our bikes back toward home—back to our women.

Feeling lighter than I have in a long time, I join my woman sitting around the bonfire and the rest of the family. Standing, Piper passes her baby brother to Promise and makes her way toward me. Taking a seat in one of the lawn chairs, I tug her onto my lap. I rest my hand between Piper's knees. Fender sets a cooler down, opens it, and starts passing ice-cold beers around. I twist the top off and throw it into the flames. I sit for a long time listening to the conversation flow. My sister is on her phone, probably texting her arsehole of a boyfriend. Mum and Dad snuggle closer together, acting like two teenagers, and I can only hope Piper and I keep the flame alive like they have all these years.

"Hey, Tequila," Fender calls out. "I noticed you hadn't touched a drop of alcohol tonight." Chatter around us stops, and all you hear are the tree frogs croaking in the background and the wood crackling in the fire. My eyes cut to Wick, who has a shit-eating grin on his face.

Tequila rolls her eyes. "That's because this big lug here knocked me up." She crosses her arms and does her best to hide a smile.

"Oh my god! You're pregnant!" Tequila's niece, Sydney, jumps from her chair. "Finally!"she shouts, throwing her arms in the air.

Wick grabs Tequila's face in his hands, kissing her hard as congratulations pass around, and beers rise in the air. I sit back in my chair, thankful I'm here to watch The Kings family grow.

Someday that will be Piper and me.

"Penny for your thoughts?" I feel Piper's eyes on me, and I look at her.

"Thinking about how much I love you," I admit.

Piper smiles, and my heart skips a damn beat. "Oh yeah?" She leans in, her warm breath fanning across my ear as she whispers, "Show me."

I sit my beer on the ground, stand, then hoist Piper over my shoulder. "Challenge accepted."